Diamond of the Desert

D.A. Wray

SWITCH

"Behind every big lie is an even bigger truth, and it is only the Truth
that can set us free"

Diamond of the Desert

D.A. Wray

2025

*"A rare story of Western Australia's colonial history that doesn't hide
from the truth – the first of its kind"*
Rohan Collard, Ballardong Wadjuk Maaman
Dooga Waalitj Healing

Reviews and recommendations

"Noting there is currently little in the way of 'truthful' colonial fiction on public record about the early years in Western Australia, The Diamond paints an engaging and compelling story of the 1850s to build respect and educate readers - many of whom are still ignorant to those truths of this boodja." Rohan Collard, Ballardong Wadjuk Maaman, Dooga Waalitj Healing

"An entertaining, informative and thought provoking journey through the early years of white settlement in the Swan River Colony and beyond - thoroughly enjoyed." Tim Finucane

"A genuinely thoughtful, character driven tale that draws the reader in with identifiable and thought provoking elements such as genuine hardship and family bonds... This is a truly enlightening journey into a rarely publicised period of Australia's not too distant historical past." Richard Connery

Published by SwitchPub
an imprint of SWITCH Consultancy Services
Noongar Country
Western Australia

9781763827110 (ebook)
978176327103 (paperback)

A catalogue record for this book is available from the National Library of Australia

Cover design by Christopher Burrows: www.christopherburrows.eu
Map images from: www.oldmapsonline.org

Diamond of the Desert

Part one: The north

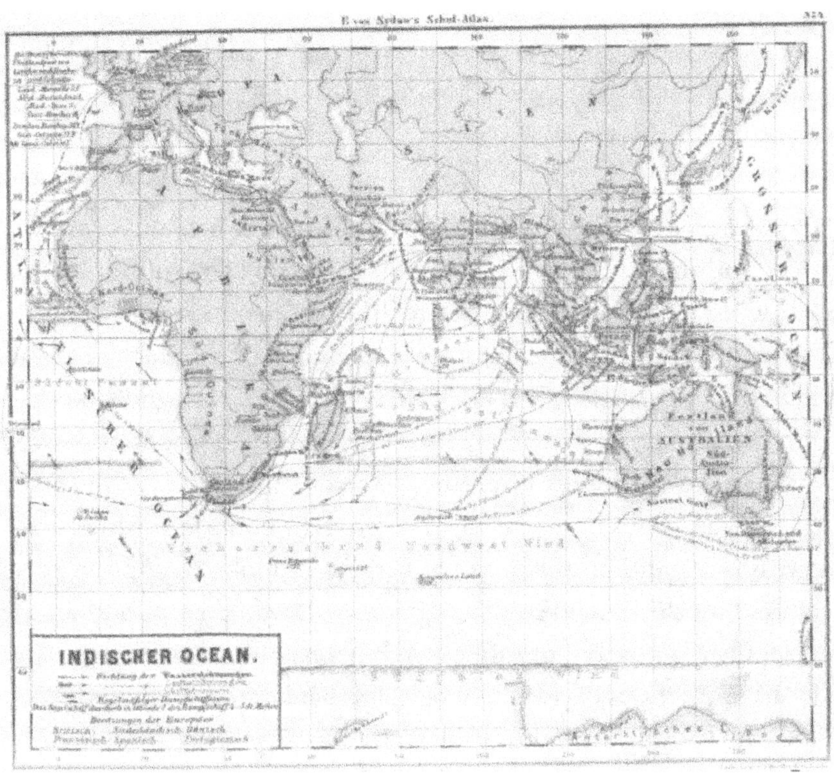

Maggie, 1844

Margaret O'Brien ran, in bare feet and joy. The boat was coming in and this day, like many others, she would help unload the fish. She had no memory of a time before the boats, before a time when her father would return as he did this day, the smell of fish thick in the air and caked to her father. She loved that smell, could imagine no other. And she deeply loved her father, a burly, bearded man who would sweep her up and tell her of his adventures – the one that got away, the many that did not. It was only rare when he brought home less than a dozen large fish in addition to buckets of herring and lobster, and she knew from her mother that even that, a poor haul, would keep food on the table for her family. But this time, her father had been out for three days and she knew it was likely to be a big haul that he would land today.

She ran through the streets toward the rocks where he would bring in his boat, the *Mary II*.

"Watch yourself there, young Maggie!" a neighbour called out in friendly warning. "You'll not be wanting to fall, and your father will get in no sooner for you having broken the school race records, nor your ankle!"

"I'll not be tripping so don't worry yeself, Mrs Ward!" she called back in reply. "And those fish'll not be swimming up here themselves!"

She loved this place, the little village of Blackrock in Haggardstown, Ireland. People said it was still new and full of hope. There were less than 500 villagers here, including nearly a hundred children like her, and many of the other families were also fisher-folk like her and her father. Everyone knew her as Maggie, and she couldn't imagine a happier place.

The Haggardstown area, an outer area of the bigger town of Dundalk, County Louth, was growing and thriving. New businesses were springing up and the rich alluvial soils of the area allowed plentiful crops and grazing lands, while her new fishing village to the south was frequented by the wealthier folk of Dundalk. There was talk of the need for holiday infrastructure in her little town. A national railway had even commenced a year or so ago which would join the great cities of Dublin in the south to Belfast in the north. The tracks would eventually meet right in the middle of Dundalk sometime around 1849.

Her days were shaped by the tide – days like today where the tide was high before or after school meant she could be at the rocks to greet and help her father. On other days her father would be home already while she sat in the school room, soaking up the lessons of the day.

The things she cared about were all here, in this little village by the sea. Her school and the teachers that she so deeply loved, her little house up the hill with her mum and dad and her siblings; surrounded by neighbours she knew and loved. Best of all, the fish and other sea creatures she found on the tidal flats as she roamed after school. Digging up cockleshells and walking the long distance to the water's edge to find all sorts of creatures caught in exposed rock pools. She wouldn't take them – her dad would provide enough. But she loved to study them, to see the weird ways shells attached to the rocks, the small tubes that would emerge between bivalve shells and she found too that there were many different types of fish. She found fish, shrimp, even lobster stranded in shallow rock pools from the retreating tide.

Last week she had found a large octopus hiding in its rocky pool. It retreated as she looked down upon it, changing colours to match the reeds that curtained its rocky home.

"Hello little fellow" she spoke aloud. "My you are an artist. Such beautiful colours! You needn't fear me though my many legged friend. Perhaps you'd share your stories of the sea?" and she imagined its reply, transporting her now to the depths of Dundalk Bay where she saw the fish her father brought in each day – schools of herring, sturgeons slowly nosing through the sand, sawfish, sharks with rows of teeth.

The Mullaharlin National School was to the north in the 'Old Massehouse' of Haggardstown and had opened only a few years earlier. There were only two small classrooms – one for the younger children and the second for the older children like her. The first of her primary years were in a 'hedge school' run by one of the local Catholic parents, as her parents and most others in Blackrock simply couldn't afford private schooling accessed by many of the Protestant families. The opening of the Mullaharlin National School had changed everything, and Maggie was proud to be one of the first students who would graduate at year 10 level. She loved school lessons, her friends and the two teachers - although there seemed to be a lot of time spent on needlework and other such 'home duties', and an *awful* lot of time on religious education...

As one of the older students, she would often help out the younger children and dreamed that one day, maybe she too could be a teacher. The education was basic, but it taught her the essential skill of reading and had triggered a lifelong obsession to read whatever she could. "An inquiring mind" her teacher had said. Though she wasn't too keen on mathematics – *just enough to get by* she thought. And now in her tenth and final school year she was regarded by teachers and peers alike as a brilliant student, with her dad joking that she was the top student ever to come out of Mullaharlin.

Her real love was reading, and she would devour any book or newspaper she could get her hands on, and from that would seek out and research other books and articles on the topics that interested her. And there were many.

Having been at the school since the very early days and having been such a talented and eager student for all those years, Maggie had developed a special relationship with her main teacher, Mr O'Hara, a bright and enthusiastic young Irishman who despaired that his lessons were too often dictated from far away England. He noted such instructions followed a familiar theme – that England is all powerful, all great, all knowing, and that the Irish were naught but privileged to share the glory. So he tried to work around the themes he was instructed to teach, spending hours at the library sourcing books, journals and articles that might at least inspire the imagination of his students.

He didn't need to worry about Maggie's engagement though – she was always keen. Often the first to arrive, the last to leave as she helped him tidy and asked incessant questions about the topics of the day. She often acted as his assistant, helping the younger ones with her eager delight and bright smile – *a teacher in the making*, he felt sure. For her enthusiasm didn't stop in the classroom and his trips to the library often ended up sourcing Maggie's own list of requested topics, which sometimes outnumbered his own! As a female, she of course wasn't allowed to enter the Dundalk Mechanic's Institute library so she pestered him to get her the books and articles she craved. He would go regularly and present her list of current topics alongside his own, in the hope they could source just one or two articles or books for her to read. The library could barely keep up.

Two weeks before, the school administrator had passed on an instruction to O'Hara that Mullaharlin and other national schools were to provide lessons on the expansion of the glorious Empire - designed of course to remind Ireland's own native peoples of their place in, and below, the world's greatest power. O'Hara had been down to the library that same day and found a newspaper article describing the life of an Aboriginal boy before the settlers had arrived. He decided to start the lesson with that newspaper article and have one of the students read it.

"Children, today we are going to learn about the expansion of the glorious British empire to countries all across the world" he began, choking back the words just ever so slightly. "Did you know that England has colonies in the Americas, Africa, Asia, and even the wild and exotic new colonies of the Antipodes, Australia and New Zealand?

England is bringing civilisation and God to all the primitive peoples of the world," he said. "God's children though Godless."

He showed the newspaper to the class, opening it to the article he had found of greatest interest. "Well today we are going to learn a little about those colonies and to start I've found here a nice little story set in the very newest colony of them all, Western Australia."

As he spoke he moved to the wall and a large map of the world, and he traced his finger slowly across the seas that separated first England from Ireland, and then the British Isles from the far distant Australia.

"Imagine you're on a boat" he began. "A great sailing ship travelling off to the Great Southern Land!" As he spoke his finger moved slowly south, over the seas and away from Blackrock's quiet shores.

He named the English colonies as he went – a bewildering number of places across the distant shores of Africa, Asia and beyond. New nations and wild and exotic lands, all claimed by the British Empire.

"On the west coast of Africa, here" he pointed. "Gibraltar, The Gambia, Sierra Leone, Gold Coast, Togo, British Cameroon..."

Seemingly forever south his finger continued, naming a further ten colonies of southern Africa. But the Southern Land was still half a world away. His finger moved north then, around the Cape of Good Hope and through even more countries: the colonies of Zanzibar, Tanganyika, the Seychelles, Somaliland, Socotra, Aden and Oman, naming them as he went.

His finger moved east now, sailing them past India and into southeast Asia and he continued to list the colonies as it moved over the miles of sea: "India, Burma, Ceylon, the Andaman Islands, the Maldive Islands, Malaya – and these groups of islands too – Cocos and Christmas Islands..."

Finally, very nearly at the bottom of the map itself, his finger came to rest along the west coast of Australia - a massive land, though the outline and features were still largely incomplete.

"The Great Southern Land" he said, before pausing and taking a closer look to find his target destination, a faint dot on the expansive, world-wide lands of the British Empire. "And the Swan River Colony – here. The newest colony of them all, children – it's barely ten years old, so younger than many of you here!

This huge new land so far from here is home to barely a few thousand English and Irish people now. Can you imagine the adventures they must have? The hardships they must endure, striking out a living there, at the very bottom of the world..." He paused a moment for effect.

"And it is home to Australia's Aboriginal people" he continued, his voice picking up. "So, I have found for you a story about those people, the native people of Western Australia, and I think you're going to like it. This story starts even further south, right down near here" and he pointed to Albany and King George Sound, until only a few years earlier nothing more than a military outpost of New South Wales.

Now, who would like to read it to the class?" he asked, returning to his desk and again holding up the newspaper.

He never doubted whose hand would be the first to go up. Maggie had shifted forward excitedly in her seat even as he spoke, and her eyes had lit up and her hand was in the air before the other older children had even considered the request.

So Maggie read the story of Degunbut Kanyap to the class with a smile upon her lips:

The Life Story of an Aboriginal Man – Part 1
By William Nelson

Before the lands of the south coast were turned to productive farm, there might have been seen a large and powerful community of Aboriginal people enjoying themselves peacefully among the well-grassed slopes and sparkling rivulets of the Esperance Bay district of Western Australia.

Little news of European settlement to their west and east had reached them. They knew of the arrival of white people but had little to no contact with them.

The Aboriginal people were living amidst an abundance of fish, fowl, and the native animals of Australia. They had no worries about their tomorrows. They were at peace with other communities. They had little or no trouble securing their daily food, no bosses to order them around, plenty of shade to bask in when the sun shone strongly, and an ample supply of kangaroo and possum skins to wrap themselves in when the winter's winds blew sharply.

They were a happy community living away from all knowledge and anxiety of commercial life.

In this tribe there was an Elder known as Kanyap. He shared great wisdom with his people and asked his messengers to send word to distant communities and invite them to come for feasts and corroborees at times of the year when food was plenty on his county.

Kanyap was married and had a son. This son was known as Degunbut Kanyap, and to all appearances was no different from any other Aboriginal baby as he coiled up in the kangaroo skin swung over his mother's back as she went about her daily tasks.

But the career of this baby is worth more than a passing thought. He has not for years past been known by his original name Degunbut Kanyap, but now answers to the more British name of Fred McGill.

Up to the time he was seven years of age he had never seen a white man. In the distance he had at odd times seen a whaling vessel beating its way up the bay, but he was not permitted to view it at close quarters. As soon as a vessel made its appearance, all the women and children went into the hills far from the coast, and the men only, fully armed, cautiously approached the beach to see the white men land to replenish their water barrels.

On such occasions communication between the white men and the Aboriginal men took place, and sometimes the white men gave their Aboriginal brothers bread and bacon. But these presents were for some years thrown away or buried as soon as the white men were out of sight. The bread was regarded as a vile slab of pipe clay, and the Aboriginal people did not want to eat unidentified meat.

McGill's early life was spent entirely in the Esperance Bay district, and there with his people he was as much a child of Nature as any of them. As soon as he was able to run about he had opportunities of seeing how his elders secured their daily food. Their food consisted chiefly of fish, ducks, young magpies, young crows, hawks, butcher birds, wallaby and kangaroo, all of which were at that time abundant in the district. The lagoons swarmed with ducks, and duck eggs being very plentiful, they also formed an important item in the menu. But the eggs of the magpies and other non-aquatic birds were left to hatch.

The ducks were systematically driven by the men into the narrow necks of the lagoon, where other people were ready to spear them, or kill them. The fish consisted mainly of mullet and whitebait in the streams and lagoons connected with them, and the method adopted for their capture was for a number of men to get into the water some distance apart and wade through the water, beating the water with sticks as they went. By this means the fish were startled, and they rushed off before the men until they found themselves entangled in the nets made of wiregrass, which were cunningly placed for their capture.

The fish when caught, were placed in vessels made of bark, and carried by women to the camp, where they were roasted in hot ashes. Occasional trips were made to the bay, where schnapper, groper, and other large fish were plentiful.

The method of catching these was different from that adopted for the smaller fish. The bait used for these large fish was crab or other large shellfish. These were broken up and dropped into the water off the rocks, on which were stationed the spearmen. In a little while the fish were thus enticed to come well in sight, when they were at once speared and dexterously landed. It was the aim of the hunters to spear these fish in the back of the neck, and if the spear struck the spot aimed for sudden death was the result.

Every now and then a raid would be made on the kangaroos, which were fairly plentiful, and McGill has a vivid recollection of the method's adopted for the capture of these quaint-looking animals.

In this the women took a very active part. The first thing to do was to ascertain the position of a herd of kangaroos, and that being done a cordon was quietly drawn round them by the women, who with torches soon had a wide ring of flame round the unsuspecting marsupials. Outside this ring of fire the men were stationed with their spears and waddies. By and by, when the smoke had mostly cleared off, and nothing left in the cordon but hot ashes and cinders, the women started off into the centre and with gesticulations and much yelling, drove the kangaroos outward towards the men.

Emus were often stalked and speared and the Aboriginal people considered them very good food. Ring-tailed possums were also regarded as a delicacy, and much ingenuity was often exhibited in their capture.

Of the vegetable food the Aboriginal people were able to obtain, the one most highly valued was the seed of the wattle tree. These seeds they called 'quannerts' and in the autumn they were able to gather large quantities of them. Seeds that were not required for immediate use were sewn up in kangaroo-skin bags, and reserved for later or saved for distant communities, who would be invited by message-stick to come and get them.

The mode of preparing these seeds was to spread them out on a stone and hold burning sticks over them until the husk cracked and peeled off. The seeds were then ground up between two stones and the ground seeds mixed with water into a stiff dough.

The dough was not cooked, but eaten at once, and was considered by the Aboriginal people to be a sustaining and palatable food.

The fruit of the Zamia palm, called by them "'quining," was also extensively used when it could be obtained. But the outside covering was used and not the kernel. After soaking the fruit for days to remove the toxins the quining was much relished.

A bulb reminiscent of an onion and known as a 'cockun' was another addition to their list of vegetables, as was the "jobuck". McGill describes the jobuck as a vegetable very like a potato and adds that to this day his people call potatoes "jobucks".   *...To be continued...*

Despite her enthusiastic and eloquent reading, Mr O'Hara had spent much of his time shushing the class and he could already see most were already restless and not particularly interested in hearing any more.

But Maggie hadn't noticed, and her reading had continued unabated. Well before she had finished she was already captivated by these exotic people, the Australian Aboriginals and as she read, she was transported by her imagination to the south land by the thought of Kanyap's peaceful life, of rich fishing grounds and of an abundant land.

But mostly, from that imaginary sail across the miles of sea and exotic lands, she was intrigued by the idea of the pioneer itself – of making something from nothing, of striking out alone. So a wide smile rested upon her lips for the remainder of the class, as she dreamed that she too may one day be a pioneer in this exotic, far away land.

Later, as she helped Mr O'Hara tidy up after the class had been dismissed, she pestered him if there was anything further she could read on the great southern land. As he always did, he of course relented to her pleas and allowed that she could take the newspaper home to read through the pages, and he promised to get more books and articles for her to read over the coming days.

Just as her body was changing, so too was her mind - expanding as she devoured the material her teacher presented; but as she read those pages over the following days, her earlier fascination had turned to concern. For as she scanned the letters and articles of the papers hoping for further stories, she had found no more references to the happy life of young Aboriginal boys, but rather a debate that raged as to the rights of the native people in Australia and the other lands of the British empire.

The consensus of opinion seemed to be that the British were unwelcomed invaders to those far off lands and should do everything in their ability to both co-exist and to acclimatise the natives to civilised and Christian ways.

She found a copy of Australia's own *Sydney Freeman's Journal* from some years earlier particularly concerning. The Freeman's Journal was disturbed by what it called "the systematic destruction of the Tasmanian Aborigines" in Van Diemen's Land and boldly wrote:

"England has far surpassed all other European nations in their attempts at colonizing distant and uncivilized regions for the last hundred years. Wherever England has undertaken this work of colonization, there the Aboriginal races, the Lords of the Soil, have almost totally disappeared in the course of a few generations!"

A naïve but inquiring mind, Maggie saw a hypocrisy in the author's very next statement:

"The only consideration to justify any State or Nation in seizing whole tracts of uncultivated lands occupied before by the rude children of Nature must be drawn from the fact of such state, undertaking by every reasonable means within its power, to improve the condition of those untutored beings whose natural inheritance they have thus usurped."

So that is, Maggie realised they were saying, *the English way was the <u>only</u> way and while decrying the destruction of a people in the name of England, it was all ok if those people are indoctrinated to become 'civilised'.*

More like them - less like they once were.

An inquiring mind, her teacher had again commented in response to her incessant questions on the topic over that fortnight. Perhaps it was exactly because her young and inquiring mind had not yet been constrained by convention, but Maggie saw hypocrisy in the words on those papers and nothing she read, nor the soothing words of Mr O'Hara himself, was able to redress her confusion and concern.

So feeling unsettled, she had resolved to ask her father what would become of the Aboriginal people. Her father, though schooled for only a few years at a hedge school was a balanced and philosophical man who had seen enough of the world of men to have opinions, and Maggie eagerly sought them out as a foundation upon which to build her own.

2

The Maguires

The Maguire family spoke proudly of their Irish roots, though they had few traditional links to County Louth. Rather, it seemed they hailed from Dublin and perhaps had spent much of their earlier time abroad in England, where James and Patrick had both attended exclusive schools. They were Protestant, and old Thomas spent much of his time supporting or involved in the Dundalk Corporation, an affiliation of local businessmen and English aristocracy.

Ireland was controlled by the minority Anglican Protestant Ascendancy via the Penal Laws, which discriminated against the majority Irish Catholic population. Mirroring other boroughs around the country, Dundalk Corporation was a 'closed shop', consisting of an electorate of freemen most of whom were absentee landlords. The Earl of Clanbrassil controlled the procedures for both the nomination of new freemen and the nomination of parliamentary candidates, therefore ensuring the local populace of Catholic workers were deprived of both the opportunity to have a say in their affairs, and the means to get ahead and ever earn that say. Indeed, many within the Corporation had lobbied against National Schools such as Mullaharlin, stating *the peasants were hard enough to control without getting an education*, which they reasoned would only stoke the flames of dissent.

Thomas Maguire had worked hard to position himself both as a freeman and as a wealthy and respected businessman. He had interests across the country, but over half his major assets were here in Louth where he owned many small farms and a half dozen large farms of around 15 acres, in addition to commercial properties and houses in the growing outer regions of Haggardstown and Blackrock. There was excellent soil in parts of Haggardstown and he received a particularly lucrative return from farm lots, in which he equally invested for improvements. He lectured to his sons "treat your tenants well and they'll work well for you – as the good book says, *so you shall reap as you shall sow*". His investments had indeed resulted in a higher yield, with some of his farms outperforming those of the absent landlords by nearly double for the land size.

But of course, he also ensured that his rents were equally high, and his tenants regularly struggled despite the bounty they produced. All of the tenants in the smaller farmlets took seasonal employment abroad or in the cities to get by, and relied heavily of what they could grow for their own food. The potato was a firm favourite, around sixty per cent of cropping in the district and almost exclusive on the farmlets, providing a cheap and rich source of nutrition for those poor families.

Today, as the fifteen-year-old Maggie contemplated the rights of the Indigenous people in lands around the world, the fifty-something year-old Thomas schemed to grow his family's wealth even further. He had organised a meeting in Dundalk of some of the minor freemen and Patrick Dare, a wealthy English merchant who was visiting to talk about exports from the area to Plymouth and beyond. Patrick had set himself a mission of ensuring a regular stream of potatoes and Haggardstown was well known for its healthy crop. He had singled out Thomas to arrange a consortium of landowners, promising a 25 per cent cut of nett profits if he could secure enough support to guarantee the volume needed. Of course, he was equally clear that the price of the potatoes would need to be set at 10 per cent below the local market, in return for which he would ensure full demand – a matter of both convenience and scale.

The meeting had proceeded over fine foods and wines, and by its end all three of the major landlords of Haggardstown had agreed to convert to potato production and force their tenants en-masse to cease other crops.

Thomas had worked hard to position the result in advance, and he was confident it would position his own family well for the future. Though some of the experienced farmers later expressed concern at the wisdom of a single-crop strategy, the ease and promise of income quickly convinced all of the merit of the 'Maguire-Dare Potato yield contract'.

Meanwhile, he had sent his son James off to collect the rent from the Blackrock tenants. He felt James was a good-natured young man, handsome and with a happier disposition than his older brother, Patrick, but lacking his 'instinct' and business acumen. He doubted he'd amount to much independently, though granted him an important role as his emissary - and to align with other interests.

He considered his handful of houses in Blackrock more as investment than an income, a hobby really, though of course again he ensured a sizeable profit through his rents. He saw great potential in the little seaside town as a holiday escape for the wealthy and had personally led a consortium to build a stone esplanade along the shore, which they expected would be followed soon enough by hotels and restaurants on the seaside land they now owned.

It was as a result of that venture that around a year ago he had first met a wealthy English Lord, John Fielding, who had specifically sought him out with a plan for a sizeable hotel as soon as the esplanade was complete. The two men had got along very well in fact, meeting several times over fine Irish whisky as they discussed progress of the esplanade and designs for the hotel, alongside a multitude of other plans and investments across the County. So they had discovered soon enough that they each had unwed children of around the same age, and jointly lamented that now in their late-20s, both should have been married off much earlier.

It only took a little more conversation, and a few more whiskies, to agree their youngsters James and Elizabeth should meet, and with God's blessing and good fortune that perhaps the families may be linked henceforth not just by land and business, but also by marriage.

3

Growth

Maggie's father was in the *Mary II*, a sturdy and large wooden boat with a bright calico sail that she could spot well out to sea. She had helped him build it just a year earlier and knew the boat almost as well as he. Previously he had relied on a much smaller 'currach', a simple boat crafted from reeds, canvas and tar which was only suitable for shorter distances. Mostly he still fished close by either in the curragh or a smaller row-boat and would be out for only the day. But in the *Mary II* he could stay out for two or even three days at a time, if the winds were right to take him towards the Isle of Man and the home of bigger and more exotic fish. He would store the fish and lobster he caught in well-smacks in the boat and they could last that way for a few days, while others he would clean and salt while still out to sea.

Maggie would occasionally go with him, though not as much as she would like to. He had taught her to fish, to sail, and to swim – *an important skill* he said, *if you want to spend time with the fishes but aren't yet a fish yeself!*

Her younger siblings were less interested in fishing and boats – preoccupied as they were with childish things. *All the better for me*, she thought, and the time and special bond with her father that this time provided carried her through the days without a thought for the hard and messy work she did when not at school.

And so, Maggie was her dad's 'little fish', and now as she ran towards the boat he thought to himself, though not for the first time, that this little fish was growing everyday. Maggie was 15, a pretty girl rapidly blossoming into a beautiful young woman and he saw how the eyes of the young men and those of men old enough to know better would follow her movements. She was so like her mother, Sarah, with her long curly brown locks bouncing around, her beautiful smile, and those stunning green eyes that demanded attention. But where Sarah fretted over money to pay each rent and agonised with the other women of the illnesses or misgiving of their children and half the town, Maggie seemed to float – nay, swim through emerging adulthood with a graceful indifference. She was innocent, yes - but he knew too she was something else – she was *smart*, and able to find her path. He prayed both she and the path she trod would never change.

So now, on the shore at high tide in the little town of Blackrock, he took a moment to watch her as she gazed with still-girlish happiness verging on joy at the haul of lobster and the several big fish he had brought home. She would closely inspect each fish as she placed them into the baskets kept above the tidal range, which she had dragged down to the boat.

She was amazed by a small sawfish, its line of jagged teeth lying parallel to its body on a long nose. He explained to her how this fish would thrash its head from side to side as it moved through a school of fish, tearing fish and then leisurely picking up the pieces and the now terminally slowed fish. He laughed as she imitated the action and before long he too was thrashing his head and laughing in joy in the gathering dusk.

Just as quickly, she changed tone and asked him once more about the articles she had been reading. He'd already had several short conversations with her in the past fortnight and knew she was still preoccupied by the colonies of Australia, and anxious about the Aboriginal people there.

"Pappy, one of the letters in the paper says it's wrong to take land that is already owned. But most of the letters say that the Aboriginal people have no right to land that is undeveloped!" she started, alarm present in her voice.

"And you're wondering which is right, Maggie?" he said, quickly picking up on the theme. "What right does any man have over another? But this is the way society works or so it seems – someone is always claiming their rights are more important than others, that they know more or better – that they *are* better. And while they'll bleat on about rights and equality quick enough they'll decide that their own situation is the exception and that those rights no longer apply for the others!" he replied.

"But we're all equal upon God's green earth Maggie. Greed for power and for money – that's what I've seen. Greed sits at the heart and blackens the souls of men."

"So, the Aboriginal people will lose their land..." Maggie reasoned, her eyes down-cast; her girlish exuberance replaced by descending worry, her smile no longer present. "But it's not right!" she exclaimed, her head raised and a defiance now burning in those bright green eyes.

"What's right and what's wrong are questions with answers only found between each of us and God, Maggie, though I'd wager how God might see it! But it seems to me that most people always want more than they have and much more than they need. Look at ol' Fergus there – he's brought in more fish than he can sell – it'll only drive the prices down for the rest of us and we'll all have to go out that bit further tomorrow.

I'll let you in on a little truth I've learned over my 40 years Maggie – with true wisdom, you learn how little you need, not how much.

But now for a 15-year-old girl, perhaps you shouldn't be so worried about things on the other side of the world at any rate."

So Maggie let the question lie unanswered, though it continued to haunt her for weeks ahead. Over time though she moved on to other subjects, inspired when Mr O'Hara passed on a new series on astronomy, and her thoughts literally turned to the sky.

Her father's worries were more mundane. His landlord's son was due to drop by and with luck he would take some fish in lieu of a week's rent. These he kept in a tub, while the others – a good catch – Maggie and he would clean and place on salt, and Sarah would sell to one of the mongers who frequented the town for the cities of Dublin and Belfast. He didn't expect much – Fergus and the others like him who took too much would see to that. But he would get what he considered a fair price for his days at sea. It would keep his wife and the children fed, housed and clothed for another week at least.

As he pondered such good fortune, Maggie happily and skilfully cleaned the fish he selected for her. She marvelled at the colours and each difference between the species – this one had a bigger mouth, that one a wider tail – and she wondered on their diets and how each had differences to suit. To the observer, she was a simple fisherman's daughter diligently going about her work, but in the world within – in that space behind our eyes where each of us dwell in private contemplation - she wondered at the very substance of life.

Nor was she ignorant to the looks and stares of the boys and men in her town. They didn't concern her, but she knew enough to steer clear of risky situations – certain places and company her mother had said she'd best avoid.

Indeed, the only boy she had found herself looking at was a young man one or two years her senior, himself a fisherman who even now was cleaning fish not 100 yards away. She'd noticed this young lad, Declan, before and now as he took off his blood and gut stained tunic, she certainly noticed him enough to take her mind off the fish at the end of her blade, and she very nearly sliced her finger. With a face that was handsome and fine, and a young body that showed off well-defined muscles as he lifted the weight of his catch, she surprised herself to find her mind no longer at the bottom of the sea, nor in the depths of space, but firmly right here, at the end of the beach in the small fishing town of Blackrock.

She quickly looked away before he or her father noticed, but his image remained. There was a quickening in her body as well as her mind, and she knew things were changing and would soon change forever.

4

James Maguire

James Maguire was a pleasant enough young man, and the O'Brien family knew him well and welcomed his visits, in as much as any Protestant landlord might be welcomed. He was the second son of old Thomas Maguire, a wealthy merchant and landlord of several properties in the Haggardstown area, including their own. The O'Brien's preferred it when James came by to collect the rent as he did this day, rather than his older brother Patrick or old Thomas himself. James at least made pleasant banter and nor did they feel belittled as they did with Thomas, or belittled and also somewhat intimidated as they did with Patrick.

James happily greeted John and Maggie as they walked up from the shore, past the area he knew was earmarked for the esplanade.

"Well hello there Mr O'Brien, and to you too young lady!"

He stole a look in young Maggie's eyes, though quickly diverted his thoughts to the mundane, and to O'Brien, the burly man looming over him.

"I see you've had a successful outing – those are lovely fish."

"As fine as any the North Sea turns out, young James" he replied politely. "Greetings to you. I trust your father and brother are well, and like yourself glowing with health?"

James knew his father and brother were not well liked by many tenants in the area, and actively promoted how he was different to ingratiate their loyalties.

"Ah, they'll be dreaming up some new scheme for the area no doubt, Mr O'Brien. All for the betterment of Haggardstown I'm sure. As for me, well yes, I feel in good health and I pray that you and your beautiful Sarah and Maggie are as well?" Maggie again glanced a shared look – she was not immune to such compliments.

But he didn't wait for a response – money was never far from his mind. "Now I'm sorry to get straight down to business Mr O'Brien, but I was just enquiring with your lovely wife as to the monthly rent and she said I should talk to you. She mentioned something of a fine large fish that I might like to grace the Maguire's table at the next business luncheon?"

"Oh, and did she now?" John replied, pleased Sarah had guessed at his plan. "Well I guess she may have referred to this fine sturgeon which Maggie had planned to prepare for our own table. But I'd be happy for it to grace your own family's table if indeed that is what you'd fancy, perhaps for a week's discount on that rent?"

"Ha, Mr O'Brien – always the negotiator!" James laughed. "But I appreciate that fish like rent does not come freely. I'll tell you what, send me back to Sarah with both those lovely fish cleaned and I'll discuss that sizeable discount with her."

John nodded, never doubting that outcome. It was a dance he played with James alone – old Mr Maguire was as soon to want the fish served to him in a swanky hotel as labour the thought of handling a wet and slimy fish. And his brother Patrick would insist that several more fish were warranted, and then go home to tell his father that the rents should be increased in Blackrock as they 'clearly have fish to spare'. But with James, he felt he had got a fair deal, and James meanwhile would be happy to have the servants prepare and cook the fish in a wine sauce for his father guests while he bragged of how he had secured not one but two fish for the measly cost of a quarter rent. At this, his brother Patrick would fail to suppress a grunt of disapproval; and his father might spend a moment more reflecting on how James would never negotiate real business deals, such as he himself had done so successfully today.

"Well now, I guess that seems fair" John conceded, assuming a somewhat beaten tone. "And seeing you've deprived us of both fish and our dinner tonight Mr Maguire, perhaps you might join us for some cake before you head home. We'd be pleased to share your company and news if you might spare some time?"

"A splendid idea!" Maguire quickly replied, stealing another quick look at Maggie, who had already started off to clean the fish. As she left he noticed the way she was filling her dress, before gulping back his gaze and leading Mr O'Brien back to his house with a guiding and gentle hand upon his shoulder.

Simple folk these Catholics he thought to himself. *Good, salt of the earth types but they wouldn't last under English rule without the likes of me, the Irish Protestant to prop them up.*

For this is the enduring burden of privilege in the 19th century he thought. *Superior men must always stand up for the interests of those lesser, who lack even the ability to know their own needs.*

Sarah quickly prepared the simple cake for the men and subtly passed an envelope containing three week's rent to James with his piece. She turned back to sort the main meal for John and the children as Maggie came back in and presented her the fish scaled, cleaned and wrapped with a little salt to further reduce any chance of contaminants on the ten-mile journey back to Dundalk.

"Well show young Mr Maguire!" Sarah exclaimed, loud enough to ensure the landlord's attention. "I've frankly seen enough to do without further acquaintance!"

So Maggie came to the table and proudly presented James her work with outstretched arms.

"Fine to be sure" James replied, though Maggie noticed he wasn't looking at the neatly presented fish at all. She blushed a little as she met his eyes with her own, but dismissed the attention just as she did with most of the men in Blackrock whenever she did an errand or indeed walked to school. James was already an old man in her eyes – 28 years and thus nearly double her own age. He did have a handsome face though, and he was always impeccably dressed... but she certainly didn't see him in the same wicked way as when she had glanced upon Declan earlier at the rocks.

"Well now, I have some other good news to tell you." James quickly changed the conversation so as to divert his eyes. "I'm very pleased to announce that I'm to be betrothed and will marry later this year to Elizabeth Fielding, she of the Fielding estate in Durham county and heir to some English title or another so it is said." He looked for Maggie's reaction then, and felt sure she had betrayed a slight blush. He continued with a smile: "Yes, this is good news for her family too as they are interested in investing in our own little town here in Blackrock through development of a hotel, for which their family are well known elsewhere. It may be some years off of course, but my father and her father are most excited by the prospect. I'm pleased to say I've had the honour of Ms Fielding's company, and I feel both blessed and happy."

"Well congratulations James!" Sarah exclaimed from the kitchen. "That is the best news I've heard for many a time." James was only a few years younger than she, and she was herself quite taken with his fine manners and pleasant appearance, transporting her to a life she had once wished - before she had met the strapping young John and forgotten all else. But sometimes she still longed secretly for fine dresses and foods, and in some small way had hoped that, perhaps, Maggie might have such things with a man such as James.

Maggie meanwhile looked awkwardly between James and her mother, and then to her father and back again as Sarah gracefully somehow turned the men's attention back towards each other. For Maggie had felt just a most distant sense of loss at James' announcement – perhaps an odd and unwelcome jealousy she realised – and she had blushed. Ashamed that she should both feel this way and more so that she should allow some visible outward sign, she turned quickly from the table and made her way back to her mother to help prepare the evening meal.

"Now Maggie, don't be so quick! Tell me what you've been learning at school" ventured Maguire, keen to keep her company for just a while longer. John had already recounted the strange conversation about the

Australian Aboriginals to him as they walked, and so he was prepared for the conversation.

"We've been learning about the antipodes, Mr Maguire" she replied politely.

"Australia?" he enquired. "Why, we have some relatives out there in a place called the Swan Colony, which is on the western side. It's a very new colony as it turns out. I was reading a letter from my Aunt Philomena just recently – a very interesting tale of the hardships of the early settlers there. Perhaps you'd like to read it?"

"Er, yes!" she said awkwardly, masking her excitement. "I would like that very much, thank you Mr Maguire. Mr O'Hara mentioned it in our class, and I should like very dearly to learn of this Swan place". She had again turned quickly towards the door, but remembering her manners turned back to James and her father. "And congratulations on your impending marriage good sir" she added with a curtsy, keen to reinforce that news like a screen before them. "May marriage bless you with happy children and a happy home" and with that she curtsied again, nearly tripping over herself in a hasty retreat.

James smiled to himself - another win today. He felt certain that earlier blush betrayed a tinge of jealousy for his news. However, he suppressed the thought of the beautiful Maggie O'Brien just as quickly. She was below him – a peasant Catholic - and clearly too young, and he was to be married to Elizabeth, a fine enough woman though herself in fact a year older than he and not nearly as striking as this pretty young girl he had seen bloom into a woman over the years.

Yes, he had always been pleased to collect the rents in Blackrock, and even now looked forward to his next visit.

5

A letter to home

Only a week later, James returned with the letter as promised. He was disappointed that Maggie had not yet returned from school, and so James passed it to her mother with the message that he "hopes Maggie enjoys a first-hand account of Western Australia, and that he would need to collect it soon and looked forward to discussing her thoughts on it then".

The letter was indeed of great interest, and Maggie devoured it in a single sitting.

13 December 1843

My Dearest brother Thomas

Thank you for your recent letter and news from our forever home and England. It is hard to believe that it is now over a decade since we were last there. I miss you and our family terribly, but I am now regretfully reconciled that the view of Dublin from our retreating ship shall be our last of that great land. The Swan River Colony is our new home now and we strive to make this place a little more like home everyday, in the hope that you or our fellowmen may join us soon. As you know, I was devastated to hear of our mother's death last year and though of course it was inevitable, it has reinforced the great distance between us.

I hope that one day, you or your boys may be able to visit us here at Toodyay Farm. Our farming community is east of Perth and Guildford, over the Darling Range that separates us from the coastal settlement. I have realised in writing this now that I have neglected to tell you much about this place, and so I would like to do so now in the hope that you will recall, there is a home here for you should you too ever find the pioneering spirit that so infected my husband Sean and I.

Though it wasn't immediately that way. We landed in Fremantle on 6 August 1833 and my first comment to Sean was that perhaps we should turn back, or continue on to Albany which is a more established town. Fremantle was a dreary and unkempt place, where dwellings and gardens were unruly and where many of the men seemed to be permanently drunk, or perhaps just stupid. But Sean was clear that we had come too far, and that the promise of this new land outweighed the inevitable hardships we must endure.

The town of Fremantle is situated behind a little promontory of limestone, at the mouth of a large estuary called Melville Water into which the Swan and Canning Rivers flow. These rivers allow inland navigation to a considerable distance, but the opening of Melville Water into the sea is so choked with rocks that it is only passable for boats in fine weather. Our boat therefore disembarked at a jetty in a small bay to the south of the town.

Fremantle resembles some of the little coastal villages on the limestone of county Durham, but it is even whiter than they, and it is greatly inconvenienced by the constant drifting of sand. The population in Fremantle was and remains today at about 200, all living in houses made of local limestone. Many of them have been left unfinished in consequence of the seat of Government having been removed to Perth, which is further up the river. These houses as well as those that are occupied are all going to decay, so you can imagine my initial dismay!

Much of the country around Fremantle is limestone covered with sand; it is unproductive of herbage and unlikely to yield anything for the support of a new colony, though with a little preparation it is said to yield good vegetables. In particular potatoes are excellent, and in some situations produce three crops in a year. Vines and figs also thrive, even in the town where the limestone rock is covered with little but soil fragments and sand.

Yet it is clear that industry is not great in Fremantle, and much of the land will yield nothing without it.

We took a walk on Arthurs Head, the promontory at the mouth of Melville Water, the top of which is rough, stony and covered with scrub. There we had some conversation with two people who have known much of the Colony from its settlement four years earlier, and who consider that it has now struggled through its first difficulties. One of them joked that he believed the whole population would have left it had they been able but were prevented by having invested their whole capital in it.

We proceeded to Perth in a passage boat which reached that place in about two hours thanks to a fine sea breeze. The sail up Melville Water was very pleasant, with a cooling breeze at our backs, the weather being hot. This estuary widens in many places into large bays. The limestone hills on its margin are covered with trees and scrub and are broken here and there into picturesque cliffs. There are several shoals one must be careful to avoid as navigation markers are yet to be installed, though in most places the water is both deep and wide. Numerous schools of fish were sporting in the sunshine, and multitudes of jellyfish of great beauty were floating just beneath the surface of the water.

We were greeted by the Acting Governor, Lieutenant Frederick Irwin and stayed in Perth for some days before surveying further upstream to Guildford and our allotted farmlands. Sean had acquired a very large allotment for a very small price via the English land titles office, and we made our initial home there with some success alongside our enduring friends Alfred and Elizabeth Waylen, before moving to Toodyay Farm where we have now been resident for a very good four, nearly five years.

At Perth, we became lodgers in the homely dwelling of the widow of a Colonial Surgeon, in whose house seven other persons were also resident. The bedrooms were without plaster on the walls, or glass in the windows, and fleas were numerous. But we of course gratefully acknowledged the endeavours of our landlady to do her best to accommodate her guests.

The town of Perth consists of several streets, in most of which there are as yet but few houses. Some of these, as well as the fences about the gardens, already appeared to be going to decay. The streets are of sand mixed with charcoal from repeated burning of the scrub which formerly covered the ground on which the town stands. The principal street has a raised causeway, slightly paved, by which the toil of wading through the grimy sand may be avoided.

Along the banks of the Swan there are narrow alluvial flats of good land that are chiefly cultivated with grain, sufficient to supply this little Colony. However many of the agriculturists being needy were obliged to sell their corn to the merchants, who appear to be a class of men ready to take every advantage to enrich themselves. This Colony suffers chiefly from selfishness and discord – perhaps even to a greater extent than the other Australian colonies.

Along with selfishness I might add alcohol is also a blight on the colony. Many labourers are paid one-third of their wages in spirits and the rest in credit at a shop that sells not much else but spirits. I was surprised to learn this was enabled through an Act of Council as common practice had previously been to allow workers two glasses of rum daily and said workers who had thus developed a strong appetite for stimulating liquors would frequently leave their work to instead go to a public house. The Act ensured this should only happen in their own time! We are amongst too few in the colony who pay our workers cash, but this pernicious law is still in force across Melville Waters.

A key problem of the colony we feel is that Holders of grants of from 5,000 to 100,000 acres have little stock of any kind upon them. Such grants are consequently of so little value that land is sold from as low as from one shilling and sixpence to two shillings and sixpence per acre! Had these settlers set aside funds to import sheep as did we ourselves, or perhaps had land grants been smaller, it is probable that land might now have been ten times its present value. Greed in obtaining grants that are too large have paralysed the country, which is not as fertile as it was presented.

Sean's decision for the family to move to Toodyay was ultimately a good one, though of initial great cost. Toodyay is in the York district, a grassy country beyond the Darling Range and upon the Avon River, which is identical with the Swan, and many of the settlers now have flocks of small size. However in driving our sheep and cattle from the Perth side of the Darling Range across that mountain territory, numbers of them were taken ill suddenly, and died almost immediately it is supposed from eating a species of Lobelia. Thankfully no accident of this kind has occurred in driving fat stock for sale from the better lands of the York district, to the inferior coast country. I am pleased to report that we now have possibly the largest flock of sheep in the Colony, around 800 head, and the whole stock of the colony is not more than 12,000. The whole of the sheep-country, thus far discovered, is computed to be able to support about 200,000 so there is great promise for production. East of the York district there is a great range of extremely sterile country, almost destitute of water upon which the Bush Turkey hatches its eggs in hillocks of sand. However, promising lands to both the south and north have recently been chartered and to which survey teams will soon depart.

And so dear Thomas, we are thriving relative to others, even as the Colony is too poor to import enough sheep to stock its extensive lands. Despite the hardships, there is great opportunity in this land, though so very far away from the green fields of Ireland in every way. I have presented here an open and honest account in the hope that some of our family so prepared may join us here one day soon, and assure a most hospitable welcome and our whole-hearted support in establishing your new home and new grazing lands for the colony! If I may I would also encourage you to mention this place to others in your circle and those so placed, that we might encourage the colony to grow and with it, the wealth of the many.

Your loving sister,
Philly

Maggie finally put the letter down two hours later, having read and reread the content and absorbed it to both head and heart. And so satiated, she finally went to bed and dreamed once more that she too may one day be a pioneer in this exotic, far away land.

6

Richard Williams (1844 -1848)

Richard Williams was in many ways both the product of English antipathy towards the poor and working classes, and the antithesis of it.

Richard was the younger son in a single parent family and felt the constant blame of his mother having died in his birth, thus sentencing both his father and older brother to become his carer even as they worked to survive.

Deprived of any support from both state and church, his father, Daniel, worked greater than 12 hours a day every day to raise him and his older brother, Robert. The family had at least received some charity in his early years, but the review of the English Poor Laws in 1834 had put paid to any inkling of both help and sympathy. That review had placed the blame for poverty firmly at the feet of those impoverished, and promised not only a withdrawal of any supports, meagre though they were, but also active punishment for any who disobeyed by providing charity. Those desperate for help were sent to workhouses, harsh and uncaring accommodation in which both spirits and backs were broken and in which countless died. Access to charity, it was said, had led men to become lazy and women to become immoral. So churches which once had at least provided clothing and meals now provided nothing but the cold stare of disapproval. Though in some ways this was better than the previous Act which placed the burden of charity on local parishes, and which had resulted in forcible removal of single mothers from their locale.

Daniel was a stonemason and builder who worked long hours on large projects throughout the Staffordshire district, and then for private clients when he could. He was a large man, caring and devoted to the memory of his late wife in bringing up their boys as best he could. But life was tough and getting worse with each passing year.

There was a time early on when he felt he couldn't go on – his beautiful young wife dying tragically in his arms as Richard came into the world and she exited his. She had held him up; her love and her cheer made the tribulations of life worth enduring. But then suddenly ripped from his life, for a time he felt he could no longer go on. For a time he drank away his sadness and hoped that each of his fights might be his last; that he too could be taken from this world and reunited with his loving and lovely bride. But in a moment he could only describe as 'miraculous', she had appeared before him one alcohol soaked night, just as clear as the day she had gone forever away, and told him that he had two boys to care for, and that he had best get on with the living lest face her wrath in death.

And so he and they had endured, and he had spent the last seventeen years working for their boys' futures, in the memory of a woman he loved and lost. Now in his mid-40s he realised he no longer had the stamina of the younger men, but he was still well-regarded by them and equally by his employer, whose clients sought him out on direct request and word-of-mouth recommendation. He knew he was good at his job, taking pride in seeing a finished product that would remain standing long after he had finally joined his beloved wife.

He would often do small jobs after work directly for clients in the Betley district, and these paid better than his meagre wages at the construction house, to the point where he dreamed that one day he could just do those jobs and quit the back-breaking tasks given him by his employer. Once his boys were settled, perhaps with wives and children of their own, he could join in the work of the church once more and while-away his days with only the occasional job to keep food on his table. His needs were small and once the boys were out of his hair, he could finally look forward to a simpler life.

Richard however shared little hope for the future, instead overwhelmed by the feeling of a great burden to pay back his father and brother, for an act in which he had no say, only to prove to them that he would repay that debt and support himself.

As a result, he was fiercely independent in both his intentions and actions. Little could sway him from his course, and he regularly said the words that were lacking in his mouth, through his fists. At 15 he was tall, strong and fit, and had a reputation as a fighter that ensured most kept clear of him. He regularly got into fights - he would win most even against men much older than he, and his brother Robert kept his skills honed with regular beatings. These fights were the most vicious of all, regularly involving weapons and he already bore the scars of a man well used to violence.

He had received only the most basic of education, expelled from school at 11 for fighting, and more recently apprenticed to a trade that his father had negotiated – Richard was to be a carpenter. This had caused upset to his brother Robert who felt deprived and jealous that he had not had the same privilege and had instead been forced to work in the coal mines, hard and filthy work that had hardened him beyond his years. When he wasn't working, Robert would often be causing trouble of some kind or another in the nearby large town of Stoke-on-Trent, and folk were wary of him.

But Richard was devoted to his father and brother with a fervour that mirrored the guilt upon which it was formed. Each beating from Robert was like a lesson in becoming a man, and he would smile stupidly even as his blood gushed from some open wound or another until Robert would eventually leave him alone in disgust. He had already worked diligently in his apprenticeship for nearly three years and hoped that in only a couple more years he would be able to find paid work with a local builder or perhaps a shipyard in the nearby coastal town of Liverpool.

In the meantime, while he drew a meagre allowance from his master he was dependant upon the incomes of his brother and father, so took on all the homely responsibilities to ensure a clean home and food for them. Indeed, he had assumed this domestic role for years now, and with increasing responsibility handed to him from his father, who was freed to do more paid work.

Richard's days were governed not by tide but by the guilt that came from his false childhood conviction that he was responsible for his mother's death and so must make amends. It engendered a great sense of sadness along with shame, and it occasionally emerged in anger. But the anger was never, ever directed to his father nor to his brother, despite the simmering resentment and outright terror to which he was sometimes subjected. Nowadays these times were more frequent when Robert had been drinking, but sometimes simply just when the opportunity presented itself. For Robert took a sense of delight in torturing his younger brother – a real resentment never far from the surface. Richard had the scars to prove a tough childhood; and the dedication of a man much older than his years.

Richard tried to keep to himself in between his work and home duties, though occasionally he would still see one or two friends. These lads he felt had not had it quite as easy as he. Arthur, a small red-headed and freckled lad ill-suited to the work had been taken on by his father as an apprentice blacksmith, while his other friend Peter worked in the mines and increasingly shared his brother's dim view of life. Peter was over six foot already and loved to drink, often with older boys including Richard's brother Robert, though he liked the quieter company of Richard and Arthur. The three of them would linger over a smoke if they could obtain a pouch of tobacco, or some beer and rum from the local when they could afford it and they would talk about the local girls and what was happening in their families.

It was in one of these conversations that Richard first heard about Australia – Peter's older brother had been convicted of an assault and sentenced to three years transportation.

"He punched his supervisor right square in the nose when he was told to work back after his shift was already done!" exclaimed Peter. "It was the third time in three days! Blimey, Dad reckons that was fair if stupid, but the supervisor had it in and pressed charges. Dad says that three years prison is a bit harsh."

Richard thought so too – in three years, he planned to have finished his trade and be earning a good salary.

"Still" Peter continued, "he says at least he'll be free to return when it's over, and that it's better'n sitting tight in the old hulk."

Confused in Richard's mind, Australia also became a large prison hulk, like the ones in Liverpool harbour that he had seen but much bigger and newer. In his mind, he pictured this massive ship perhaps a few days sail from Liverpool, out beyond Ireland even and perhaps somewhere near the Congo that he had heard about from his brother.

In his mind's eye, Australia then was just a large floating prison to which he had no desire to ever visit and which he hoped very much to avoid. The Congo on the other hand sounded like a place a young man could make his fortune, and he wondered if one day he might be able to go there.

All he knew of Ireland was that it was part of the English Empire but full of Catlicks and that thousands of them had made their way to Liverpool and even out to his little town of Betley, where they were resented by the locals for taking jobs from proper English folk.

The three boys only occasionally got up to any real mischief, but when they had a few too many drinks their loud and raucous laughter often attracted the attention of the police, known to the locals as 'the Peelers'. More than once, as they walked to the outskirts of the old town prowling for trouble, they'd scale a wall or two and pinch some juicy apple or orange to savour in quiet delight. Fresh fruit was a delicacy

Richard's family rarely got to enjoy. Richard would do small shopping trips to supplement his father's weekly trip to the market, but it was only ever the staples of flour, eggs, sugar and the like that they could afford, and he'd look longingly at a pile of apples or oranges in the market stalls with an unquenched desire. *One or two from the orchard wasn't going to hurt anyone* he reasoned.

But last year, as the boys groaned with juicy delight on one such occasion, they were caught quite literally red-handed by the orchard owner, Mr Patton, and three of his burly men. To Richard's great embarrassment, the boys were hauled up to the local Peelers.

They were given a fair hiding and locked in a cell overnight and his father came to collect him the next morning, much to Richard's disgrace. Luckily, because of his age they were all three let off with a warning: "We'll be watching you boys. Any more trips to the orchard and you might end up in the bum-end of the earth like Peter's no-hoper brother. Men have been sent away for less so don't think you won't be too".

Richard avoided walks by the orchards from that day on, though he still looked enviously at the fruit at the local grocery. But he had no intention of ending up at that floating prison out near Congo and worked doubly hard at his trade and domestics to reinforce the point.

And work he did – he loved making something useful from the shell of a fallen tree, and though much of his learning to date was focused on cutting and plaining the wood to the dimensions required by his master, he had watched carefully and learned well. He was precise with his joins and was already helping his master with design work for ornate pieces that would sell well in London and the big cities. He was sure that by the time his apprenticeship was complete, he'd already be a master turner.

He also liked talking to his father about stone masonry and accompanied him on jobs whenever he could. He knew the alignment that existed between the two trades and dreamed that he could perhaps even combine them in his future work – *that would really set me apart* he thought. His father, Daniel, wasn't as strong as he used to be, though he'd never admit it, and Richard would spend an hour or so on his way home to help with any physical tasks left to him.

In turn, Daniel appreciated his son's help and took great delight in seeing the boy fill out and rapidly become a man. He had a temperament more like his own, and a level head that reminded him of their mother - unlike his brother who he feared would fall foul of the law before long. *Yes, Richard often had scuffles and he'd been in the sights of the law there for a while, but he's knuckled down. In only a couple of years he'll be a qualified carpenter, and there is work aplenty.*

The years passed in Betley as Richard grew from boy to man. England entered a recession and the work dried up somewhat, making it even tougher for the family to get by. By 1848 there were lay-offs at the mine and Robert was one of the first to lose his job, predictable as he was not well regarded by his employers, reputed as a malingerer and troublemaker. Still, he had picked up other work and miraculously kept out of reach of the Peelers, though Daniel knew his trips to Trent-on-Stoke were becoming increasingly frequent and, he feared, nefarious. Robert would often come home with coin gained from some card game or fight, but there were other items too – a diamond ring, a necklace, a lady's silk purse... Daniel suspected these were ill-gotten, not won in a contest as Robert claimed.

The arguments between them became more frequent, and it was inevitable they would reach a crescendo.

That time came in late 1848, when Daniel was forced to take Robert to task when he learned he had dragged young Richard along on one of his 'ventures'.

"What were you thinking, you young fool?" Daniel started, subtlety never his strong point. "I know what you get up to with your scungy mates, though I'd rather not. I'm not as stupid as you might think, Robert. I've seen the things you bring home, and I hear the gossip. But you're a man now and you'll lie in the bed you make, filthy as it may be. But you'll not be dragging your brother in with you!"

"Oh your angel Richard!" Robert fairly screamed. "Things were fine before he came along; but still you behave like he's some sort of gift from heaven"

"You're both gifts, lad, don't you see? When your mother died, I was lost but it was caring for you both that brought me back to the path. You've hardened over the years, I don't know why, but Richard has promise – don't drag him into your den of thieves."

"Well I guess 12 hours down a mine each day since I was 11 will do that. All so I can support your precious Richard as he completes the apprenticeship I was never gifted. But don't fret, Richard is a coward and was an embarrassment to me – he turned tale when his moment came."

That confrontation six months ago had ended in blows, Daniel himself predictably losing both the fight and a tooth, and ultimately his son who stormed out in a huff. The now 21-year-old Robert had kept away since then, though they heard stories that he had moved to the dodgy parts of Liverpool where was drinking more frequently and involved in a gang.

The physical effects of that fight also seemed to speed the onset of Daniel's physical decline. Less than ten years ago Daniel had begun to notice the first signs and symptoms that he had dreaded would worsen – shortness of breath, a harsh dry cough – the onset of respiratory disease known to afflict stone masons and which had taken his father before him.

The symptoms had progressed over time, and though he had tried his best to hide them from his sons and work, his appearance and demeanour betrayed his worsening health and in the six months after the fight his state of ill-health had become clear to all. Approaching 50, he was regularly experiencing chest pain, throat hoarseness and he had begun coughing up blood. He increasingly had trouble sleeping and became ill-tempered and had lost his appetite and with it muscle mass –

and he knew that within years he too would go the way of his own father, though he had already outlasted him by several.

Richard had finally finished his apprenticeship and was sought after
by people in the industry, spurred along by Daniel's bragging tributes
and shameless recommendations. He wasn't earning much as a first-year
tradesman, but his income thankfully and for the first time in nearly 30
years allowed Daniel to reduce his hours, actually taking Sundays off to
join in church meetings and again socialise with neighbours and friends
gained over the years.

However Daniel's health had already reached a point of no return.
Within short months following his conflict with Robert he was unable
to do the harder physical work anymore, and although his employer
tried to keep him engaged with supervisory work, soon enough his de-
clining health robbed him of even that and he dragged out his days
around the house with only occasional work or income.

Richard did all he could to keep the house running, but between
work, domestics and caring for his father it became clear they were going
backwards. Although they owned their house, they could no longer afford amenities and food became harder to obtain and afford.

Now 17, Richard was a strong and capable young man, pursued by
the local girls. At over 6 foot he was taller than most, without an ounce
of fat and had developed a strong physique, musclier than even his father. He had long brown hair, brown eyes, a dark complexion and a
strikingly handsome face which ensured he was rarely without some girl
or other by his side, and was known to knock around with two or three
girls at a time. But relationships never lasted longer than a few weeks and
only on a couple of occasions got serious.

But around the time that Robert left and his father's health issues
worsened, he fell deeply in love with a girl around his own age. Perhaps it
was due in part to the troubles caused by Robert, but in addition to having a tremendous and shared sexual appetite, she was someone he felt he
could talk openly to, and he found himself craving her presence and dis-

cussing his troubles and future hopes more and more. Within months he was besotted.

As is sometimes the case, the same was unfortunately not true for her. She liked him enough, but where she had felt attracted to him by his physical appearance and stayed with him for both the envy of the other girls and for the fun and intimate times they shared, his constant talk now seemed to her like whining. As both his father's health and the family's financial situation further declined, so too did her attentions – there was a smell of decay about him, and Richard's increasing responsibilities were all too serious for the fun times she sought. She began to make excuses for not meeting him, and then one day – seemingly out of the blue for Richard – she declared she had met someone else.

Richard was devastated. He felt abandoned and alone, and from that experience came to mistrust all the women who came into his life, instead preferring to break off any relationship before it might blossom.

He was determined to never be hurt again, to never again share truly or deeply of himself.

7

Irish summer 1844

The days passed into weeks and the weeks to months in Blackrock; Maggie running between home and school, home and store; home and shore. She didn't spare a further thought for James, though Declan and she shared glances with increasing regularity – he always seemed to be nearby.

To her great embarrassment, one day she had quite literally ran into him while running a bucket of fish heads and guts back to shore. Declan had been sorting ropes and stood and turned too quickly for her headlong rush. He in bare chest and long pants, was to say striking in youthful vitality. Yet Maggie fair crashed into him and the bucket with fish offal spilled onto his chest, pants and her hair.

"Oh my dear lord!" she exclaimed in surprise. "I'd swear you weren't there two seconds ago and now you here you are, wearing my fish in place of your shirt!"

"Well that's fine enough Maggie O'Brien! Shouldn't make me smell much different, though the same might be said of you even without a fish eye sitting in your hair!"

"Ha, 'tis a fine bauble!" she joked, and awkwardly brushed her fingers through her hair. "But you wear it well – perhaps even an improvement I think it might!"

"Ah you'll make someone a great fish wife someday, Maggie. Your husband will smell no different from the sea like yourself, and the fish'll not see either of you coming. And anyway, tisn't just a fish's eye in your hair, but I see there are many others including me own over other parts of you!" Maggie was two parts shocked, three parts flattered by his impertinence, but it turned to embarrassment as Declan continued to explain himself: "You're comin' undone Miss O'Brien!" and he glanced down towards her midriff.

And Maggie looked down to find with some horror that her blouse had come undone from just below her breasts and her midriff and the curve of her bare breasts were showing to all the world, and right now to Declan who she had wanted more than anyone to impress. Her blush was vivid, as was her hurriedness to do up the buttons.

She turned in embarrassment and quickly started to leave, but Declan called her back. "Now don't you be worrying, I do believe you came undone in our collision and only I've had the pleasure of seeing your fine belly, which is how I'd like it to stay if you don't mind me saying Miss O'Brien."

Maggie's blush turned an even brighter shade of red, and Declan too flushed at his own indiscretion. And so he laughed and in an effort to make light of the situation showed off his own belly in a stance that showed his young body at its finest angle. *Perhaps it was deliberate* Maggie thought later. But either way that image stayed in her mind for some nights to come and when they next met, the spark was firmly ignited.

Meanwhile her studies both in and out of school continued with no less abandon. She learned from her teacher that several of the farms had diverted from grains and invested heavily in potato, which was a staple in her house as it was in most others. This triggered an interest in agriculture and she spent weeks reading books on cropping. She learned potatoes were a sound food crop and highly nutritious, though were mineral intensive in cropping and depleted the land in multiple rotations, particularly in early cycles. They were primarily a summer crop taking only weeks to form tubers and then a couple more weeks for the leaves to wither at which time they were ready for harvest. This meant that there could be three or even four harvests over the summer months and tubers would remain in the frosty ground ready for the next season.

But the low leaf cover also meant that cropping carried a constant risk of soil loss from ill-weather, while mistiming the cycles could lead to crop failure.

She learnt too that there had been a potato crop failure in the 1820s right here in County Louth and several others over the years, and that some of the farmers now shifting their crops exclusively to potato feared this might just as easily happen again. In 1844, newspapers also began to express concerns that a potato blight in America could spread to Ireland and Europe.

But it was the summer of 1844 and for a 15-year-old girl, things were good in Blackrock and County Louth. The future beckoned brightly and it was hard to imagine that anything could go wrong.

Almost impossible to imagine the tragedy that would befall County Louth and most of Ireland in the summer ahead, a time to be known forever more as 'The great famine'.

8

English struggles, 1849

It was twelve months after Robert had left, and Richard and Daniel were struggling to keep afloat. Daniel's health had deteriorated rapidly and he spent most days in bed or barely dragging himself out to do some small amount of housework. Thankfully, some parishioners had realised what was going on and would pop by to help and to chat, but Richard carried the full burden of caring for his father and maintaining and running the house through his small income. He worked tirelessly, often 12 hours a day and also made items of furniture for sale when he wasn't working – beautiful pieces that at other times would fetch a good price, however the overall state of the economy meant demand was poor.

On one of the rare occasions that allowed him some time for socialising, he met up with Peter and Arthur and the three of them enjoyed an afternoon of too much beer and rum.

"Cor, look at those!" Arthur exclaimed, pointing shamelessly at a girl, barely 16, who hurriedly crossed the road and rushed to get away from the now drunken louts.

"Steady on, Arfur!" Richard drawled and staggered to his feet to perform a clumsy bow. "Pardon my young friend dear lady – I do believe he's drunk! Perhaps come join us so I can show you not all of us are quite so uncouth!"

Peter roared with laughter, but as he stood up to join in the bow lost his balance and crashed over the table, sending glasses everywhere.

"Right, you're out" boomed a voice behind them, and they turned to see the proprietor pointing the way.

"Sorry, Mr Warren" Peter half said, half laughed. "Put it on my ledger!" and the lads got up and left without further hesitation – no one wanted to be banned from Mr Warren's tavern.

"What ledger are you talking about?" laughed Richard as they got out of earshot.

"Well I ain't got one yet, but hopefully he'll at least start one now!" and the three of them again roared with laughter.

"Right then" announced Arthur with a sharp clap of his hands as they started to walk. "I reckon I'm feeling like a couple of juicy apples me self – any you buggers game to join me?"

And the boys were both stupid and drunk enough to agree.

They walked to the edge of town, laughing and joking as they went. When they reached the walls of Patton's orchard, it was Richard who first scaled the wall, taking only a moment to check that nobody was watching.

They revelled in juicy apples and chatted about the months since they had last been here. All of the boys' families were struggling from the effects of the recession.

"Gotta admit it's been real tough for us too" Richard said when his turn came. "Dad's not well, and there's no sign of Robert. Dad reckons he's joined a gang in Liverpool and will end up in big trouble soon enough. I'm tryin' me best but I ain't earning much, and Dad's on his last bloody legs I reckon!"

The mood became sombre, so Arthur quickly changed the tone "Least you got your dad's back" he said. "My old man clipped me over the ear the other day and told me I wouldn't even make a blacksmith's butler!" and the boys laughed. "Thing is, he's right of course!" Arthur's continuing small size stood in stark contrast to his father's burly stature, borne of 20 plus years of metal work.

"Ah, you'll get there, squirt!" Peter said and patted the smaller lad patronisingly on the head. Arthur knew this was a term of endearment shared by the three, but which from any other man would be considered an insult – equally to Richard and Peter. Nonetheless he feigned insult and jumped on Peter, making a commotion.

Just then, Richard heard a faint noise and hastened the lads to keep quiet. Seconds later they heard hushed voices that sounded not too far away and rapidly approaching, and without hesitation the three were up and over the wall and sprinting to safety.

They laughed and joked at their near escape – no doubt the owner and his men had thought they had an easy catch. But as they rounded the corner, there were the four men standing before them, wielding weapons.

"You're nicked!" exclaimed Mr Patton.

"What are you talking about?" replied Arthur as he stepped forward to brush past them.

"Not so innocent we think" said the larger of the three goons, grabbing Arthur by the arm and flinging him back to the group.

"Back off you great tosser" said Peter and stepped forward, ready for the fight which now seemed imminent.

One of the other two swung hard at him with an iron bar, but the street hardened Peter deftly side-stepped and the man's wild assault found no target.

Richard, who was studying the situation from the back of the group, quickly weighed up the options. The three men were altogether too large to take on in a fair fight with just Peter to provide any real support, but Richard had already spotted a weakness in the largest of them from the way he threw Arthur – he favoured his left leg and Richard saw now that he had a visible limp in his right leg.

"Peter – go right. Arthur take the boss" he whispered, and with a confidence won from many fights he deftly stepped up to the large man then dropped quickly as the man rounded to swing, kicking out his right leg in a swift and seamless movement that brought him crashing down. In the next moment Richard was back on his feet and with two quick punches, the third man who had been silent before now was also down, gasping for air from a solid punch to his gut. The large man was trying to get up, but Richard was quicker and even as his second punch landed, he used the forward momentum to continue with a well-aimed stomp, yielding an audible crunch as bones in the large man's right hand were broken. Richard followed through with a well-placed knee to his head and the large man was down and out – mere seconds into the fight.

Meanwhile, following Richard's lead Peter was engaged in a fist fight with the remaining thug to the right who wielded a knife, and Arthur had leapt forward as instructed and had Mr Patton in a head-lock – his arms strong from hours of blacksmithing it seemed, even though they lacked the brawn of his father.

The third man was regaining his breath and Richard could see was acting irrationally – a dangerous condition in an equal fight, but one that gave an immediate advantage to an opponent who could keep calm and look for the opening that would appear. He rushed at Richard with abandon, and much to Arthur's concern took Richard down in his headlong anger. But somehow, by the time they were on the ground it was Richard who was on top, having used the momentum to swing the man's greater weight around, and the thug met the pavement with a nasty thump, leaving him bloody and dazed as Richard himself rolled back to his feet in a fluid movement. The thug unwisely stood back up moments later, and Richard responded with one final, quick and precise jab that broke his nose and landed him on the first man, who still lay grasping his broken hand and groaning on the ground, the weight removing any hope of getting back up.

Peter's attacker, seeing the two others now down for the count and his boss pathetically struggling in Arthur's iron embrace, wisely stepped back as he saw the large and strong Richard ominously turn towards him. "Boo" said Richard and the man dropped his knife and held up his hands in a conciliatory motion, as if to say the fight were no longer fair. The moment of hesitation was all Peter needed to land a well-aimed blow to the gut, followed by a left hook and right uppercut that crashed the man unconscious on to the pile.

Arthur loosened his grip on the old and fat Mr Patton, allowing him to survey the situation which had clearly not gone the way he'd imagined.

But he was still defiant. "Why you little thugs! I know you stole my apples - you'll get your comeuppance!"

"Like I was about to say, Mr Patton - don't know what you're talking about" said Arthur, releasing him now from the grip. "We're just out for a walk."

"And anyways we wanted to thank you for the last time we were here – don't you remember us?" added Peter with a menacing tone to his voice.

"We was just 15, and you sent us up the Peelers without a second thought, and we coped a right hiding for the sake of a few of your precious apples. But we're not so helpless anymore, are we Mr Patton?" and he gestured toward the pile of his fieldhands. "All growed up like, you see, and we're not going on up that way again, are we? So we wanted to thank you for doing the right thing now that you didn't back then, and instead just going back to your comfortable home and your fat ol' wife and fat little children... maybe get these three seen to first mind – and don't even think about callin' the Peelers, right?"

"Why you..." stammered Mr Patton, already making his retreat.

"Coz, Mr Patton" Richard stepped forward "you'll not be wanting to see us again, right?" and his icy tone made Patton's blood run cold.

"Well, you just make sure that's the case!" he stammered, and as he turned to make a hasty retreat he stumbled and almost tripped as he rounded the corner and headed towards the gate back to his property.

"Ha!" Arthur laughed after him, though Peter and Richard supressed their laughter.

"We'll not be having any more trouble from him thanks to you!" said Peter as he turned toward Richard. "Where in God's name did you learn to fight like that!" and the boys made their way back towards home, laughing and joking as they went.

9

The Great Famine, 1845-51

Things in Ireland had taken a dramatic turn for the worse.

As the first potatoes of 1845 were pulled from the ground, it was immediately clear that a dreaded blight had taken hold. The crop that had done so well had developed a fungus that had spread rapidly across the nation from potatoes imported from America, just as Maggie had read.

Where once there were fields of productive land, now there were barren fields.

Potatoes had been a reliable and cheap source of nutrition for much of the Irish population for decades, and the failure of nearly half the crop that year was devastating. Many Irish lived on small plots and potatoes were the only thing they could grow that provided the nutritional mix needed for their families. In the countryside farms and townships, emerging poverty and starvation was palpable as increasingly, the weakest, the oldest and the poorest began to die.

Yet the bulk of the wealthy, residing mainly in the cities of Dublin and Belfast, hardly noticed the impact of crop failure, at least during that first year. Also unnoticed were the pleas of the farmers and all those across the country who sought relief from the Government. The English government were in some ways unaware of what was going on - the Lords were both distant and indifferent – but the Poor Laws ensured that little support would be forthcoming. One hundred thousand pounds worth of largely inedible maize, and a program of public works was all the help that came from England between 1845 and 1847, at which time it was already far too late.

When over half of the crop again failed in 1846 and then 1847, the sustained losses were devastating. While there was a merciful respite in 1848 as the crops returned, the blight returned in full swing in 1849.

"It's like throwing a rope to a drowning man and then snatching that rope away as he reached the boat" Maggie overheard her father saying, with tears burning in his eyes.

The Irish came to know this time as 'An Drochshaol' – The Hard Times - but in truth this was an understatement. Over the seven years of 1845-1851, over a million people died and simultaneously the era known as 'The Great Migration' began, with over two million people leaving Ireland for greener pastures.

The population was reduced by a quarter as the Irish left their island in droves. First the richer landowners who could still afford travel, and then the poor who may only have had enough to sail to England, Scotland and Wales. In arguably the darkest year, 'Black '47', three hundred thousand left for the nearer British Isles; one hundred thousand went to Canada; and over a million went to the United States.

Tens of thousands also migrated to far away Australia, with the effect that by 1871 the Irish accounted for one-quarter of all foreign-born settlers, half a planet away on the opposite side of the world. One in six did not survive the crossing - about the same odds of surviving the famine.

For fishing families like Maggie's, the loss of the staple potato affected nutrition but more so it disrupted commerce and trade across the nation. While fish were in plentiful supply, the family struggled as merchants put up the prices of other goods in the demand vacuum created by the potato, and yet the prices fishing folk gained remained the same.

Maggie had finished school and had taken a job with the Maguire family, arranged through James' direct petition. She gave all the proceeds to her mammy, and it made that bit of extra difference so that the family continued to manage, hard as it was. She would often see James when she worked at the manor, and occasionally also his new wife, Elizabeth. On these occasions James would give her a cheery smile and the couple would continue on their way, chatting about one purchase or another or some upcoming holiday. When he was alone however he would always find time to stop and enquire after her and her family.

So Maggie's family struggled through the Hard Times, but in the realisation they were far better off than many in the County and their friends and relatives across Ireland. Fish produce increased in demand, but not in price as the markets John traded in were typically linked to those least affected by the famine. As is so often the case, the famine was felt hardest by the poorest and weakest, particularly affecting country and farming folk and simultaneous as England entered a recession.

Maggie's family helped out their farming neighbours wherever they could by providing any excess fish to those families needing them most, and increasingly families would turn up at the rocks hoping for help, having already scoured the shores for whelks and any other kind of shellfish or edible seaweed. Ironically of course, the English Poor Laws meant that they would be breaking the law if they gave these fish openly, and so Maggie would 'accidentally' leave some fish behind as she cleaned them.

The family was both saddened and spurred on to help their neighbours whenever and wherever they could. Though the family wasn't in a position to do much more, at the local market she and her mother would often slip in an extra fish or ensure a larger portion than charged to those they could see were suffering. But as the famine escalated, Maggie was horrified to see that people now would lurk and await the discarded fish remains they left behind at the rocks. She saw firsthand that many people got ill from this, and they heard that people had even died. Those poor people had little thought for hygiene, ripping into the guts and bone equally as they would the fish flesh they left behind. Soon enough Inspectors were posted to the docks to stamp out these acts of 'charity', under the added priority that the practice was not only dangerous to the moral health of the poor, but also to their physical health.

"Not that they care enough about the Irish to provide food, nor fret at their health as they lie dying of starvation..." muttered John, and

Maggie began to see the ember of dissent grow in her otherwise cheery father. "All the help the Irish get is Peel's brimstone and unaffordable bread!"

It was inevitable this flame would catch and grow in the Irish population. In many ways, as the famine worsened England's bad policy decisions did indeed make the crisis worse. For one, there was unquavering belief in 'laissez-faire' government – that the government should not interfere in the free market - and so trade policies continued with no thought to the condition of the local population. Angering the impoverished most was that grain and other food exports continued to leave Ireland with no attempt by the British government to first feed the locals. Food was still available at market, though at three times last year's prices.

Beyond this though was a belief, enshrined in the Poor Laws, that the poor were responsible for their own misfortune. So in July 1846, the newly elected Whig government stopped all relief, leaving hundreds of thousands of people without access to work, money, or food. However within weeks, as the poor streamed into the remaining filthy and disease ridden workhouses, Russell's government hastily backtracked and introduced a programme of public works which had already employed some half a million people by the end of that year.

Thus began the year remembered forever as *Black '47*, arguably the worst of 'An Drochshaol', the seven dreadful years of The Great Famine. The public works introduced hastily in the previous year quickly proved impossible to administer, with the multitudes of starving now forced to work on un-needed roads and fences, outdoors and in the horrible winter of 1846/47 there were many deaths attributable to what was clearly bungling mismanagement.

And so in the spring of 1847 these public works were stopped altogether and to continue to receive any form of relief the poor were instructed to travel many miles in bad weather - of course large numbers perished along the way.

Eventually realising the extent of the problem, the government reverted to a mixture of "indoor" and "outdoor" relief through Poor Law workhouses and soup kitchens - but it was too little too late. Protestant church groups such as the Quakers ran the soup kitchens and while providing much needed help, it often came with 'strings attached'. In some cases, children were offered haven in mission schools in return for their re-education under Protestantism. Often, many refused soup because of these abuses, and as few as those abuses may have been, those who did take soup were called "soupers", and the name remained in use for over a century, being those Catholics prepared to forsake their faith to get ahead.

Such was the volume and cost of the relief effort that in June 1847 the Poor Law Amendment Act was passed which forced the costs on to Landlords through increased rates and taxes based on the number of tenants, rather than the rent received - the principle as stated by the British aristocracy was that *Irish property must support Irish poverty.* The English newspapers reported at the time: "*Britain has permitted in Ireland a mass of poverty, disaffection, and degradation without parallel in the world. It has allowed proprietors to suck the very life- blood of that wretched race*".

These amendments thus presupposed that it was greedy landlords who had created the conditions that led to the famine, and so landlords themselves must contribute to the solution. It was a radical repositioning, for the first time saying that wealthy landlords were at fault rather than the down-trodden poor - but of course it was also a convenient blame that protected the wealthy English merchants and others who were profiteering from the misery of Ireland's countryside.

The Amendment achieved little for the poor and starving – to the contrary it resulted in hundreds of thousands now becoming homeless. As tenants were no longer able to pay rent, and the land taxes were now based on occupation and not income, the simple method of choice to reduce Landlord tax was tenant eviction. Further, the Amendment prohibited a tenant who held more than a quarter acre of land from receiving relief. In practice, this meant that small farmers were forced to break lease and deliver up all their land to the landlord before being able to receive any relief. This resulted in nearly 200,000 small landholders being forced to resume their holdings to their landlords, and plots under 5 acres dropped to one third their pre-famine number while those of 30 acres or more tripled in count.

Rather than providing relief, there were now hundreds or thousands of both starving *and* homeless Irish.

In contrast, the calls for action from the Irish themselves were simple enough: open Irish ports to foreign produce; and retain Irish produced foodstuffs for local consumption before export - just as the Dublin parliament had successfully done during the food shortages of the 1780s.

But with their policies of laissez-faire government, the English of course continued to ignore this plea and so the call for help grew into a shout for Irish sovereignty. During the early 1840s, the movement to win political independence for Ireland by repealing the Act of Union was already in full swing under Daniel O'Connell, who had harnessed a mass movement of farmers, artisans, and the clergy that the London press labelled The Young Irish. Following the outbreak of the Great Famine in 1845, a radicalized Young Ireland parted ways with O'Connell's constitutional approach to Repeal, and anti-imperialism was a common theme in the columns of their newspaper. The Irish came to hate the English.

Against this backdrop, Haggardstown suffered but weathered better than other parts of the country. It at least had the fishing industry to fall back on, and many of the farms continued to grow crops that were in high demand. The broader County was spared the worst effects of the Great Famine through cereal-based agriculture, new industries, construction projects, and the arrival of the railway. Nevertheless, so many people died in the Dundalk Union Workhouse that the graveyard was quickly filled and a second graveyard was opened which is known to contain over 4,000 bodies from that time.

However, the Maguire farms and those of the aligned landlords faced insurmountable odds and the planned Dare-Maguire potato empire ultimately failed. Their 1845 crop was always going to be lean with so much of the land turned over only recently to potatoes, but the losses sustained were 'uncomfortable' to Maguire and as the blight continued into its second and subsequent years, Thomas reluctantly came to accept that his potato empire may not eventuate, perhaps even for many years yet to come.

Yet although the plans had failed and the Maguire family income thus affected by reduced and breached rents, it was still manageable to the family. Fortunately the plans had only barely begun, and they had a number of other interests and assets outside of potatoes and the handful of big farms to fall back on. As is the standard for hard times it was the farmer tenants on the Maguire properties who bore the brunt of the burden of the Hard Times, while the rich continued on their way. The Poor Laws prohibited his charity, but Thomas Maguire initially reduced rents and supported able-bodied family members to find other work in his business empire. Generous sole that he was, he of course could only offer wages half that of his other staff, some of which were sacked shortly afterwards - and the wages were at any rate returned to him as rent.

But as the famine drew on into Black '47 and as the Poor Law Amendments came into effect, some of his tenants were no longer able to even afford the rent, and so Maguire began the unusual practice of 'sponsoring' some of the younger men and women in these family to emigrate, under the expectation that they would pay him back when able. Others in the Dundalk Corporation scoffed at the practice, and many of the absentee English landowner members were far less caring for the suffering of their long-term tenants, choosing eviction as their first and only course of response. For them, the Poor Law amendments meant that leaving them in situ would only cost money they did not have, with tenants now unable to afford rent. They would prefer to leave the land vacant and fallow, waiting for better days.

For Thomas Maguire however, cool logic suggested that sponsored emigration would serve to reduce his land taxes and to support his struggling families for whom he did genuinely care – a 'win/win' as he explained to his boys, although Patrick was clearly unconvinced. Thankfully the crop of 1848 was sound and his decision to not evict provided much needed relief and income to all, but in the following year the blight was back and reluctantly, Maguire also began to evict smaller tenants and resume their land.

It is said that the best of businessmen make money regardless of the direction of the market, and so it was for Thomas Maguire's family, despite those lean years. With a mix of good planning and good luck, the family's fortune was maintained and progressively surpassed those of his rivals. Even early on Thomas knew he could sustain the losses, and he schemed to benefit – one of his two business partners, a fellow Irishman by the name of O'Shaughnessy, was too heavily invested in the potato contract and by the end of 1845 was already showing clear signs of financial distress. Thomas cooly waited for the right time to make an offer to buy him out – at a quarter of the price he paid for his own land of course – to alleviate the poor man's suffering.

And to his great happiness, he found by as early as 1848 that his practice of supported emigration was providing a significant return - many of these former tenants were now drawing good wages in their new homes and returning significant sums to their Irish relatives, who in turn were now again able to pay rent and remain on their plots. Similarly, due to the Poor Law Amendments he was able to combine the smaller holdings of many evicted tenants into single larger and more viable farms, which at Patrick's prompting he progressively turned over to cattle.

Thus, although the Potato empire had failed to eventuate through unpredictable changes in the environment, by 1852 and as the famine finally ended, the Maguire family were in much the same financial situation as they had been in 1844, while many others in the Corporation were markedly worse off. Indeed, the family now owned even more land aided by the discount purchase of O'Shaughnessy's land, and their wealth grew as they pioneered the creation of amalgamated lots to create cattle farms across the county.

10

A plan for James

Inspired by the successes of those young Irish tenants he had supported to emigrate, Thomas schemed a new plan for his son James. While Patrick had become increasingly involved in the family's interests, successfully modernising land holdings through conversion to cattle production, James and his wife Elizabeth had swanned through the Hard Times with long holidays abroad at her family's estates. While James had assumed the lead role in progressing plans for Blackrock's new hotel, the famine had inevitably postponed commencement and so, as he reflected, Thomas came increasingly to believe Patrick should take the reins while James should take on a whole new venture.

And while Patrick and his wife already had three healthy young children from their four years of marriage, both families were disappointed that James and Elizabeth had still failed to produce any children after three years, and feared that time would run out with Elizabeth's advancing age – Elizabeth was already in her early 30's.

The fathers continued the healthy respect and regard from those years earlier, and over dinner and several bottles of French wine one evening on a glorious Dundalk evening in the Autumn 1849, they found themselves discussing Thomas' success with supported migration and the tremendous potential that the new world held.

It was soon suggested that their offspring would be well suited to extended travel and could cement both families' fortunes in the new world, while perhaps also forcing the two closer together. Thomas relayed the stories of his sister in the Swan Colony, Australia, and Elizabeth's father was suitably impressed; and as easily as that it was agreed that James and Elizabeth should travel to Western Australia for a period to speculate on property and other interests as may emerge.

Once agreed, correspondence was made with the Maguire relatives, and the plan shared with James and Elizabeth in due course.

Their initial response was one of acute alarm and they expressed their dismay in no uncertain terms, particularly Elizabeth who was used to the finer things of life and not at all convinced this would be continued in the undeveloped antipodes.

But they were eventually convinced that it would only be for a short while and was both a great adventure and an important venture to secure both families' fortunes in the new world.

Further, to sweeten the deal old Mr Maguire suggested and it was hastily agreed that young Maggie O'Brien should be released from the household and 'invited' to join them on their voyage as their servant.

"She shall be a great support to Elizabeth." James nodded sagely, rising to leave as he tried to muffle his glee. "I shall speak with her and her parents when the time is right."

Thomas nodded his agreement as James left the room, but Mrs McGuire bid Elizabeth to stay – there were still important plans to be made.

"Now Elizabeth" continued old Mr Maguire, "we have of course discussed the matter with your parents and have their wholehearted support. But they stressed that is conditional that you should agree to this great adventure. You shall arrive in the Swan River Colony which is a developing though still very small town, and while we hope you may find some minor investments there, it is in the North that we are most interested in investing.

You see, we have in mind that James should travel to areas to the north of the Swan River Colony where my dear sister Philomena feels there is promise for vast grazing lands. We should very much like to extend our holdings and install tenants to grow cattle for export, and where it is viable also suitable crops for local consumption."

He hesitated a moment before more firmly broaching the issue of grandchildren. "So you understand, Elizabeth, that it shan't always be a comfortable expedition, should you, ah, become 'indisposed'. We feel this may be too much for your, ah, delicacies, and should it perhaps be necessary that you may need to curtail your travels – that is, if the timing is right, we wish you to know that our family in the colony will ensure your comfort for the short period James travels north."

Seizing her moment, Mrs Maguire, until now a passive observer interjected "What my dear husband is trying somewhat clumsily to say, Elizabeth, is that we must also enquire of you as to your intentions, and I ask on behalf of both families you understand... A delicate subject I'm afraid... but I must be frank... We wonder at our grandchildren you see."

"Oh my!" stammered Elizabeth, embarrassed to be discussing such a thing with her parents-in-law. "Well it's just not happened yet, I'm afraid. I can't explain it. But I'm sure with God's good grace I shall produce child one day! Perhaps the sea air and Australia's green fields will act in our aid?"

But the truth was, Elizabeth had avoided any chance of falling pregnant these past three years. She disliked sex with James, finding it awkward and ensuring it was minimised to those times she knew she was not ovulating, and sufficient only to provide such services as a good wife should, or so she had been told. At other times, she lied to James that she was 'having her period'. The inexperienced James didn't know any better, and though he wanted children, in truth his own experiences with Elizabeth were at best 'stilted' too – it felt like a transaction, a mechanical act devoid of any real emotion, and he found with some shame that he didn't lust after her attentions. They did enjoy travelling and parties together and could even be described as 'friends' he thought; but they spent most of their time either apart, or surrounded by others.

It was in truth little more than a marriage of convenience brokered by their parents, and though neither of them were resentful, their relationship felt more like a cordial business transaction through every exchanged word and each time they lay together, than the affair of passion that James craved.

Arrangements commenced for their travel in the spring of the following year, 1850. James was given a total 5000 pounds from both families – close to a million dollars in today's currency and sufficient to buy a good amount of land to the north and to make initial improvements before installing tenant managers. He was also authorised to make 'promissory notes' back to his father as soon as other suitable lands were identified.

But all involved had seriously underestimated the vast distances and time involved in the endeavour. Used to thinking of the travel between regions of the Irish and British Isles – from Dundalk to Durham for example being a comfortable two-day journey – they all miscalculated that the entire adventure to Western Australia would take less than a year.

11

Wisdom

Late in the autumn of 1849, James returned Maggie to her Black-rock home as he often did, arriving as the family sat down for supper. Naturally, James was invited to stay and gratefully accepted. Though the food was humble, he greatly enjoyed John's conversation and Sarah's attentions and hospitality, and it gave him a chance to spend further time with Maggie, for whom he had developed a deep fondness.

Tonight though he had a most important matter to discuss with both Maggie and her parents.

Maggie was now 18 years old and had worked in his employ for nearly three years, taking on increasing responsibilities. His father too had been particularly pleased with Maggie, both her beautiful face that cheered up the place, but also her clear intelligence and capability and he had also grown fond of her, seeing a potential role perhaps as head of domestics or even a business proprietor, though a most unusual role for a woman.

As they finished their light supper, the younger children were excused and James asked if Maggie might stay on to join in more "adult conversation, some of which concerns her".

The conversation turned to the famine and the great despair of the Irish people.

"It's been tough for our family too, though we have no doubt that our own situation cannot be compared to those of the poor folk" James said. "You know, one of the young children in our tenancy up Dunbin way died just last week, the third in that wretched family" he relayed, genuinely upset as he talked of tenants who had become friends over the years. "We've done what we could for them and other tenants over the years of course as you also know, helping their family with paying their rent through other work, as has been the case also for young Maggie here – and to which our family are equally grateful as her help is fine indeed" he flashed a smile her way, and she quickly averted her eyes and blushed.

"But the Government have changed their policy you see, and landowners such as my father are asked to shoulder the cost of charity to pay for the horrid workhouses and soup kitchens, through increased tariffs you see..."

John and Sarah suspected this conversation was leading to an announcement that their rent would go up and shifted uneasily in their seats – another increase could cripple them. Sarah knew too that John had become increasingly angry and outspoken about the British, even attending rallies of O'Connell's The Young Irish. One of the O'Connell's policy demands was that landlords should in fact *reduce* rents in lieu of improvements made by their tenants – a topic not likely to sit well with young James.

"I heard a saying about the British and the famine last week that I think runs true" Sarah quickly chimed in, hoping to find the common enemy lest John should rise up and insult the handsome young man. "T'was in the paper and Maggie relayed it to me – oh, I've forgotten it now... how did the saying go love?"

"*The Almighty sent the potato blight; but the English created the Famine*" said Maggie.

John and James both nodded their agreement. "Ay, the Whigs leave us little choice in our own affairs 'tis true" said John, and James added a courteous Irish nod. "But we're struggling too" John continued "thank the Lord not as bad as that family you've mentioned, but strugglin' none the less... We're grateful for your help to our family James, and I know Maggie also enjoys the employment from you and your family, and the company of all your servants too". He threw in the latter to reinforce the relative hardships between them. "But..."

"It's hard times for us all I'm afraid" said James, quickly cutting him off. "Supporting our fellow Irish is the important thing now don't you agree?"

"*Aye, and to be sure that the rich are no worse off*" thought James, though he was too polite to say so, just yet.

The adults lowered their eyes, knowing the next thing said would be about rent.

Maggie had listened to the conversation and she suspected where this was going too, but taking her father's cue wasn't about to let James off lightly nor encourage the anger she saw rising in her pappy.

"I've been thinking through this situation you know" she said, and suddenly all eyes lifted and were upon her, the strikingly beautiful young woman who said the most remarkable things.

"I read that back in the 1780s, before the Act of Union, Ireland had a famine then too, though 'twasn't as bad. The Irish Government acted quickly and imposed trade restrictions to ensure the locals were fed first, before food was sent overseas; and they opened up the ports to foreign goods to ensure plentiful supply. It worked for a time as you know. People talk about that now of course and say that if we had our own independent government like we did in that time, that we would stop our foods being shipped off shore and we'd feed our own first."

All the adults nodded, this was the commonly held and growing belief among many Irish. Even James, of the Protestant Ascendancy and therefore closely aligned to England, had little trouble in aligning himself to Ireland when the occasion permitted.

"But you know what? The most uncomfortable thing I found when I looked into some books and newspapers about that time..." she continued. "Back then, it was we Irish who strongly opposed that measure and soon had it stopped. It wasn't the English, no – it was Irish merchants who stood to lose money from trade. It was Irish farmers who feared their prices would be lowered. Pappy, it was even Irish fishermen who were afraid the cost of fish would go down if we weren't supplying some other country!"

The adults were shocked, looking about them, trying to find some response. But Maggie continued without hesitation, seizing the moment.

"So, it strikes me that now just as then, our troubles are very much the fault of every single one of us who refuses to stand up for and to do what's right. Every person who knowingly perpetuates inequality – British and Irish Landlords, British and Irish merchants, and any man who seeks to take advantage of his fellows at the markets by increasing prices of every other good.

It is greatly convenient for us to reduce it to a single cause, to point the finger of blame. But the blame isn't just with the English, not solely, though it suits us to say so. Yes, English policy has shaped, allowed and even aggravated the poverty and inequality of the Irish; but it is the greed and self-interest of every-man that has caused so much suffering."

She looked deeply into James' eyes as she drove home the point.

"My pappy has always said he can't understand why people want more than they need. Why have two houses? You can only live in one. Why take more fish than you can sell? It'll only drive down prices and harm future fisher-folk."

As the room fell silent and the older adults contemplated her words, James looked back into Maggie's eyes with only a mild shame – rather, he was stunned at the inner beauty shining behind those eyes, and he couldn't help but fall a little further into them. And so the next thing he said came a little easier.

"Oh Maggie, such deep thoughts for such a young mind. But I'm not so sure it's greed that drives evil into the hearts of men – perhaps each of us is just trying to get by and protect the loved ones around us, and so they want more just to ensure that future?"

Maggie moved to respond, but James quickly cut her off.

"Anyway, look that brings me to what I wanted to talk to you and your parents about perfectly I think" he said, and drew a breath. "As I mentioned, times are tough for all of us including the Maguires, and my father has come up with a plan that involves me and my Elizabeth, and you too Maggie if you and your parents are willing."

This was not what any of them had expected. Now all eyes were on James, and he had Maggie's full attention.

"Elizabeth and I are going to go on a trip to Australia for a wee while, and we seek to further our land holdings there. Large tracts are being sold for very little you see, and my father wants me to find the best land and purchase it and then install productive tenants. And what he wanted me to ask you all is if Maggie might join us, fulltime as our servant you see and for that, my father will see that Maggie is well paid and that your family is compensated." He paused to look for their reactions. "I know it's a lot to take in, so of course none of you need to decide immediately. But I'll likely be leaving for Western Australia in only a few more months and I'd very much like Maggie to join us - and thus to also avoid the rent going up as I fear it otherwise must."

Maggie was shocked, proud, angry, frightened all at the same time. She had dreamed of Australia for some years now, and this would indeed be a great adventure; but that James had not first spoken of it with her felt insulting; and that he had now linked the request to a thinly veiled threat of increasing the rent made her cross. She couldn't help but give him a scowl to show her displeasure, and she watched him cringe a little under that gaze as he thought she was about to refuse his offer.

But simultaneously, she was curiously excited by the opportunity of taking such a long journey, and at James' side. Innately aware of James' attentions and likely *in*tentions toward her, she felt an edge of sexual excitement at the prospect which she found unsettling. She had known for some time now that she also found James physically attractive, and that attraction had matured somewhat these past years of service as she had found in James a kind and well-mannered man – who was also strikingly handsome and quite fit thanks to regular sports. And the age difference seemed so much smaller now she was a woman – nearly nineteen; he still in his early thirties.... He had treated her well for many years now, and she had felt a growing closeness. Privy to all the household's gatherings and rumours, she had seen that Elizabeth was somewhat cold towards him, and she felt sympathy and even an odd anger that James should be treated so.

As she looked into his eyes, it was a sexual excitement that had welled up below all her mixed feelings, threatening to overwhelm her otherwise rational head, and without realising it she finished her scowl with a smouldering look that James certainly did not miss. For his part James' alarm turned to hope and he sat back a little with a gentle smile forming on his lips, shared only with her. To have young Maggie along for the trip! And his glance moved down, towards her exposed shoulders and the curve of her well-formed bosom...

But Maggie was a smart girl, and rational thought never far from the surface. As she watched his gaze drift she seized the opportunity.

"I'll be needing triple my current wages of course, given I'll be helping out round the clock" she said while regaining his gaze, just as quickly as the look had passed between them. "In addition to full board and lodgings of course. And we'll make that for two years, with 25% payable in advance directly to my parents who you'll also assure there'll be no further rent rises for that time."

James looked a little shocked, and John and Sarah exchanged surprised glances. "Er, I'll need to confirm that with my father" he started. "Why Miss Maggie, you drive a hard bargain!"

"Not from greed you understand" replied Maggie, her gaze now penetrating to his soul. "Just looking out for those I love."

12

Caught and nicked

Richard thought he had seen the last of Patton and his thugs after their encounter, as he continued with long hours of work and caring for his father and the house.

But too soon, he realised his few drinks had cost him more than the price of the grog.

For full of pride and avarice, Mr Patton had investigated to find their names from the police register – Peter having revealed their previous encounter – and then contacted his business associates to exact revenge.

The only one of the three within his grasp was Richard. His remonstrations ensured a major contract with Richard's employer was cancelled, and that the employer should hear that it was because of Richard.

And just like that, he became unemployed.

Things seemed hopeless – with only occasional income from items of furniture that he could build and sell himself, their situation soon deteriorated from bad to dire. He looked around desperately for work, and his father still had enough pull to get him occasional short term and contract work, but the income was well short of what they needed and within weeks they were in ruins. So he took to stealing things where he could – opportunistic items that he could use such as food or money, or items he could easily fence such as clothing and tools. He was careful for the most part, but as time progressed and desperation grew he increasingly took risks.

It reached a peak one night as he strolled the streets and came upon some chickens, not yet back in their henhouse. He saw the opportunity for a meal, but not the farmer who raised merry hell with a whistle he kept for just such occasions.

He quickly had a chicken in his grasp, though it flapped and clucked in fright and so he ran – straight into the arms of two police, who had been following him without his knowledge. His headlong rush knocked one over but the other quickly had him in restraint and within minutes, he was up at the police station charged with stealing, resisting arrest and assault on a public officer.

"Ah, young Mr Williams!" declared the sergeant in some delight. "We've been expecting you!" and Richard wondered what he meant.

His father sent a message to say the church congregation would help out and not to worry, but Richard was worried, and frightened beyond any relief.

He languished in the cell for weeks as the case against him was prepared, and when the time came to front court he was given no legal counsel nor opportunity to prepare.

The charges were laid out as he stood scared and alone in the dock – stealing, assault and resisting arrest – supplemented by a new and unexpected charge of aggravated assault brought on by Mr Patton's goon, 'Mr Newton' - the same large one that Richard had so nearly crippled that afternoon some months ago.

Richard saw fat Mr Patton sitting at the rear of the court, smiling and chuckling to himself as the charges were read.

The farmhand provided the most damning evidence, presenting a character reference from Mr Patton and playing up to the judge by claiming his assault was unprovoked and his injuries life altering – that he had a limp that restricted his future work opportunities as a fruit picker, and a damaged hand that had already ended his season.

The judge deliberated and formed his opinion in less than a minute.

"Mr Williams, the evidence against you is clear, the charges serious. You have been caught red-handed with stolen goods, and you have assaulted one of his majesty's police servants in your attempt to get away. It seems these offences are not isolated, and that your transgressions have extended to assault on members of the public also, with Mr Newton an innocent victim. Do you have anything to say for yourself?"

"Well I guess I stole that chicken, but those other charges are bull – Mr Newton there went to clobber me and I was just lucky to get him first" he tried his best to explain. "And all that happened after that was I ran into the Constable, nothing else to it."

"You admit to the charge of stealing but continue to deny the other charges, despite the evidence of credible witnesses." The judge shook his head in a patronising show of disappointment, looking askance to Mr Patton who also shook his head in mock dismay. "Mr Newton's character has been assured through his employer, Mr Patton, who has also corroborated his account. Ironically, if you had sought to be as industrious as Mr Newton, seeking work rather than relying on crime, you should not now be in this predicament.

Nonetheless I shall take your account of the incident into consideration, and on the charges of assault of a police officer, I find you not guilty."

Richard felt a glimmer of hope. But it was just as quickly quashed.

"However, on the more serious charge of aggravated assault of Mr Newton, you are found guilty and sentenced to 5 years imprisonment. On the charge of stealing, you are found guilty and sentenced to 2 years imprisonment. Both terms to be discharged concurrently." And he slammed down his hammer with a cracking sound that made Richard jump.

Richard's heart sank – his years in prison would be a death sentence for his father.

The judge continued. "Mr Williams, you shall be transported and will serve out your sentence in the Swan River Colony of Australia."

Richard thought back to his discussion with Peter and Arthur, his vision of Australia as a huge hulk anchored somewhere off the Congo and cried out "No! It'll kill my father!" as he felt his spirit crushed.

"Once there you will be eligible for a reduced sentence through your service to the empire and to the settlers of Western Australia. With good behaviour you will serve just 12 months under supervision and then shall be granted ticket-of-leave status for a further period, after which you may stay in Australia or return as you may wish."

Richard again felt some relief and even uttered a "Thank you" to the judge, even as he saw the nasty old Mr Patton shift uneasily in his seat.

"But I stress to you, Mr Williams" the judge concluded "should you return you shall have made every endeavour to reform for, as I believe you said to Mr Patton: *"You'll not be wanting to see me again, right?"*

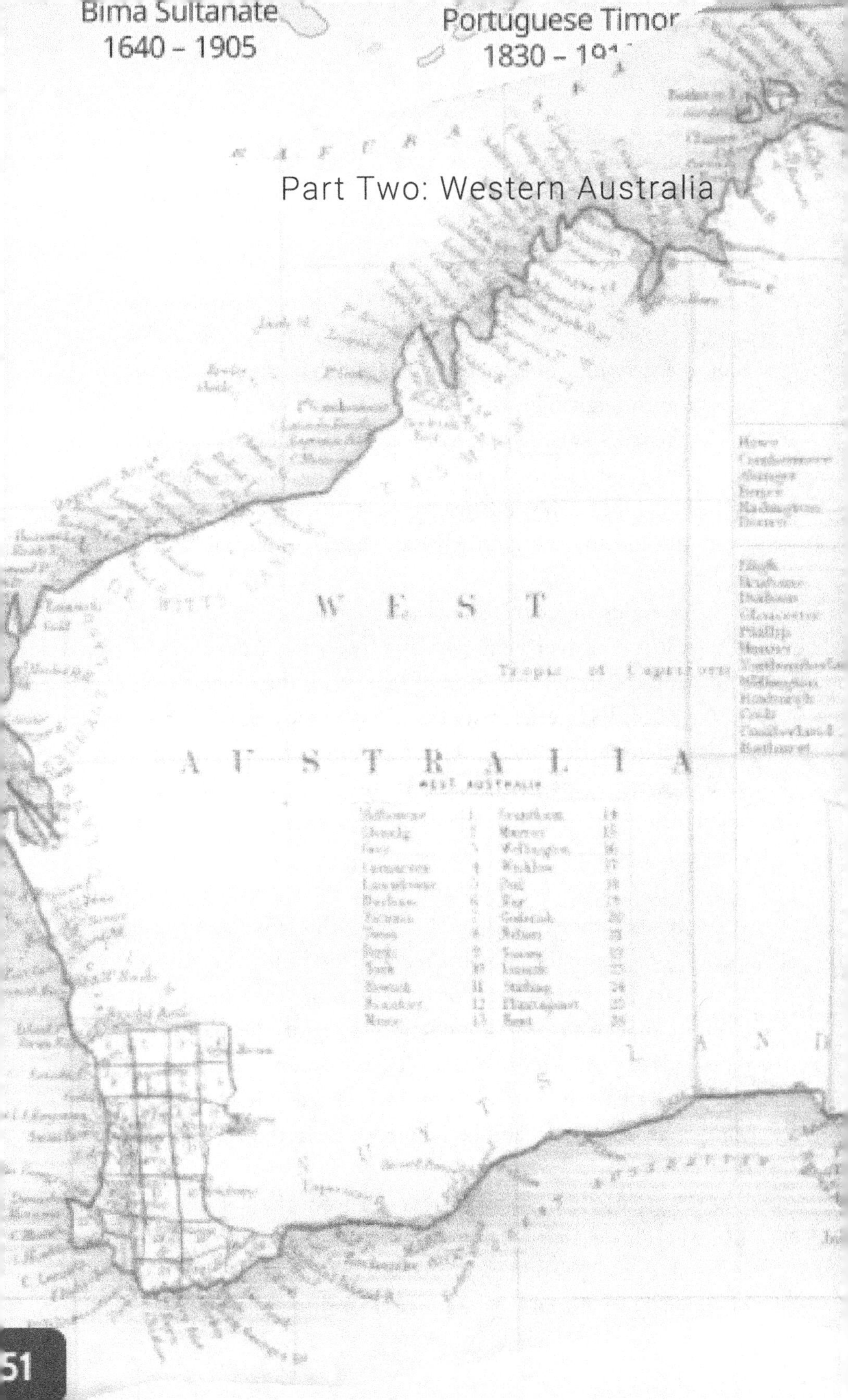

Bima Sultanate
1640 – 1905
Portuguese Timor
1830 – 19
Part Two: Western Australia
WEST
AUSTRALIA

This land at the bottom of the world is like no other.

As the hot desert inland and the long, cool Indian jostle for calm, it breathes. Long, deep breathes punctuated by night and day, the cooling and heating of each mass. This breath has continued, every day, every year through millenia.

As the tides swell to staggering depth, it pulses. The endless ebb and flow of water as the moon calls to the land – the romantic moon, ever seeking the earth's embrace. In the north, the call is strong and the earth stirs, moving, writhing below as the sea rises and falls at the lover's beckon.

Its thoughts are slow forming, spanning decades and even centuries – more a dream than a thought. But assuredly, it dreams – of rivers coursing through hill and plain; of mountains that reach to the sky. It dreams of endless green forests, stretching to the coast and of the white sands that greet them there. This land dreams of turquoise waters, rich coral ecosystems and great fishes that prowl the abundant sea; of hot desert plains that span the arid interior and where life yet struggles, survives and abounds under the savage sun.

And as flora and fauna live and die on the vast expanse, so it feeds. Stretching back nearly 2000 million years, this land has seen countless species come and go. Dinosaurs roamed 120 million years ago, megafauna followed for hundreds of thousands of years; the unique Australian biome trod and shaped by Aboriginal people for tens of thousands of years. Modern humanity, its weapons, machines and technology have been here too, but for mere decades. It, they, we live in a blink of an eye passing and becoming yet again the very land that was trod.

And as these newest inhabitants tear from the soil its rich ore, so it bleeds. This is a land rich in resource of every type, of wide plains and sunburnt hills abundant in earths both rare and those most sought. Mountains torn asunder by the passage of time and the lands heaving breathe, scattered across the plains hundreds, even thousands of kilometres away. Now torn away through dynamite and chisel, yet still but a scratch on the vast tapestry. A land this ancient provides up the minerals that man's unrelenting hunger claim; steel beasts score the earth, tearing minerals rich and rare, converting the ancient plan to the products of man's industry.

Sitting in the sun for an eternity, it is ageless.

The Indigenous people of this land know its dream, following its seasons, its pulse and have breathed with it for generation upon generation. For tens of thousands of years - they feel it as much as know it and they revel in its depth and majesty.

From western coast littered with reef and islands and all manner of life; to the deserts of the east baking in the sun, yet rich with life and beauty for those who seek it. The great forests of the south, trees reaching to the skies and the network of plants and animals seeking safety and nourishment in the branches and undergrowth; to the north of this great state stretching across two and a half million kilometres – a third of Australia, and yet alone greater than ten times the land mass of the combined United Kingdom.

It is a land unique beyond measure. Long ago, it is said a clash of continents resulted in its unique landscape, with regions distinct not only in geography but in form, soils and land-type. Yes, the very earth had heaved to spawn lands of such diversity, and those lands had merged to form this unique place, Western Australia.

This diverse land is the home to the Aboriginal peoples. Multiple nations, languages, dialects with trade, housing, agriculture. People of many Aboriginal nations – the Noongar in the southwest where the settlers first arrived; the Yamatji in the mid-west; the Wajarri and Martu to their East; the Ngurrara and Juburara in the Pilbara; the Wongi and Ngkatha to the east; and across to the Ngaanyatjarraku in the desert; Ngarinyin Country to their north, in the ancient lands of the Kimberley. Each unique nation scattered through a diverse environment; perfectly adapted to it. Hundreds of thousands of people, living in balance with nature through shared knowledge passed down through each generation, culture and beliefs transmitted not in letters but in song, story-telling and art; a culture changing only as need demanded.

The Kimberley of Western Australia was where these first humans landed, as long as 65,000 years ago, following a great sea voyage to this new and yet already ancient land inhabited by forest and mega-fauna and ancient mountain ranges that broke the sky in their upward quest.

Western Australia dreamed for an eternity; the Aboriginal people captured those dreams, recorded them as stories of creation, art and songs to carry down the generations. Great beasts that shaped the land; the very heavens above showing the way to and across their homelands. The Aboriginal people too shaped the land, using fire as a tool to manicure places for human habitation – a veritable supermarket of foods, medicines and every item needed for a full and healthy life. Large family-based groups swelled and expanded to skin-groups, clans and nations as they expanded to all corners, shaping, growing as they went. They established trade routes across vast distances to exchange goods and items unique to each nation. They created irrigation, farming and housing as they rotated across their unique territories; a semi-nomadic life that ensured regrowth for areas that had been used, and which reflected the seasons and environment.

It was of course not always peaceful – there were conflicts, and women taken whether by agreement or force. Skirmishes and transgressions were of course not unheard of, but rich cultural lore and tradition ensured these were few, and largely the people lived in peace and prospered in a land supplying their every need. Transgressions would be settled swiftly and firmly and so there was strong compliance with duty to family and to the land. The cost, if it could ever be called that, was to stay in your own country, demarcated through loose landmarks that allowed only so much trespass. Stay in your place; share. And so naturally, a close affinity between people and their home grew to a point where land is its people, and people were and remain today that of the land – connected, symbiotic, a whole. Symbiosis of land and intelligence.

And so this great land at the end of the earth dreamed in peace, a slumber filled with art, dance and song; of beauty and terror that could take your breath and your life away. Mountains rose and fell, their soil spread across the lands over tens of thousands of years to form vast plateaus and flat lands scoured with both life and death. A whole, connecting.

Seas rose and fell, creating islands lost in time and reefs both rich in life and full of danger to those foolish enough to trespass. Western Australia's ruggedness and remoteness kept its dreams hidden and known only to the few, the tens of thousands of Aboriginal people who had become one with the very soil of their home beneath the stars. A whole, connected.

This was also the place of the last European pioneers. A mere 200 years ago, even as the neighbouring nations developed thriving cities and industry, as industrial powers fought and traded for wealth and expansion; as every land on every continent yielded to modern man, still this western side of Australia lay 'unclaimed' by the great powers. Humanity elsewhere had grown in a different direction. Science, religion and, it must be said greed provided the new tapestry where those with the means could take and shape to their own desires. The Europeans were at the forefront, but nations across the world adapted to a new world not of dreams, but of cold hard fact of science, technology and, alas, of boundless selfishness – a culture of individualism where it was seen as good to take the bounty of nature and turn it towards 'profit' – not just taking enough to survive, but taking more than enough, to treat it all as if it were only ever there to be taken. Technology enabled, the world was changing rapidly, had already moved from the pitiful struggles of despot kings and chieftains of only a few generations earlier, to mighty wars now raging between nations and empires.

Against this backdrop of rapid change, growing technology and weaponry, of nationalism, power and wealth, of growing greed and of individualism that came at the expense of the whole, Western Australia still slept.

Land to the modern humans was a commodity; something to be consumed and used for more – more profit, more power. And as those who profited the most ensured expansion; so too did every man and every woman as they looked inward for the dream that the Aboriginal people knew lay outward, in the land and in the skies that give us birth.

And so while the dreamtime dies across the world, the story of the invasion and colonisation of Western Australia in the 1850's only now begins. Isolated from the European powers that spawned and then spurned it, the tiny settlement on the banks of the Swan River was already a failed and failing colony, claimed by the British in 1829 only for fear of French expansion and then promptly forgotten by its Government on the other side of the world. The Swan River colony did not flourish. It did not live up to the promises of the individualists, of those seeking their riches, of developers; nor did it measure up to the ideals of the late colonial era who pontificated of a 'civilised state bound by the laws of God'. By 1850 there were still less than 6,000 settlers in an area one-third that of Australia, with most of these in the southern coastal areas.

The Swan River colony, the new capital of an emerging State called Western Australia and later to be named 'Perth', struggles to find arable land, and the colony fails to find any trade or innovation to take it forward.

The Noongar people live uncomfortably alongside the invaders. They are a kind people who tolerate and live alongside settlers in their 'contained' areas, as was the policy of that time. Indeed, it was only through support of the Noongar Menang that the NSW outpost colony of Albany, founded three years earlier and 500 kilometres to the south, had survived at all in those early years. The relations with the Noongar Wadjuk people around the Swan River are also largely amicable for twenty years. Yet there are conflicts too as the Noongar see these strange new people gradually expanding upon their lands; killing animals wantonly; committing brutal murders; taking their women. On occasions, they sought and found retribution for such acts only to have it metered back three-fold upon them, and upon people innocent to the act judged only by the colour of their skin. The horrific massacre of the Binjareb; other atrocities inflicted by the early administration under the guise 'they need to fear us before they can love us'.

And within a generation, the colony would start to expand, to swell the dreams of the world's poor for a better life; to swell the pockets of the rich – and to end the dreamtime in this remote corner of the world.

Throw in good people. Some bad people. A clash not just of cultures, but of core beliefs. Men and women of both intellect and moral goodness. Many more people of poor education and dubious moral character. And good people who did bad things.

This is the time and place into which the last pioneers stumbled, acting upon the people, the animals and the breathing, pulsating and glorious land of Western Australia itself with their own dreams of building a better life for themselves and their children. Most knew no better – their beliefs shaped by a culture on the other side of the planet, and of dreams that screeched only 'more, give me more'.

13

The journey south, 1850

*D*earest Pappa and Ma

I am sitting at my little bed in the steerage of The Hashemy. We are three days into another period of great calm, in which The Hashemy has moved not an inch and so I should love to tell you a little about our voyage out, a great adventure that shall endure with me forever.

I may not be able to write again for some months, and I imagine that even when I do I will be largely unable to send it to you over the miles of sea between us.

So here is a slight description of a sea voyage of some 14,000 miles – can you imagine it, Pappa - performed in nearly four months now since we left Liverpool.

We set out to sea at one o'clock in the afternoon, and proceeded with a fair wind which carried us rapidly from the shores of England, and I sung in joy when I glimpsed what I thought was the Isle of Mann and wondered if I should see your sail therein, my darling Pappa.

At the end of three days, however, it blew a slight gale rather contrary to us for about a week, and we made little headway. After a time the wind again became favourable, and we soon got into the Bay of Biscay. This we were a week in crossing, during which time a mighty storm blew up and many of the passengers became quite unwell. Sometimes we appeared to be mounted upon the top of a wave, at the next moment we were sinking gradually until we were surrounded by great waves breaking upon us. Then the vessel would seem to pause, owing to her being buried so low in the sea that you would fancy the wind could not reach her sails, but in an instant the waves would rise under her again and then she would mount majestically, with the wind howling through the rigging—and then we knew we were at sea. It is a most grand, awful, and beautiful sight, though we were quickly locked away in steerage to ride out the storm.

There was a terrible commotion below decks—many poor little children were dreadfully sick and half dead with fright, while their mothers were too ill to attend to them. Some of the grown-up passengers were absolutely crying with fear and agitation; others, from the rolling of the vessel, were thrown into all positions about the decks, two women badly injured from the rapid jolts upon us. One of these I helped and in time have come to friend.

When we crossed the Bay the wind subsided into a favourable gale, at which we were very thankful, for now the water was smooth in comparison with the tremendous sea we had lately experienced. And now the passengers became more intimate with each other, and we mutually communicated our plans and intentions, and the means we possessed of carrying them into effect. And so it was with no small surprise that I discovered not one passenger in ten knew anything about farming, nor fishing or indeed supporting themselves in anyway, although they all professed their object to be the acquisition and occupation of land. Several of them resided in London and other large towns and had known nothing but the army all their lives, and scarcely knew wheat from barley. How these persons who have been brought up in trade are to succeed in the management of land I cannot conceive.

The wind now continued favourable for some time, when we came in sight of the Island of Madeira, but we were very much disappointed in not having a clear view of it owing to our not nearing it until the evening. Strong winds now prevailed, but fair. The ship went steadily nine miles an hour, which was considered very good sailing, for she was loaded dreadfully heavy and therefore of course was deep in the water. We continued steadily on our course until we reached the Tropic of Cancer, where we were becalmed six days: the wind at last sprung up, and carried us favourably to Mayo, one of the Cape de Verde Islands, where we put in to replenish our watercasks.

A small American brig was laying here, waiting for a cargo of salt with which this island abounds, and is shipped from hence to all parts of the world. We remained only three days at this place, and then proceeded with a fair wind until we reached the Line, where we were again becalmed for six days. We found it dreadfully hot between the Tropics, and here, for the first time, saw a great quantity of flying fish to me quite a novelty though perhaps not to you, pappa. Some of the strong ones will fly nearly 100 yards at a flight when they are pursued by large fish of prey. We sailed well for a fortnight, but then there was a dead calm for another ten days.

The wind afterwards got up, blew hard, and quite a-head, and so continued for several days which drove us within two days sail of Rio Janeiro, well outside our intended route. The cabin passengers tried their utmost to prevail upon the captain to put in at that place, but all to no purpose.

The wind now became favourable, and so continued until we came within the latitude of the Cape of Good Hope. We met with good weather in rounding the Cape, but afterwards it began to rain, and blew tremendously for a fortnight; and much of this time we were all battened below decks. We were permitted to have lights, but were obliged to buy them.

The wind shifted and became less boisterous, and we saw several whales and a large fish called a sun-fish, massive in size and weight – one of the strangest fish I have ever seen, even more so than those you would catch to show me, Pappa.

We made St. Paul's in due course: it is a little rocky barren island, about midway from the Cape of Good Hope and the Swan River; it is said to be uninhabited but its shores abound with fish.

We proceeded rapidly for a week, and have again becalmed for three days now. Here we have seen a great many whales once more but nothing else. No sail, no land – only blue horizon before us, and blue skies above. However we understand that the Western Australian coast is now within days ahead and so I take this opportunity to pen these words.

I look forward to telling you the next leg of my adventure soon, when we arrive at the Swan Colony!

Yours faithfully
Maggie O'Brien

14

The REAL journey south

Somewhere west of Africa, the world came tumbling down.

The boat had sailed for a fairly uneventful two weeks when the first of the storms hit, and now, sitting at the galley table near her bunk that was her only private space on the ship, Maggie felt the world turn upside down. It was a strange sensation, she thought inwardly, as there was little sign of the outside turmoil in the steerage section that she shared with 130 other second-class passengers – men, women and children. But the results were unmistakeable as plates, cups and belongings rose up and then crashed about the cabin. Maggie herself was sitting at the table and though she felt the violence of that rapid motion in her gut, she was fortunate to have not been standing like several other passengers who now groaned on the floor nursing bruises and cuts. Two women were badly injured, one of them lay unconscious and the second was screaming in pain.

People milled about nursing various injuries and caring for those close to them, but Maggie quickly realised no one was coming to the aid of the unconscious woman. So she dashed to her, fearing another rapid jolt could cause her to be crushed or to hit her head once more. Maggie heaved her up into a bed, where she would at least be secure, and then she set about helping others as best she could. Moments later, the boat rolled violently again, lurching to port before righting itself with an equally violent motion, like the settling of a pendulum. Maggie guessed the sea was coming from the East and that these large swells were around twenty seconds apart, directly hitting the side of the boat.

People began to vomit, and the wails of infants and the screams of many women and some men made the scene in steerage nightmarish. They had been warned that rough seas were coming and it had been getting progressively worse, but most of the passengers had continued on their routines with little regard.

The ship adjusted sails and course but the storm was violent and settled in like this for a full three days before sanity and calm returned. During this time, life in steerage became horrific, and Maggie learnt the lady who had been screaming had died.

Like most of those plying the route to the antipodes, this small ship The Hashemy, had not been built with the transportation of people in mind. What had been cargo space had been hastily converted to 'bulk' accommodation, badly overcrowded and with poor ventilation. Rats were common. Sea water seeped in through hatches so it was constantly damp below deck.

The galley provided meals, but preservation of food was difficult and consequently meals were boring and monotonous. The menu consisted of salt meat and salt bacon, fish, cabbage, potatoes, beans and peas, in various combinations. Passengers had to collect their food from the galley and take it back to steerage to eat.

'Steerage' accommodation was essentially one large room that acted as dormitory, dining room and common room all in one. It was dark because there were no windows and the few dim lanterns hanging from the deck beams provided the only light. Passengers' beds were crammed into bunks, stacked one atop another with barely enough room to even turn over. The Hashemy had only two common toilets on the upper deck for the steerage passengers, and people would shower in a sectioned area with cold sea water drawn up by crew. Most people it seemed preferred to not shower at all, or at least to leave it for a couple of weeks.

During the storm and the several more that followed, the crew would 'batten down the hatches', which for the steerage passengers meant that they would be locked below in an attempt to ensure their safety and to minimise water intake. However, this meant the toilets were now inaccessible and so they had instead been provided with pails which were to be emptied only when the conditions permitted. Of course, several pails were not secured and so with each violent roll, somewhere down below one or more buckets would tip, spilling their contents across the floor. Vomit, urine, faeces seeped into cracks and crevices. With no ventilation the smell became unbearable but worse, laden with diseases, and it wasn't long before diseases spread, including cholera. The rats which had previously skittered past had become more brazen, and much more numerous. Barely anyone escaped without some form of illness – trenchmouth, ulcerations, scabies and headlice were common as the unsanitary conditions set in, and with the body lice deadly typhus too set in.

In this, their first encounter with rough seas, a baby who had already been quite sick had also died and a dozen or more people – men, women and children – remained below as they were simply too sick to move.

Only the fit and young escaped the worst of it, although they too suffered illnesses. Maggie herself felt ill but continued to tend to the fallen woman for days, as it emerged she had fractured a rib in addition to a nasty head wound, and Maggie knew she needed to minimise her motions for at least four weeks. The woman had roused soon enough, and immediately began wailing from the pain, and desperately inquired after her two children who Maggie found cowering in a nearby bunk. Maggie did what she could to comfort them, and as the days continued she engaged them as much as possible in helping their mother by playing games and reading to her, providing water and small amounts of food and ensuring she was as warm and comfortable as possible. Maggie her-self would help the unfortunate woman with toileting, which could only be described as a harrowing experience for them both. Afterwards, Maggie would empty the waste to a bucket which she secured against a post.

Now, as the worst of the storm passed it was clear the woman would pull through. She managed to sit up a little in bed and was taking more of the soups and rations provided by the galley, but as importantly, she had lifted in spirit and now smiled at Maggie as she told her story.

Maggie learned the woman's name was Hazel, that she and her husband had decided to set out for Australia together, however her husband had been billeted to the single men's quarter. There was something about the woman's telling of the story, her nervous eye movements and disconnects in the story line that made Maggie wonder what was really going on, but Hazel wouldn't provide any further clarity, only that her husband was aboard but unable to assist her until they reached the shore.

She decided against pursuing the matter further and busied herself with talking to and helping Hazel and other women and their families. There was a family of six, a couple in their 30s with four children under six years of age and now expecting another - in a matter of days or so Maggie thought. The woman's name was Sandra, and she welcomed Maggie's help, with one of her children quite ill with a stomach upset the toddler had acquired in the last day. Not far from them was another family of three – a couple not much older than herself who were both badly affected by seasickness and struggling to care for their toddler, a delightful girl of two who spent much of her time singing and dancing. The woman's name was Louisa and Maggie learned they were travelling to Albany in the south of Western Australia.

Maggie soon became a well-known and liked passenger, and through her some of the other passengers began to form connections as well. Louisa's girl started playing with Hazel's two children which was a relief to both families; and steerage became more social as people began to share their stories and where they were going. Maggie was surprised to hear many migrants were Pensioner Guards – returned servicemen and their families who had been enticed to migrate with promises of land and wealth. Some planned to land at Fremantle, others at Albany to the South. The common belief was that other areas held greater promise.

To her delight, she also found through these conversations that there were two other single young women such as herself who were travelling to Australia as servants. Both were around her own age – Patricia from London and Caroline from County Down, another rural part of Ireland. She sought them out, and the three soon became good friends and would enjoy whatever chance they had to sit together and share stories of their homes, families and work. While Patricia was headed to Melbourne, Caroline had been brought over to work as a house-servant to a property in Guildford, forming an instant common bond with Maggie and they became very close, the best of friends. Caroline was excited and relayed with a giggle that she understood there were already several eligible young men awaiting her arrival, or so said correspondence with her from relatives of her employers.

When they were finally released from steerage, Maggie made her way up to Mr and Mrs Maguire's first-class cabin. The day was quite delightful – clouds remained but it was sunny, the seas had flattened, and a firm breeze carried the ship along. Giant birds wheeled in the sky, their calls cutting through the air. A group of people had gathered around a litter of newly born kittens, and a young man struck up a jaunty tune on his violin. Adults and children both danced and laughed as the kittens mewed loudly, their calls joining the sounds of the violin as if the kittens themselves were singing. People laughed and joined in the gaiety and the numbers swelled. Caroline and Patricia were there and beckoned her over, but she pointed towards the stern and mouthed that she would return a little later.

A short way on, she found a smaller and much more sombre gathering and realised she was witnessing the burials of the baby and woman who had died in the preceding days. Their bodies had been shrouded and burial at sea hastily arranged. One of the passengers, a lay priest, officiated with passages from the bible. Then the bodies were cast somewhat unceremoniously overboard, whereupon the requiem sharks that followed the ships would sate their ravenous appetites, even as the bereaved of those departed looked on in horror. Maggie rushed past as one young girl cried and screamed at the shark to let her mother go.

James and Elizabeth were in a private cabin towards the stern, alongside the captain and first mate, and other private cabins for the first-class paying passengers. Maggie had carried their bags to the room as they boarded, and thought the little room looked lovely with its wardrobe and comfortable bunks. There was even a little desk and a chair, and the window let in a lovely stream of light and could be opened for welcomed fresh air. She was bemused then when Elizabeth had turned her nose up at the sight of the room, which she expressed was far too small and 'musty'. James had consoled her with mention of the forward lounge and Officer's galley which they could share with the other first-class passengers, and that there was also a toilet and shower which, though also shared with the officers and other passengers, was only two doors down.

Now, she knocked on the door and James immediately opened it to reveal a room in some disarray. Elizabeth, he reported, had been violently ill during the storm and was yet again in the ship's head, much to the chagrin of the first mate who had relayed the complaints of both the Captain and other passengers of whom she had thus prevented entry. Maggie set about cleaning the room, as James settled himself at the writing desk and a full glass of whisky. He explained he was writing to his father and brother and was delighted to have Maggie's company and conversation.

"Elizabeth isn't quite cut out for this type of travel it seems" he said, looking for some sympathy. "I seem to spend a lot of time alone!"

Just then, Elizabeth re-entered the room and James' mood immediately turned. Elizabeth glanced at him but barely acknowledged Maggie, commenting that the room was a mess and without a word of welcome or thanks to Maggie who had already been doing her best to tidy, instructed that she should clean it immediately, starting with the bed so that she herself might lay down. Maggie put the cloths down that she had been gathering, and quickly adjusted the bedding so that Elizabeth could lay down, whereupon Elizabeth lamented the horrid conditions she had to endure.

James interrupted after a few minutes and asked how Maggie was faring in steerage, and Maggie relayed only that it was comfortable if cramped and that she had met a great number of lovely people and made some friends. As she continued to clean the room, she told them about the Pensioner Guard families, and her friend Caroline who would be sequestered to a household in Guildford, the upper reaches of the river that they had read about in Philomena's letter. James nodded his acknowledgement.

Maggie laughed and blushed a little as she relayed how excited Caroline was that there would be many eligible young men, catching James' look of disapproval. Elizabeth muttered something about 'the young whore' and louder, that she supposed such behaviour would only continue despite being on the other side of the world.

The room fell a bit silent at that, and Maggie – keen to finish her work and return to the festivities back on deck – mentioned her friend Hazel's situation, and how strange she had thought it that her husband had been put up separately.

Much to Elizabeth's alarm, James explained that there were no separate men's quarters on board, other than for prisoners who were being kept in the lower hold.

"Probably the unfortunate wife of one of those scoundrels I dare say, Maggie" he declared knowingly, and flashed her a mischievous smile. "I understand there are perhaps a hundred guests of his Majesty, sent to expend their sentences as servants of the Crown in the new Swan Colony" he explained. "Only the second such muster to travel to Western Australia you know. Yes, Philomena has written about in in her correspondence to my family: apparently the authorities had been adamant against prisoner intake these past twenty years but have now realised that without it, the colony may fail." And he necked the last of his glass and poured himself another.

"There are some in the colony that will be looking most forward to their arrival. Though I dare say the women folk should be a bit more apprehensive!" and he looked towards his wife.

"So, watch out ladies" he said mischievously, making a strange face and shaking his hands and arms. "Vagabonds and miscreants abound on board this fine ship, and they shall as soon take your life as your liberty and honour!" He turned directly toward his wife who now looked pale once more, her eyes wide at James' tale. "Particularly a fine lady such as yourself" he said, and then gave Maggie a little private wink.

"Oh my Lord!" exclaimed Elizabeth. "I shan't go to the toilets alone again! Maggie, fetch us a pale! And don't you look so horrified, James" she continued "you shan't be in the room when it comes time for me to use it!" and James now turned a little pale himself, realising he had just scared his wife out of leaving the cabin for the remainder of the journey, and that his retreat was now to be a toilet for as many hours each day as Elizabeth had occupied the ships privy.

"Ah, well I guess that private lounge will be my new haunt more often then..." he joked with worried dismay, before adding in a belated attempt that the prisoners were all well-guarded.

Maggie suppressed a laugh and smiled to herself at how James' attempt at humour had backfired. However, she was herself also concerned at James' revelation - though she had read enough to know that most of the poor prisoners sent to Australia had only committed minor crimes and had received their sentences for the convenience of the authorities on both sides of the planet, she was worried what this might mean for Hazel and her children.

"Oh, poor Hazel!" she exclaimed. "She's been sentenced alongside her husband in effect, to leave her family and home behind and set sail to a new and unknown world where they'll forever be under the eyes of the authorities!"

"Don't you worry too much there, Maggie" James soothed. "I expect her husband will be a strong labourer or have some trade or skill in demand to be even able to afford that his family came along, and in only a very few short years he will be a freeman. The prospects for families such as those are doubtless in fact much improved than remaining in the current despair of England or our own beloved Ireland!"

"In fact," he mused "I shall have to inquire as to the skills of our prisoner batch with the Captain – it would be a boon to us to be assigned an appropriately skilled young man...". He took a deep draught of his glass and turned once more to Maggie. "Who knows, perhaps it will even be the fellow of your woman friend, what did you say her name was, Sadie?" Maggie quickly corrected, "Hazel" but James continued "That should be a happy coincidence wouldn't it, for Sadie and all the family to join us on our expedition?" and he laughed.

Maggie found Caroline and Patricia enjoying themselves alongside the crowd of steerage passengers who now danced and sang alongside the violin and kittens. It was a joyous occasion, everyone much relieved to have fresh air after days locked down below and no-one wanted to leave. One or two crew even joined in, pulled from their duties by Caroline and Patricia to join them in a jaunty jig. Caroline was a particularly attractive young woman, and shone with joy in the beautiful spring weather - the centre of every man's attention as she twirled and danced, her smile and laughter infective.

Everyone laughed and enjoyed themselves and Maggie felt happy, though she contemplated the prisoners held down below. As the dancing continued, she wandered over to the side of the boat to enjoy the waves and freshening wind. So she was all alone when she spotted a young man in leg irons, bare chested as he emptied a bucket of water over his head. Maggie flushed and couldn't help but look, his strong body muscular and defined – a man of stunning masculinity, more so than the boyish charms of Declan, the love she had left behind. As she stared entranced by his muscular torso and handsome face, she realised there were other prisoners too, overseen by two guards who stood nearby, holding guns but chatting nonchalantly. As the prisoner tipped a third bucket of water and smoothed back his long brown hair, Maggie was temporarily transfixed in the moment as she felt a wave of desire. But she quickly looked away as she realised now that he had caught her eye and that he was looking directly at her. Though at a distance, their eyes locked for a mere instant before she forced herself to look away and rushed back to the celebration, her heart beating fast and her mind full only of his image. She was swept into a dance by Caroline, and the moment was all but forgotten.

Up the deck, the young man watched her go with a jolt of unfamiliar emotion. He watched tenderly as she returned to the crowd and danced happily on the deck and felt the woman's own joy as she was swept away in that dance. This young woman he had seen for but a moment, was a striking beauty to be sure. But he had known many other beautiful young women. No, there was something about those eyes and the look they had shared that had instantly distinguished her from the many other girls he had known. He felt drawn to her, somehow impossibly linked and he started forward involuntarily, but the chain on his leg held him in place and then the guards leapt forward threateningly, pointing their guns and directing him towards the hold that he shared with 99 other prisoners, a room barely large enough for two thirds that number. He cursed them but moved, the young woman now a retreating memory.

Though he felt sure he would remember that face, her long brown hair, but mostly those startling green eyes forever.

As Maggie twisted and turned in a dance with one of the excited sailors, she looked back in the direction she had come from, just in time to see his muscular back and shoulders disappearing around the curve of the boat, the guards cursing and prodding him along. She felt her heart quicken again, but as she was swept into a dramatic movement, the moment was gone.

Elizabeth's long periods in the cabin with bucket by her side did at least encourage James to get out a little and explore the boat and meet some of the passengers.

He had an interest in boats and spent many long hours with the Captain who happily told him all about the ship and how it was built, how to navigate, how the sails were best operated, and the weather conditions. James was genuinely enthralled in the conversations and became a regular in the chart room, and the Captain was equally keen to have a willing and enthusiastic listener. Through their conversations, James also learnt about boat builders and the burgeoning businesses in the colonies to supply their expanding needs. Encouraged by the Captain's tales, James revealed he was looking to invest and keen to explore boat ownership and trade further, and so the Captain provided him with some local contacts, should he wish to pursue it on their arrival.

There were a few other first-class cabins on board the small boat, and James met the occupants during long hours sitting in the private lounge, writing to his father and brother. One of them, the Bruce family, included six noisy children scattered across two cabins. They kept to themselves, however James uncovered that they were the family who had Maggie's new friend Caroline as their servant.

Another were a young couple who James was surprised to learn were travelling to settle permanently in a largely unsettled area far from the Swan, as they simply didn't seem the type. They were well mannered and well dressed, with no knowledge of farming, and only minutes into the conversation began talking of the church and God's intentions for the God-less natives, in which they would play a part. James discovered they intended to establish a native mission in the southwest of Western Australia, to support the 'wretched native children' there in finding their true path in God. They seemed decent, Christian folk and though James wasn't particularly enthralled at the conversation, which seemed to invoke God and God's Will with regular monotony, he was genuinely interested to hear about their plans to establish the Mission and to gain Government sponsorship for their work. They were, they explained, sponsored by her extremely wealthy father, who it emerged was an ardent man of God and as it happened also part owner of the very ship they sailed in now. Their plan was to build a house in a coastal area to the south, where a nearby waterfall provided abundant fresh water, and to establish a garden and perhaps a small flock of sheep and goats maintained through native labour. The native children themselves would be transported to their Christian care and education through the authorities, together with an annual fee for their upkeep. The couple expected operations would break even within a few years and that in time, the older children would continue on as their paid servants. They were also particularly excited to lead the small community nearby in construction of a Methodist church and had gathered generous donations through her father's business connections to present to the local priest and congregation, with whom they had a steady stream of correspondence. James was taken in by the romantic promise of their story and wished them every genuine success. He promised to write to his own father to seek a small donation for the church, to which the couple were both delighted as they swapped contact details.

Next door to James and Elizabeth was an older and rotund couple who turned their noses up at any conversation other than their constant complaints about the food, service, and the unruly passengers in steerage who 'cavorted on the decks whereas they should be permanently secured below'. Through some persistence, James learned a little about the man – enough to realise he would not wish to pursue further contact. It emerged that he and his wife were on a short return journey to 'represent certain interests in the directions of certain concerns', and to ensure these interests were 'well understood' by the Colonial administrators. James couldn't guess at either the business nor the English interests the man represented, but he correctly guessed he was a high-ranking English official – possibly a Magistrate – and that he would be using both legal and other threats to ensure the interests he represented endured. The man was extremely pious and radiated a sense of arrogance and self-righteousness which even James found irritating. Shifting subject, the man pontificated about the poor state of Government affairs, giving James and his own wife a long lecture in how the poor only had themselves to blame and that aid to them was a disgrace both to the hard-working classes and to God himself. Watching James' reaction, his diatribe culminated in his views about the Irish and that the Protestant

Ascendancy were a poor replacement for proper English Lords, who would have far better kept the population in its place and brought Ireland closer to England. James got the clear impression this was itself quite deliberate and targeted at him, the message: *"Know your place"*. Not once did he ask about James' own family nor indeed even allow him an opportunity to provide it. James contemplated getting this man on side – perhaps over a few brandy drinks– but he really couldn't endure too much more of the conversation, and so made his farewells with a pleasant wave, as he vowed to avoid engaging the horrid man in conversation again.

Elizabeth felt a wave of nausea come over her once more, like a storm front moving across the ocean. Even though the weather and seas had been calm for a second day, she still felt poorly, and she knew this was an illness that would not pass.

She had seduced James frequently in the weeks and months since her 'chat' with his parents, determined that she should fall pregnant before they left with the hope that she in fact would remain. But for those months his seed had not caught, and she had begun to think that at nearly 34 she may have left it too late.

But now, as she dry retched into the bucket in her room, she knew she was pregnant. Her period was over 3 weeks late.

It hadn't worked out the way she had hoped, though she was pleased that she was able to get pregnant at all. She had feigned lust for the man almost daily in those many weeks while she would be most likely to take seed, and for four months nothing had come of it, though James had willingly complied. Now they had been on the boat only five weeks and they had only had sex a few times as she had genuinely left seasick.

"It's the ruddy fresh sea air after all!" she thought wryly to herself.

She had thought if she got pregnant before they left, that they wouldn't have to go at all, or perhaps that just James would go alone. She had plotted that the Maguire girl would then stay at home - and that they could increase the rent as it should have been in the first place. She wondered again at the thinking of James' father, and of James himself in anointing the blasted young woman to their journey. It wasn't that she wasn't capable, nor even that she wasn't pleasant enough – though Elizabeth found such mannerisms grating. *"Butter wouldn't melt in her mouth!"* she had joked to her own mother, as she expressed her distaste for the girl and that she would be travelling with them.

No, the cause of her concern was that she felt certain the two silly men were simply taken in by her beauty, which Elizabeth herself could not doubt. Though he was careful to not betray it, she felt James light up when Maggie entered the room, and she had certainly noticed how kind he was to her, never admonishing her even though her work was so often sub-par. Though she felt certain the girl was far beneath his station, she realised her youth and beauty was beguiling to the lesser sex and had little doubt the whore of a girl would try her best to take him away if only she got the chance. *"Men can do stupid things when they think with their willies!"* she laughed to herself, and vowed to ensure those chances should be minimised.

She calculated the course of her pregnancy silently between the waves of nausea.

I shall be giving birth in the southern summer, four months after we arrive... I'll tell James the news in the next week or two, and that I shall take up the Maguires offer to stay with their relatives while James can do his trip alone – I'll be sure to point out my distress such that Maggie will have to stay with me.

And I'll also be sure that she permanently parts ways with the Maguire family by the time James returns!"

Life onboard for both Maggie down below, and James and Elizabeth up on the top deck, continued with a monotony punctuated only by storms and social dramas as passengers fought and argued over some minor issue, and by the deaths which continued and worsened as the weeks rolled into months. Of course, illness and premature death were common on land too in those days, so the expectations of the travellers was not high - but the hardness of those four months cannot be underestimated even though Maggie sailed through it without major illness.

When she could, Maggie called by daily to help Elizabeth and James, but for the first time in her life she had many long hours of leisure which she occupied with helping others, reading, or chatting with her new friends.

She and James also shared walks around the deck, and she joined in one or two of his conversations with the Captain, wherein they were both surprised to learn she knew quite a bit about sailing, and even basic boat building. They had cordial chats as they strolled, and their mutual fondness grew. Maggie enjoyed his company and she thought they even had some good intelligent conversations every now and then, when James wasn't talking about his travels or his dreams of endless guises. But her physical attraction to him she firmly supressed – she reminded herself he was too old, and that she must never act on her ever-growing feelings towards him.

James too kept his feelings in check, though took every opportunity to spend time alone with her. Impending fatherhood was like a dream come true and until recently at least, Elizabeth had satisfied his desires. Though he occasionally fantasised that it was Maggie in her place; and though his desire for Maggie had only grown through their increased time together, he was sure his feelings towards her were bound now by a plutonic love, like that of an older brother.

Elizabeth had told James her news after a few more days and sure enough, he was gushing in his joy - fairly dancing around the decks and telling every poor soul the news whether they wanted to listen or not. She found it quite endearing really.

"Why do you realise, our little bundle shall be born in Australia! Good lord, perhaps he'll be born with a boomerang and shall play with the native children!" he had announced to the table of first-class passengers and senior crew over dinner that night, and everyone laughed and congratulated him once more.

"He'll be a first-born son of that brown land that is our destination - a true Australian!" the Captain had said. "They call them 'the Lads and Lasses' you know, these first-born generation of free Australians" and James and Elizabeth both contemplated that reality.

"Well, this Lad or Lass will be there for only a few months though" Elizabeth hastily added.

And when Maggie visited their cabin the very next day, Elizabeth made sure she heard the news directly from herself and not from James. "Has James told you our joyous news?" Elizabeth enquired, locking the girl's eyes so as to gauge her response. "I am with child! You shall help us to raise our own little Australian!"

But Maggie gave nothing away, rather she looked genuinely pleased and quickly swept Elizabeth into a hug, which Elizabeth had no choice but to reluctantly reciprocate.

"Congratulations!" she said, and she gave James a quick hug too. "Such wonderful news! Your father shall be pleased too, I'm sure."

"That he shall" James replied. "I've already written him the news, and all our family will know even before our little boy is born."

"Oh and it's a boy, is it?" Elizabeth jokingly scalded him, and James looked a little embarrassed. He had hoped for at least a little jealousy from Maggie, but he had seen none and now the girl had set about tidying the room as if today's news was of no particular import.

Maggie meanwhile was genuinely pleased at the news. She had been having confusing feelings towards James. She enjoyed James' company on warm evening walks and realised those feelings had intensified - perhaps since she had seen that prisoner on deck. Elizabeth's news reminded her that here was a bridge that must never be crossed. No, her feeling towards James were but fallacy, and the news should be welcomed! Or so she convinced herself.

There were several more storms, one or two as bad and even worse than the first, and though passengers had now adapted to the routine, the damage had already been done. More and more passengers fell ill and several died as typhus and cholera spread – all of them the elderly, infirm and perhaps most tragically, young children and babies. And needless to say, all of them in second-class steerage or amongst the convicts.

This included the sick child of Sandra's family, and Maggie herself was there when the child finally passed. Sandra was distraught and wailed and flailed at her husband in her distress, until in his warm and loving embrace she finally settled to a resigned sobbing. Maggie thought of that tender union, the strength he gave her and she him. But in so many ways, Sandra's quiet sobbing was much worse for the other passengers, who couldn't help but be caught up in her raw grief. While the others avoided her and her husband, when she wasn't helping the children Maggie would simply sit with Sandra and hold her hand sometimes for hours at a time as she read a book, and Sandra seemed to eventually respond to this with each passing hour until one bright and sunny day, Maggie noticed the sobbing had stopped. She turned and found Sandra looking deeply into her eyes, no longer the distant and withdrawn look that had occupied her for the past days. Sandra stared deeply, as if finding a strength alongside the kindness that lay within, then she stood up, patted her heavily pregnant belly and shook herself off as she called upon one of her children to stop running around. It was as if the past days were finally done with, or perhaps had never happened at all.

"Thank you" she said simply to Maggie, and as suddenly, she was again a mother, moving on with life. Her husband too saw the transformation and moved immediately to her side, helping to settle the children as he gathered them around her in a family embrace, where they were all together in this moment of solidarity in grief and family.

In all, there were 20 funerals over the three months of travel – around one in six of the passengers in steerage.

But still the boat ploughed on, pursued by the wraith-like requiem sharks which were never far behind. Maggie continued to help out other passengers wherever she could, and became firm friends with Hazel as well as Caroline, both of whom she knew were bound for the Swan Colony. In time, Hazel told her the truth - that her husband Henry was indeed a prisoner. "Oh Maggie, it is my great shame! Please don't tell the other passengers!"

Maggie held her hands and lamented that she should have to leave her family in England.

"Oh no Maggie, I'm quite alone" Hazel replied with genuine clarity. "My family are all scattered around England and our parents are now long dead too you know. No, I shan't be missed and I shan't particularly miss them neither - though I'd have loved to see them one last time.

But no, my place is at my husband's side. I do so love him, despite what he done."

She looked embarrassedly away, collecting her thoughts before she continued. "He was convicted of robbery you see" she said in a whisper. "He's always gonna be 'enry the robber and I'm always gonna be 'that robber's wife'!"

Maggie didn't pursue the story – it really didn't matter what set of circumstances had led her husband to crime - but she relayed James' belief that the Colony held promise for families such as Hazel's, and that they'd be much needed as the colony grows. Hazel's mood picked up a little "Maybe it will be ok?" she enquired as much to herself. "It ain't like our shithole in London held much for us anyways, which is why Henry got himself in that trouble in the first place..."

"I'll tell you what, Hazel" Maggie offered "When we're both there and settled in, let's catch up? Maybe I could visit. Though from what my master James has told me, I'll be heading north with him and his wife for a wee while. But perhaps when I'm back, you'll already be in a fine manor, and you'll be the Lady of the house in your fine dress and not even recognise a lowly servant such as myself!" she joked.

"Oh, la de da!" Hazel giggled, for the first time now thinking positively about the possibilities before them. "The lady of the house! And a pioneer too don't you know!" she did a fancy little curtsy before turning back, and looking Maggie directly in her eyes. "But one thing Maggie O'Brien - you shan't never be forgotten, not by me anyways."

Despite rough weather and storms that lasted for days at a time, there were many good times on the long journey south, and a comradery developed between the steerage passengers as the weeks passed into months, and they realised their destination was at last drawing closer. They shared hopes and dreams for the future, formed enduring friendships and made promises to keep in contact. Each of them had set out with a dream, itself a collective dream for a better life; a better future for themselves and their families. These pioneers, the multitudes that flooded from the old world to the new, to these fledgling colonies of the old powers on the very edge of the world.

Together, they would eventually build a nation. A new colony thousands of kilometres from their homes; a place forgotten in a rapidly changing world. These and the thousands of others that followed would be the pioneers of Western Australia, the newest of the colonies and with huge, unexplored tracts of land, resources and promise. They brought new dreams and new technologies, and through their sweat and determination Western Australia would one day emerge as a beacon of hope and democracy; a place of tremendous wealth - and though also tremendous inequity a place that would be characterised by notions of 'a fair go'.

They did not set out to destroy the dream of creation held by the peoples of those new worlds – mostly these pioneers were good people. A few with wealth and power; many more who had neither.

The ship they travelled on was a microcosm of broader English society: The few rich and the privileged on the top; the multitudes of middle and working classes below; and the convicts sitting at the very bottom, the bilge of society.

The upper deck comprised of just a handful of families and individuals. Some like James carrying the privilege that their forebears had attained, seeking either fortunes or their place in heaven; a well off and large family setting off to greener pastures; and a couple who plotted to ensure the English way and English power should prevail, half a world away.

Steerage comprised a mix of pensioner guards who had served the Empire at risk of their lives and other working-class English and Irish, each family overwhelmingly suppressed and escaping the abject poverty and misery of their islands; the English working class driven by poor living conditions and little chance of change; the Irish by poverty, starvation and religious discrimination.

And crammed into the most squalid and poor conditions of all, prisoners drawn from across both lands. Just that same year, 1850 had marked a major change in policy when Western Australia elected to change its status from a free colony to a penal colony. The first 75 convicts had arrived from England in June that year aboard the Scindian, and the Hashemy would arrive in October, the second of 43 ships to transport convicts over the next 18 years. Around 9,720 British convicts were sent directly to the Swan River colony. Towards the end of that period, many of these convicts were more hardened criminals who were convicted for more serious crimes than stealing sheep and picking pockets, as comprised most of those on The Hashemy.

Simply, the prisoners supplied a source of cheap labour to local settlers, and the policy change also came at a time when the eastern states were shutting down their penal settlements and once again Britain found herself without an offshore dumping ground for convicts.

There were indeed serious criminals amongst them – a few that even now plotted for power and money, and others who for the course of their lives had turned bad and were destined forever to a cycle of doing bad.

But the worst criminals of all were typically not in that crammed hold, but on the upper deck - men that were used to riding rough shod over the lives of others through abuse of wealth and power. They rarely had to worry about being 'caught' – their deeds were celebrated by a culture that pivoted on wealth and power as a central aspiration.

Common to the early pioneers was their capitalist culture and with it came a strong sense of conviction - of their own importance and beliefs, that their God had given them purpose and a free-hand to impose those beliefs upon others. Class and race defined them, and they were convinced of their superiority. Their central and collective belief that the English way was the right and proper way; that capitalism, Christianity and 'civilisation' were the only acceptable ways of life.

Their privilege, and their power, overwhelmed their humanity.

These things carried them across the world, to a new land with an ancient and innocent people who had only just begun to realise the realities of the European invasion. Barely 170 years ago, a matter of just a few generations.

Compare this with the culture of people now being invaded. Wealth had no meaning, other than perhaps items that could be exchanged for other items of need; but it was need that defined this, not 'wants'. Power was equally meaningless – certainly individual people had power, but this power was contained and controlled by a deep culture and beliefs that had sustained those people as a group for hundreds of generations. Land, resources were not something that could be owned because they were as one – born of the land, returned to it.

At its heart then was a clash of cultures, the individuals mere pawns to the sweep of history. What each of them failed to see was that culture is of our own creation. Though we are shaped by it, culture is but the collective creation of those that share it. Culture is a construct designed to allow groups of people to survive and to adapt to change - and if we fail to adapt to change, it is our culture that has failed.

The reality was most people, then as now, were good people simply going about their lives. Then as now, they were shaped by their upbringing, by the dominant cultural beliefs of the time and they were both defined and controlled by it.

A culture that was reflected in everything they knew, everything they did.

15

The Swan River Colony

After 95 long days and nights at sea, they finally arrived in Fremantle on 25 October, 1850. They had left England in the northern hemisphere's Spring, and now it was mid Spring in Australia, but the first thing that caught them was the oppressive heat. This was a heat not like the hottest of the English or Irish summers, where the temperature could rise as high as 30 degrees Celsius. Here, 30 degrees was mild. The sun beat down on the half built coastal town of Fremantle at the head of the river with an intensity that seemed to suck the very life out of the buildings and poorly built streets which shimmered in the afternoon heat. While those on the ship were joyous to finally see their destination, and cheered as the Hashemy sailed smoothly past Rottnest Island and they finally witnessed the vast coastal beaches and expanse of their destination, the mood turned sombre as the town came into full sight. There were few people to greet them, and they quickly saw the town was in a poor state, devoid of trees and with only small houses scattered about.

But then a group emerged and called greetings of welcome and instruction to the crew. A small group of men assisted as the ship docked, and to everyone's great joy placed the gangplank to allow passengers to disembark. There was seeming chaos as luggage, men and their families, and much needed stores were unloaded to the docks, and James, Elizabeth and Maggie were swept up in the throng as they carried what they could. Maggie navigated the crowds to get all the luggage out and only their crates of personal supplies remained, which would follow them to their temporary residence at Toodyay Farm in the coming weeks.

| 105 |

James watched in amazement as Maggie was hugged and tender words exchanged with what seemed to be half the passengers, friends she had made along the way it seemed. Meanwhile a clearly pregnant Elizabeth sat on her luggage in a patch of shade, fanning herself frantically. James tended to her needs in between exchanges with several of the first-class passengers and the senior officers, the Captain himself explaining where they should go to get a river boat up to Perth, the still unofficial name of the capital of the Swan River Colony and the state of Western Australia.

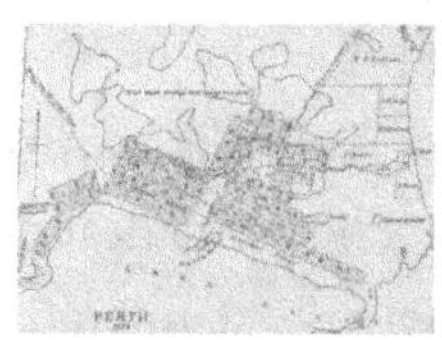

They arrived at their temporary accommodation at the capital, some 22 kilometres up-river as the last light of the day faded. James' relatives had arranged the accommodation through a friend, who was alerted by the ferry man's staff and soon came to the jetty to greet them and load their belongings to a horse drawn cart. Though exhausted, they were all excited to reach their destination. They would have one to two weeks in the townsite while word was sent ahead to James' family, who would make arrangements for the next leg of their journey to the family home in Toodyay Farm.

While James and Elizabeth chatted with their local host after dinner, Maggie, who had of course eaten separately chatted with one of their host's staff about the Colony. The boy's name was Hayden and Maggie guessed he was around 17, just a little younger than herself – she had turned 20 on the voyage. Hayden explained he had been born in the colony in the early 1830s, one of several of the first group of settlers who had arrived with James Stirling himself. He proudly told Maggie of how the colony had grown during that time, with settlers now scattered across the river plains in all directions, and some houses already to be found on the new track that joined Perth to Fremantle. He explained their cargo would likely be transported along that track in the next week or so. Hayden said his own family had purchased lands in Maylands, a

little further east, but found that the soils were not well suited to farming and they had struggled to get by so they had eventually purchased
other land on the south side of the river which they were trying to make
productive. Hayden and his two younger brothers had part-time employment in the city to help makes ends meet, but they loved working
the land. Maggie enquired if the younger boys were being schooled, to
which Hayden laughed and said there just wasn't the time, and no accessible schools anyway. He seemed a nice enough boy, clearly hard working and clever enough in his own way.

The next day, there was a commotion in the street outside and Maggie was alarmed to see Hayden running past with a group of men, each
of them armed and shouting in anger. The house maid looked on too
and explained that the town was on edge after a local shepherd had
been convicted of killing an Aboriginal man and sentenced to a term
of imprisonment. Many of the settlers knew the shepherd well, and felt
the sentence was unjust and that the courts were out of touch with
the realities of farming in the district, where the Aboriginal people persisted after all these years in killing their livestock. Maggie learned that
the Noongar population had by now largely retreated to the northern
parts of the colony, although some had assimilated and were engaged as
labourers and stock hands, for the most part in exchange for rations. But
every time there was a minor conflict, Aboriginal people as a whole were
commonly blamed and inevitably a group of local men would get in
an uproar calling for revenge. Hayden, the pleasant young man she had
spoken to the previous night, was one of the ringleaders. They would
go and harass one or other of the local workers or visitors before realising the Aboriginals responsible were beyond their reach, and then return home amidst much grumbling and cursing of the Aboriginal race.

Maggie did her best to observe impassively – she yearned to learn
more about the colony and the Aboriginal people and knew that speak-
ing out against these practices would certainly not endear her to a population whose help she knew they would need.

But already she suspected, a key problem here was a lack of education.

She explored the townsite as soon as her labours for Elizabeth and James allowed. The streets had improved a little on the earlier description she had read from James' relatives. Now there were some more substantial buildings scattered around – a courthouse, a large church, even a theatre which doubled as a marketplace. There were a large number of merchant warehouses, though few retail businesses selling those stores as barter was still the main means of exchange. And the houses now had well established gardens, blossoming with colour from both European and native flowers.

People bustled about on foot and in horse drawn carriages, some collecting supplies and others making their way to jobs. She sat for a time beneath the shade of a well-established tree and enjoyed the sights and sounds of the new colony and its people. A woman and her husband joined her, and so she asked them about the colony. There were now close to 5000 Europeans in and around Perth and Fremantle they explained, and people were excited to see new arrivals such as herself arriving with increasing frequency. Settlers had expanded up and down the river and some inland areas towards and over the Darling Range, but most of the land away from the Swan River itself was sandy and unproductive. The colony still struggled to meet its own needs, relying on imports while exports were few.

She asked them about the northern areas that James had mentioned, and the man said that yes, there were encouraging reports of pasture lands from an earlier expedition and that lead had been found in the river somewhere up there. However the greater interest, he explained, was in a new private settlement to the south, a place called Australind. He proudly announced he was a partner in that venture, and that a lovely young woman such as herself would be far better to go south than to the rugged north.

The couple moved on and before long she was approached by an older man, clearly drunk despite the early hour and so she made a hasty retreat to the main streets where she explored the handful of supply shops that had sprung up. The high prices of basic materials struck her, as did the scarcity of essentials. She was glad that she wouldn't be here for too long, realising that they had brought only enough supplies for their planned few months, along with the more substantial haul of items that had been requested by James' relatives. James was paying her well in addition to the quarter of her wages that went directly to her parents, and she had had little cause nor opportunity for purchases so had sequestered away a sizeable purse. However, she realised with dismay that even these savings - that back in Ireland would be considerable indeed - would not last long in the distant Swan River colony.

There were pretty dresses and shoes that she passed by without a glance. She settled instead upon a measure of sturdy cloth that she thought could be useful to make a few hard-wearing outfits and perhaps for repairs, should the need arise. She also purchased a heavy second-hand jacket at a good price, mindful of warnings that the nights could be cold before the summer fully set in. It was a man's size and she fairly disappeared when she put it on, but it was a good price and she figured the excess size could help in many ways.

Thus encumbered, she returned to their temporary dwelling and put her supplies with her other belongings before seeking out James and Elizabeth who she found in the sitting room.

"I've just been into town and had a wander around" she relayed to James, Elizabeth barely acknowledging her arrival.

"Things are quite expensive here you know, probably three or four times what we might pay back in Ireland. It's a good thing we're only here for a few months!"

Elizabeth smiled a little at that reminder, but James looked more sombre. "Ah, well it might be a little longer than that of course, with Elizabeth's pregnancy and all. I've already written my father to send further supplies on the next ship. I think in fact we may be here for a good six months, ladies – possibly even a little longer to get the best weather for our return journey."

Elizabeth shifted uneasily in her seat and exclaimed loudly that the primitive conditions were hardly conducive to a lady, let alone a new-born baby. "I do hope your Aunt's home is more comfortable than this... 'dwelling', James!" the latter seeming more like an order than an enquiry.

"Yes, well we shall see" he replied, before quickly changing the subject. "Now I must avail myself of our limited time here in Perth to make some enquiries as to potential land purchases. And the good Captain has given me the name of a certain gentleman who is one of only a few supplying boats locally and is well regarded by the Captain and his line. I understand we shall need to obtain passage up the Swan to Guildford before travelling overland to Toodyay Farm, so I shall make those arrangements and alongside that, I may just enquire about investment in his company! Maggie, given you surprised us both with your knowledge of building boats, I'd like that you should accompany me, and perhaps to check that the fellow actually knows about boat building! Elizabeth, would you care to join us?"

Elizabeth turned up her nose and said she would rather have another cup of tea, so James and Maggie set off to the jetty where they had arrived the previous day, to make contact with the owner. Arrangements were made for the owner to meet them early the following day, and so Maggie and James enjoyed the remainder of the afternoon strolling the town.

It was a great pleasure for them both to be able to enjoy steady land after months at sea, and to enjoy each other's company alone for a while without the hustle bustle of shipboard life, nor Elizabeth's interruptions and disapproving glances. James boldly took Maggie's arm, proud to have the beautiful young woman by his side and Maggie gratefully took it. They chatted as they walked, and the conversation turned to James' purpose of land acquisition.

"Philomena's latest letters sang the praises of new land opening up in the north, quite a distance from Perth – around a month's full ride. I haven't told Elizabeth this, so please keep it as our little secret, but it is my intention to join an expedition there and to start improvements on a selection, so that we might install tenants.

We'll likely be here a full year in fact. Maggie, I'll of course need you to stay with Elizabeth and the baby, but I'd also like you to help me while I'm away by acting as my agent for this boat building proposal, should it come about after our meeting."

Maggie was thrilled by the responsibility and the trust that James was giving her. Of course, it was not really a request – she was his servant – but the idea of playing a small role in the developing colony was far more exciting to her than the endless chores of a house maid.

"Oh James, how exciting! I must admit, I had suspected you might be thinking about boats after that chat with the Captain. And I'm sure you noticed the price of our journey up the river yesterday! It's clear there's a grand opportunity to supply more boats to the Swan colony to transport people and goods up and down the river, but the colony will also need ships to explore and supply the coast. I heard today about a new place to the south called Australind, and also that there are reports of lead ore strike in the north."

James was immediately impressed with Maggie's insight and acumen. "Yes, well let us see what the owner says about the expansion opportunities when we meet him. I'm sure the colour of my money will entice him - but I also have a trump up my sleeve, should it be needed to secure my investment."

16

Building a nation

The next day they went back to the jetty at the time agreed and found Mr Bignell, the owner of the river boat company, getting off a ferry from Maylands alongside a small number of settlers all excited to be in town. Mr Bignell invited them to his Perth office for tea, where he also produced many of his craft. Maggie was fascinated that a boat building enterprise should be tucked away in one of the main streets, and Mr Bignell proudly showed them the ratchet gear arrangement, wheels and rollers that he used to trundle each vessel along Murray Street, and down Barrack Street to the river.

He was clearly interested to hear that James was prepared to invest in his company, but also sceptical and off-hand in his commitment.

"Well, I'm much flattered that the Captain has seen well enough of me to encourage your visit Mr Maguire, I truly am. And it's true that the colony is needing boats to be built locally. But quite frankly, what with both passenger ferries and hiring my little fleet to settlers I am already doing very well, so I'm not exactly rushed to expand. Though I have been pressed on the matter by no less than the Governor - with more and bigger boats, we could certainly expand our runs, particularly up and down the coast to the newer settlements...." James looked at Maggie with a smile.

"But as I explained to the Governor" Bignell continued, "there are serious constraints you see, and I'm not sure even your money could resolve them."

He went on to explain the major hazards in the Swan waterways, which required goods and people to be off-loaded and transferred over flats and impenetrable passes. As the colony had expanded to new grazing lands further up the river, settlers had required boats to move supplies but nothing had been done to make navigation easy for them.

James was despondent, but then Maggie relayed that the colonial Government was considering dredging key shoals, and cutting a channel through the narrow pass barely a mile upstream.

"One of the locals told me!" Maggie laughed in response to James' look of bemusement. Mr Bignell confirmed that was now likely, and that having an expanded fleet ready would be of tremendous service to the colony, with demand virtually guaranteed.

"Though I'd need to move to more suitable premises!" he laughed. James was delighted to see Mr Bignell's negativity turn around, thanks to Maggie's interjection.

"However, the two biggest constraints to expansion remain" Mr Bignell continued. "What we truly lack are two things – decent wood, and decent labourers. As you might have already observed, the key skill of many of our locals is their ability to stay permanently drunk, and their uncanny ability to malinger even as their labour is in such demand! There are few skilled boat builders, and barely the same number of men prepared to put in a decent day's work!"

"Wood and labour you say" James repeated. "Well if you agree to our partnership, Mr Bignell, I have a solution to at least one of those problems" James replied.

James revealed that he had secured up to three fully qualified and experienced carpenters and reportedly reliable labourers amongst the complement of convicts on board the Hashemy.

Mr Bignell was ecstatic at the news, commenting that he had hoped the second shipment of convicts would include the more skilled workers the colony so desperately needed.

"The captain has included a recommendation in his report to the Governor, that the carpenters should be rotated to boat construction as a priority" James concluded, his trump-card revealed. "You will just need to meet the Governor to confirm the arrangement in the coming days, ahead of any petition your competitors make.

Or may I now say, OUR competitors?" James extended his hand, and Mr Bignell enthusiastically shook it.

"Now I apologise I should have made a more formal introduction earlier of my young servant here, Maggie O'Brien. Don't let her youth or beguiling good looks mislead you, Mr Bignell! Maggie was the top student at Mullaharlin National School and has been hand-picked by my father to accompany me on this business journey as both my servant and my assistant. As such she has my full authority to act in my stead during periods when I am away. As you've already seen, Maggie is well educated but she also knows a thing or two about building boats herself."

Mr Bignell looked surprised and a little put out at the suggestion that he should have to deal with a woman, and a young one at that. So James hastily explained that Mr Bignell would of course take the reins on a day to day basis, but Maggie would support any necessary business arrangements and act as James' own emissary as required for the period of time he was away. Mr Bignell seemed satisfied and shook Maggie's hand into the deal for good measure.

Maggie was elated to be included, and James couldn't help but notice a twinkle of gratitude accompanied that of pride in her eye.

"We'll need to secure some decent wood, and quickly if the deal is to go ahead" she interjected, the men turning towards her with surprise. She asked Mr Bignell if he knew of any reliable local timbers, to which he revealed that all his handful of boats had been built from imported timber, and that is what he expected to use for expansion. He explained the biggest builder and their main competitor, the Mews family, had depleted or otherwise secured most of the suitable river timber in the vicinity, and the smaller builders had no choice but to rely on salvaged supplies, inferior local timber or pre-formed planks imported from as far away as the Hebrides.

However, he also expressed that the imported timbers were far superior to the local ones, "...and safer for use" he proudly added. "None of my craft have run into trouble – same can't be said for the Mews craft nor most of the other local builders."

"But I read that there are healthy trees in the Eastern colonies and in Albany, so surely there'll be a supply closer than Hebrides!" Maggie mused, as much to herself as the others. "Let me make some enquiries while we're here – I'll see if there may be a reliable supply nearby before you have to commit to further imports."

James and Mr Bignell nodded their agreement, though as Maggie left the meeting Mr Bignell commented privately to James "I'll tell you now, we'll need to import. Give her credit for trying, but a dozen or more builders ain't yet found a suitable timber and I very much doubt your young protege will either, with the greatest respect Mr Maguire."

And so Maggie's next few days in Perth were occupied in the library and talking to builders, fishermen and settlers alike as to their experience of working with different woods. Most of the timbers documented were too hard, too gnarly or both and for a while Maggie had doubted anything would be suitable. But she persisted in her research and took meticulous notes which she corroborated through visits to the library, and finally through a meeting requested with the highly respected botanist, James Drummond, on the final day of their stay. But Drummond's office had refused to take the young Maggie seriously, and so he sent his son and apprentice in botany, Johnston, to meet her.

Johnston was visibly surprised and delighted when a beautiful 20-year-old had shown up, fussing over her unnecessarily and making efforts to ingratiate himself. He was only a little older himself.

A few days later James' relatives had sent word and their time in Perth was at an end.

Mr Bignell joined them on the ferry boat as they made their way up the river to Guildford, where a buggy would be waiting with house staff to transport them over the hills to Toodyay. Elizabeth sat in the sun, shaded by a parasol and fanning herself profusely. She glanced frequently over at the men, infuriated that Maggie sat close to James as official papers were signed and mutual congratulations extended over brandy.

James' investment was substantial at nearly 2000 pounds, more than half his available funds and to be paid in three instalments. It would allow new yards upriver at Maylands, and a projected tripling of construction focusing on a small number of large coastal trading vessels, along with smaller barges and craft for river use and a small fleet of fishing boats.

Mr Bignell announced he had already prepared a letter to his supplier to increase his timber supply and was confident he could obtain a shipment in only a few months. "Pending Maggie's findings of course" he added and their eyes turned towards her, both ready to hear that her 'research' had been as fruitless as Mr Bignell had predicted.

"Gentlemen" she commenced "I have what I believe may be a solution." The men looked to her in surprise, curious to hear what this young woman had found that the many local builders had failed to.

Maggie reached into her travel bag and withdrew a small chisel with a wooden handle, a red/ grey-brown colour with reddish streaks and presented it to Mr Bignell who looked at it quizzically. "Beautiful, but I have enough hand tools already" he laughed, and James chuckled too, slight embarrassment in his voice.

"Ah not the tool, Mr Bignell. Look at the handle! It's made from a species of eucalyptus called 'Brown Mallet' and it's apparently quite abundant to the near south of where James and I are now headed" she proudly exclaimed.

"I found this in a general store – a farmer has made a few for sale under the name 'Browne's Brown Mallet mallets'. Well the name got my attention I'll admit! But I liked the look of this wood – look how densely interlocked the grain is. So, I bought it to show you."

Mr Bignell turned the wood over in his hands, his face not betraying his thoughts either way.

"It also attracted my attention because my pappa used a similar chisel made from the same wood he used in boat building" she continued, "and so I wondered if it's also been crafted from a construction wood." Mr Bignell shook his head "No, too thick for that – this is used for coarse work."

"Yes, that's what I realised too" Maggie replied without missing a beat - "it's been made for building a house, not a boat."

Mr Bignell couldn't disguise his surprise and reached again for the chisel.

"So, I spent an afternoon in the library and found some arborist records on 'Brown Mallet' and compared them to other eucalypts that have been documented. This tree is found on the edges of wild woods and is relatively small which is why it might have been overlooked - together with the fact it is found over 160 kilometres inland from the coast!"

Without giving them a chance to protest the transport distance, she continued "Then I spoke to a York farmer who was down buying some supplies, and he was familiar with the Brown Mallet. He described it as mostly scrubby, only up to 30 foot height and that he knows a few locals use it in building construction, but he reckons its best use is on the fire!" Maggie joined in as both men laughed.

Mr Bignell passed the tool back to her once more. "So, a scrubby bush tree whittled down to make tool handles or stoking a fire – as I expected" and turned to James with mock disappointment.

"And sturdy houses" Maggie corrected as she looked down to read from her notes once more.

"So anyway, I took it to Johnston Drummond – the son of James Drummond, WA's most respected Botanist you know - to confirm the species. Well as it turns out, the Drummonds live out very near your own Aunt and Uncle, James, and Johnston knew the Brown Mallet quite well. Though I must tell you he notes it has never been used for boat building.

But here's the thing. His own records say it can grow 'as high as 100 foot in height and has a three-foot girth' – quite different to the type that fills the fireplace!

So then I checked pastoral records back at the library and found a record that described Brown Mallet as 'rather hard to work with, but one that dresses well and is both solid and *suitable for construction*'. Johnston also said it's easy to dry, and drying reduces the weight by around a fifth.

So I'm thinking if we could find a suitable source in the Avon valley, drying it there for storage and transport would make a few cart loads from one or two trees possible quite regularly, and from the pastoralist reports workability will also be a whole lot easier."

The men's demeanour changed and Maggie pushed the chisel back across the table.

"Incidentally" Maggie added as Mr Bignell again inspected the chisel more deeply, "the botanical records also note the bark has a particularly high tannin content that can be used for tanning leather and for adhesives manufacture. So, nothing will go to waste.

What do you think, Mr Bignell?" she enquired, now transferring the role of expert back to their new partner.

"I don't know" Mr Bignell said, pondering the tool. "It sounds promising I'll grant you that. But I can't tell from this little sample."

"Which is why I got this from Mr Drummond..." said Maggie and reached into her bag a second time to produce a plank over a foot in length, much to their amusement. "Why, do you know this was his only sample but he gave it to me when I smiled nicely at him." And she gave James and Mr Bignell that same smile, leaving them both with little doubt that she would get just about anything she so wished.

Mr Bignell's attention was now firmly on the wood – he could clearly see the same potential Maggie had. "Excellent work, Maggie!" James said enthusiastically and then requested Mr Bignell to run some tests and send word if he thought it may be suitable.

"Perhaps a trial is in order..." Bignell suggested. "See if you can't find a suitable stand of this 'Brown Mallet' and commence arrangements for supply."

Maggie's enthusiastic smile lit up her face, and much to her delight James gave her a secret and deep smile in return, pride shining behind his handsome face and eyes.

"It's amazing what you can find through research" Maggie commented as she left them to finalise both the agreement and their brandy, and as she walked back to Elizabeth she felt the men's eyes upon her.

"How old did you say she was?" she heard Mr Bignell ask, and she heard too James' quiet reply:

"Old enough."

17

Toodyay

Maggie was impressed by the 'farmhouse' and the farm itself called 'Toodyay' when they eventually arrived late in the day. The long jaunt over the ranges in the buggy had proceeded without any issues, though Elizabeth had needed frequent stops and had complained incessantly about the flies and the 'horrid, uncultivated lands'.

But Elizabeth's demeanour had changed instantly as they arrived at a stately stone manor, its extensive green fields fenced and dotted with sheep, cattle and wheat pastures. Philomena and her husband came out happily to greet them, and a host of servants rushed to their aid to unload their supplies. They were shown to their rooms – Maggie would share a room with two of the housemaids, who greeted her with a smile.

"How splendid that you have finally come!" chirped Philomena over coffee and biscuits, something of a rare treat. "We are most excited that Thomas has seen fit to send you, James, and that he shares our hope for the expansion of our family's fortunes."

"Ah and a great adventure to boot!" added James, and laughed alongside Philomena and her husband Sean, a particularly fat man who looked to be 80 or more, though James had understood him to be around his father's own age.

They exchanged stories of the sea voyage and news of the family back in Ireland and England. The couple were shocked to hear the first-hand stories of the famine, though delighted to hear the family were coping well.

Philomena – Thomas' only sister – had moved to Belfast with her husband Sean as a young woman and they had raised two sons and two daughters all of whom were now married and in their own established homes. Sean had a family wealth even then surpassing that which Thomas would eventually amass. James and Elizabeth learnt how they and their sons had moved to Perth in the very early days of the settlement, the excitement of new prospects enticing the young men as well as Sean and Philomena, who by then both in their 40s and quite bored had decided to go along 'for a few months to help them settle in'. That was in the early 1830s, now nearly twenty years ago. The colony in those days was very basic but they purchased a reasonable house in Guildford before moving to Toodyay Farm, their 'retirement home'. They explained good land was very cheap in those days and like others they purchased much, but they had the added advantage of vast wealth with which to quickly improve those lands. They explained that was a key error for many of the settlers who now languished on the outskirts of proper society – they had large land holdings but had left themselves little capital to improve it.

As a result of their 'wisdom', they explained, they had enjoyed healthy returns on their investments for many years now, and so had decided to stay. They were now one of the richest families in Western Australia, and by far the wealthiest in the district.

The fertile plains of the Avon River valley had been 'discovered' by Ensign Robert Dale in the same year that they arrived. Philomena and Sean had moved to this farm which they called 'Toodyay' in 1835 and were one of the first established families in the district, alongside the botanist James Drummond and Captain Francis Whitfield, their adjacent neighbours. "Yes, a mere 3 miles that way, and that" Sean laughed, pointing with his arms crossed to the north and south.

Philomena explained they had chosen the land as a country retreat as it so reminded her of the County Kerry area of her birth, and that they had been pleased that it also produced both wool and wheat of a higher quality than their other land. Their only disappointment, she explained, was the town itself and the lack of services.

"Oh this area has potential to be sure, though the town itself is taking far longer to grow than we might have hoped. We boldly call it Newcastle you know; but as yet the only thing there is a general store with little in the way of product! Though you can get a drink at least – there are three inns! But don't fret, the servants go weekly to Guildford and Perth for supplies."

Elizabeth looked pleased, and wondered if perhaps this foolish adventure to the great southern land might not have been such a disaster after all. It was very hot but yes, she could see herself in this place quite comfortably. She stood as if to look out over the green pastures outside, deliberately projecting her belly and showing her effort and displacement.

"And Elizabeth, your pregnancy is the greatest news of all!" Philomena exclaimed, taking the bait. "Why Thomas will be overjoyed! Only recently he wrote expressing his hope that you might finally fall pregnant, and of course we would be delighted that you would stay with us through the birth and as long beyond that occasion as you might wish."

"Oh, that would be wonderful!" Elizabeth replied, her relief obvious to all. "I found Perth quite uncivilised, and as for Fremantle, well the word 'uncouth' is the only description that springs to mind!"

"Well let me show you around then" Philomena offered and took Elizabeth's arm for a tour of the house and yards. As they left, James heard Philomena say she would arrange a midwife to come up from Perth when the time came.

James and Sean were left to discuss business, and Sean soon raised that he and his sons were key investors in a local consortium called 'The Cattle Company' who had secured newly leased lands to the north in the Province of Victoria – sites referred to as Champion Bay, and the Irwin River and Greenough River Flats - and encouraged that James should do the same.

James was already familiar with the history from Philomena's earlier letters. George Grey had discovered the area in 1839, returning on-foot from a disastrous boating voyage in which all three of their boats had sunk near the mouth of the Murchison River. Grey reported that the Province of Victoria south of the Murchison had exciting possibilities but that there was some 'rough and inhospitable country in between'. Further explorations of the Victoria district followed, primarily at the urging of the York Agricultural Society including Sean himself, who were alarmed at the implications of the overstocking of Avon Valley runs. By the end of 1847, seven expeditions and two official surveys had been made to the north of the Irwin River and three southward from there. All agreed that the Victoria district had favourable pastoral potential.

In September 1848, Assistant Surveyor Augustus Gregory led a 'Settlers Expedition' as far north as the Murchison River with the primary goal of finding new grazing pasture but to also watch for useful minerals, take note of plants and animals and observe the character and customs of local Aboriginal people. The party travelled the upper Irwin, examining the land for pasture and minerals and encountered many Aboriginal groups who had created tracks through the bush that Gregory's exploration party used. After riding through areas of sandy hills and scrublands, the party came across a chain of small lagoons and swamps of fresh water and grasslands. The land was promising and on return to Perth, Gregory submitted a formal report to the Avon Valley graziers indicating that the expedition was a success and there was over 100,000 acres of good grassy land in the vicinity of Champion Bay and the Irwin River.

Sean explained that The Cattle Company then promptly secured the lease of 120,000 acres from the Crown at a cost of just ten shillings per 1000 acres and championed the previous year's expedition to survey plots and to install the first herd of cattle and sheep. Just the year before, in September 1849 the Cattle Company had driven 4000 head of cattle and 350 sheep to an area surrounded by river, ready for the first settlers to arrive.

"The Cattle Company plan to sub-lease smaller lots to 'outstanding settlers', conditional that they improve those lands and then purchase and install the Company's own sheep and cattle, which the Cattle Company will then eventually export."

Settlers would sub-lease lots varying between 3,500 and 20,000 acres around Greenough River and would install stockyards and other improvements, and then the Cattle Company would move in and manage the herds in exchange for a guaranteed share of profits. For cashed-up investors and sub-leasees alike it was a good deal that would quickly open up new lands for large herds and guaranteed profits.

It was a bold plan for the time. Western Australia was as yet barely producing enough for its own meagre needs, and the Cattle Company's gamble was both that they could sub-let lands to settlers who would effectively work as their labourers; supply stock to them at a profit; and also that there would be sufficient produce to enable export to the East, and beyond.

"A nifty arrangement I'm sure you agree" Sean concluded.

After much discussion, James decided that in addition to investing 5000 pounds in the Cattle Company to match Sean's own investment, the Maguire-Fielding Family Trust would also directly sub-lease a sizeable parcel of land. This, James argued, would ensure he could personally oversee that the improvements happened quickly, and would provide him with a base from which he could select and purchase more land to the north over a few months. He stated that he would then simply move in his own tenant managers – achieving both a better and quicker return on his investment in a matter of months.

Sean agreed it was a good plan that would also speed up settlement of the area, and most importantly that it would ensure the very best lands were set aside for the family.

The cost of all this was of course considerably more than James had available in cash and it would take too long for that cash to arrive from home, so it was arranged that forty per cent would be in cash, with the remainder via a 'promissory note', which Sean offered to endorse to the Cattle Company. The note would be paid in cash by the Maguire-Fielding Family Trust on presentation to a bank in England – a common practice at that time.

This would leave James with enough money to purchase necessary equipment and labour.

Over the next weeks, arrangements for the expedition were made and a departure date in March 1851 finally confirmed. This date worked in well with Elizabeth's pregnancy, which proceeded without complication. James' sub-lease was approved and his selection of land was described as 'prime grazing land alongside the Greenough River near the river crossing and in a central location between the settlements to ensure ready access to supplies'.

The land was unfenced and so herds were free roaming, overseen during the day by shepherds and driven to stockyards at night. James' main task was therefore to oversee the building of stockyards across his lease, and shepherds' huts so that the herds could be moved in as other settlers arrived the following year. This made him both an investor and a key partner in the settlement of Greenough itself.

Maggie worked tirelessly around the house alongside the other servants and took a lead role in preparing for James' journey – it was as if she were back in Dundalk at the Maguire's own sprawling house.

But James gave her leave to also explore the area in search of Brown Mallet and after enquiries she soon found a healthy stand of large trees only 10 kilometres away, sufficient to meet their needs for one or two years at least. From their base in Toodyay Farm, labourers were immediately set to work removing a small handful of trees for the trial, sawing them to workable planks at Maggie's specifications, and then set aside in a considerable stockpile to dry. Maggie accompanied the first cartloads to Perth herself only eight weeks later, and she was pleased to see first-hand Mr Bignell's delight at the finished product. A while later they received word back from Mr Bignell that the wood was quite suitable - "difficult to work as had been anticipated, but Maggie's cut and preparation of the wood had made dressing much easier than feared".

She also made several other trips to Perth in those early days, and during these times she would inspect production of 'The Speculator' – a schooner soon to become the first locally made coastal hauler in Western Australia. James accompanied her on a couple of trips, and Maggie would be joined at other times by one or two of the servants to collect supplies and deliver wool and wheat. Of course she always took advantage of a visit to the library, and to pop in on Johnston Drummond who had now become her close friend. Inspired by her initial research, her latest mission was to learn the names of Western Australian trees, and he was only too happy to tutor her!

Their friendship deepened over many long conversations and as they connected, one day she told him of the story she had read about Degunbut Kanyap those years ago, and asked what he knew of the local Aboriginal people. So she was delighted when he replied that he had met many Aboriginal people in his botanical surveys throughout the southwest and to the north, and that his brother John was very well acquainted with groups throughout the area, and he happily relayed some of his observations.

"The local Aboriginals are the Wadjuk people of the Noongar tribe that is found throughout the southwest, and they appear to me and to all who know them as fine people of high intelligence. We estimate there are at least 6000 around the Swan settlement – many more than the settlers" he began.

"I've seen that there are many different families and groups throughout the areas I have travelled, and what I've found is that each group have clearly distinguished hunting-grounds. The boundaries between them overlap but in places they are quite definite, such as trees that are recognized as landmarks, and they are very clear to stay in their own areas unless invited by their neighbours. So my father and I always make a point of seeking out the elders when we are surveying trees, and we've never had any problems.

What has stood out the most for me is just how remarkably peaceful they all are" he remarked, a smile upon his face. "They haven't acquired a taste for tobacco, nor for the spirits that badly disaffects so many of the settlers." He laughed then as he continued. "Nor do they show a disposition to wear English clothing, despite often assisting with many odd jobs around the district!" Maggie laughed too, as Johnston revelled in her company and smiles.

"A few years ago I travelled to King Georges Sound and learned that several tribes of Noongar people assemble there once a year and hold a sort of fair; and that as different tribes excelled each other in the manufacture of weapons such as spears, throwing sticks or woomeras, kylees or boomerangs, shields and waddies, these formed the articles of exchange, as well as the red-ochre with which, combined with grease, they decorate themselves. Maggie, I know that red-ochre is only found very far away in certain localities..." Maggie looked at him quizzically, wondering what he was getting at. "So Maggie, don't you see?" he continued "There is trade, and over long distances!"

Fascinated to hear of the local people first-hand, Maggie then relayed her concerns regarding the newspaper articles she had read, noting the majority had said Aboriginals had no right to their own land unless it was developed and industrious.

"Yes, it is unfortunately very true that there is ongoing disquiet, and there have been regular unsavoury incidents over twenty years now - almost too many to mention..." he replied, his eyes now downcast as he recalled some of those dreadful events.

"I recall a short time after my family arrived, 1832 from what I can remember, that there was great unrest among the settlers at a string of murders and stock losses reportedly at the hand of a local chief, Midgegooroo and a much feared warrior, Yagan. Midgegooroo was well over 50 and very well regarded by many in the colony, however he was captured and summarily executed in cold blood by the acting Governor, Lieutenant Irwin!"

Maggie remarked that James' Aunt had written about Irwin. "Yes, well. Maggie, the pomp is his façade - underneath Irwin is a most officious and unpleasant man, seeking as he readily states to intimidate the natives into submission. Although many in the colony cautioned against him the execution of Midgegooroo in respect to the likely impact on native relations, he proceeded nonetheless."

Maggie saw a tear forming in the corner of his eye, and it rolled down his face as he continued.

"The notion exists among many settlers such as Lieutenant Irwin, and even the Courts, that *the Aboriginal people must be made to fear you before they will love you*. Maggie, I say to you that it is an ancient barbarism which does not belong in a so-called civilised society, but to our enduring disgrace, in the last 25 years many a poor Aboriginal person has been shot under this idea in Western Australia.

But you know I am a good Christian man, and like you I have been troubled by what I've seen. I recently spoke to the Colonial Chaplain Rev John Wittenoom about these horrid events and he said he believed that in almost every case that when any of the white people had been harmed by Aboriginal people, the Whites were the faulty party!"

He whispered now, leaning in towards her. "At one point, the settlers actually meditated a war of extermination against them! But an outstanding Christian man, Robert Lyons, who has become over many years now my mentor, made so powerful an appeal against the injustice and inequity of such a measure that the war of extermination was thankfully abandoned.

Maggie, I'll always remember his words when the settlers inquired what they should do instead. Lyons replied, *"Do, my dear Sirs, what our Lord and Saviour Jesus Christ has commanded."* And to the further question, *"What is that?"* he answered, *"Whatsoever ye would that men should do to you, do ye even so to them."*

The bulk of her days were spent in dreary toil at Toodyay Farm, working alongside the other house servants and solely responsible for Elizabeth and James' needs. She took care to avoid Elizabeth alone, but equally to ensure she addressed her every need and was obvious in so doing. In turn, Elizabeth cooled to her, reducing her complaints to James to barely once a day. She excused Maggie's feigning infatuation for her husband as little more than puppy love and as her pregnancy advanced, chose to believe that it could never be more.

Spring rolled into Summer, the household happy as it prepared for two momentous occasions – the epic journey north, and the birth of a child, the very first such event at the Toodyay farm.

18

A double tragedy

Maggie was in the field the day James and Elizabeth's son finally arrived. It was 20 December 1850, and the heat was extreme. As she arrived home in her little cart, she could sense immediately that something was not right. No one was around, and James was nowhere to be found. Philomena sat alone in the dining room, apparently in shock and Maggie was unable to get anything from her. Then she found one of her roommates rushing with a bag of something towards the laundry, but the girl continued past muttering only "must clean the blood, the blood".

With mounting alarm, she quickly deduced what might have happened. The child was several weeks early, and the midwife was yet to arrive. As she rushed to Elizabeth and James' room to confirm her suspicions and to offer her help, she opened the door to see a throng of servants cleaning more bloodied sheets and caught just a glimpse of Elizabeth lying prone on the bed. She screamed in alarm, and Philomena herself appeared and hustled her back out the door.

"I'm so sorry, I'm so sorry" was all she could say, and Maggie could see Philomena was trembling uncontrollably.

"What happened?" Maggie frantically enquired. "So much blood... She died before she could see the child... A great tragedy..." was the only response she received, and Philomena moved down the corridor barking orders to the servants. Then she turned back to Maggie "Don't just stand there girl" she said, suddenly remembering Maggie too was a servant, not the daughter she sometimes thought she was. "James will need help – he wandered off towards the river."

Maggie longed to see Elizabeth, to see if there was anything she could do to help – to give her dignity. She couldn't believe she was dead. But her heart called out to James and so of course she rushed to find him.

When she went outside she turned towards the river, but there was no sign of him. Logic said he would go right, towards the section of river they all commonly accessed. Or perhaps straight ahead, towards a section of rapids that was a pleasant place to sit and relax.

But Maggie's heart was in control now, and before her head could even direct her feet they turned left, towards a wide, slow section of river that was rarely accessed as it was far from the house - a rocky area shrouded in bush.

Once there, the path became even less clear but yet she turned north without hesitation, moving over shrub crowded rocks for a hundred meters before she finally saw him, sitting quietly on a rock.

She didn't say anything, just sat beside him and when he offered his hand, she held it gently. And in time he leaned into her and cried, long heaves that grew from his centre and emerged in shallow, hopeless sobs.

He told her the story of the birth, that it came on suddenly but unravelled slowly. Elizabeth had been enjoying a cup of tea when she doubled over in convulsive pain and blood suddenly stained her legs. The household quickly realised it was the child coming, though it was several weeks earlier than anyone had expected. Excitement turned to alarm as the flow of blood worsened and now Elizabeth's screams rattled the house. He helped her move to their room but the walls couldn't muffle that dreadful sound. Word went out immediately for help, but of course there was none, and nor was there any that James could offer.

Several times Elizabeth passed out from the pain, but still she rallied and pushed. The maids did what they could, he said, but there was no saving her as ruptures now took hold and life faded even as her body willed her still to push, to expel the life within. The child had eventually emerged, but too late for Elizabeth to see it was a boy – she was already unconscious from loss of blood. And then, worst of all for James who sat hopelessly on the far side of the room, there was silence. Ten seconds where there was nothing, an awful and endless time. And then the boy cried, and again there was chaos as maids rushed and the child was separated and then taken away. He moved to Elizabeth. Her womb had been packed with bed clothes in an attempt to stop the bleeding, but she was blue and unresponsive, and in his heart he knew it was already too late.

James was ashamed he had then felt an overpowering need to escape, that he fled before he knew for sure that she had passed.

"Oh James, there was nothing you or anyone could do" she whispered, pulling his head towards her."

And there they remained for an hour, perhaps more, until he roused and announced, "I must see the baby."

The household rallied to support James and the baby. The boy was nearly two months premature, and the odds of survival were against it. The urgent need of course was to feed the child, and as there was no wet-nurse available he was first put directly to the teat of a goat, which he hungrily fed at. However of course the goat was not too pleased, and so Philomena suggested bottled cow milk which proved more manageable, though the boy took to it less readily. As soon as she could, Maggie set off once more to Perth and visited the midwife, who recommended the addition of small amounts of wheat, malt flour and bicarbonate. Later that day, the boy took to the mix more readily and immediately showed improvement.

Elizabeth's funeral was arranged on the Farm itself, and James agonised over a letter to inform her parents. Their investment in the Australian venture had been a sizeable stipend for Elizabeth and a promise to reimburse suitable purchases, and James realised both now would need to cease.

Maggie became the boy's Nanny, though the task of feeding and caring for him was spread among the maids as Maggie continued to manage aspects of the timber production, amongst occasional trips to Perth.

James pushed on with his plans to join the Cattle Company overland expedition, which was still to proceed in March – now just two months away. He filled lists of clothing, food and other items that would be needed, sufficient for at least one year and the full change of seasons on advice of Sean - though he doubted he would be there that long.

Most pleasingly, Maggie joined him on several trips to Perth, taking down wheat and fleece and returning with supplies. During the trips they became very close, James relaying his sorrow and his gratitude to Maggie; she happy to listen and to bask in his attentions. They certainly didn't kiss nor even hold hands - but they were close and he felt an electricity each time she brushed against him, and his excitement for her company grew. But he kept his growing affections well hidden from his aunt and uncle – it was too early and too complicated.

It was certainly not unusual for master and servant to couple and even to marry – particularly in the antipodes where women were scarce. However, James' felt the time was not right, and perhaps if he asked Maggie to join him on the trip North, their love could blossom free from prying eyes.

On one of their trips to Guildford in February, he was elated to find a letter from home at the Postmaster's office - a long awaited reply to the letters he had sent his father and Patrick immediately upon arrival and several more since.

The letter was addressed to 'Mr and Mrs Sean Anderson and Messer James Maguire' and so he resisted the urge to open it. The rear of the letter reflected only their home address in Dundalk, but James thought it looked like his father's handwriting and seal, and imagined that his father was writing to confirm further investment, and perhaps even a visit. His eagerness to present the letter to his Aunt and Uncle showed as he returned back to Toodyay Farm, and it was agreed they should all wait to hear the good news together that night, as they reclined in the drawing room after supper. Sean was assigned to read it and dramatically broke the seal, withdrawing the letter with a smile upon his lips.

"It is my great regret" Sean commenced, reading from the short letter that emerged, his words and smile rapidly fading as he continued "to advice you all that James' and my beloved father, and Philomena and Sean's cherished brother, has passed away."

Philomena gasped and nearly fainted – it was the first news they had heard from home since James' arrival. She was brought smelling salts and then took the letter to read herself. "Thomas died peacefully at home after a short battle with cancer" she read aloud, before passing the letter back as if it were a poisoned chalice.

James took the letter and started to read it aloud, but his voice trailed off as he read it now solely to himself. Then he reached for the envelope that Sean had placed on the coffee table and passed the letter back to Sean.

"He has sent me some private correspondence" he advised, composing himself as he stood erect. "I will retire to read it, and perhaps it is best for you to be alone with Philomena to absorb the rest of the letter yourselves."

He looked at Sean and then moved to his Aunt, who sat still with head in hands, softly crying or trying to compose herself. "My heart is broken" he said and touched her gently on the shoulder. "My father was a great man, and his passing is a great sorrow to us all. My condolences to you, Aunt for you have lost too, your brother and hero to your own mother and father. May God keep his soul."

James retired to his room and opened the smaller envelope that had been sequestered away in a rush. His eyes darted across the page, and his shoulders slumped as he absorbed its meaning.

19

A different direction

Thomas Maguire had nursed his family through the worst of times, but yet he was unable to see it through. In 1849 he had developed cancer and was not expected to survive more than a year or two at most. When he first learned the grim prognosis, he told no-one but immediately escalated the schooling of his oldest son, Patrick, to take over the business. Despite his continued aggressive attitudes and mannerisms, Patrick acted on his guidance and instructions in good faith and soon became the face of the Maguire empire, such that it was a seamless transition when Thomas did indeed eventually die as the Irish winter of 1850 approached. Even as James still approached Western Australia, Patrick had already firmly taken hold of the business.

Patrick's unambiguous ambition was to grow the cattle empire. Almost immediately upon his father's death, he abandoned the residual cropping that had continued in the district and instead installed cattle. He evicted the tenant farmers within weeks, and employed a single manager working across several properties, supported by only one or two farm hands. Within months he saw a healthy return on his investment, and the Maguire wealth grew. But more importantly for Patrick, so had his influence. People in the district feared him, and he knew that with fear came respect. He was invited to meet with politicians and men of great power and influence, a pioneer himself as Ireland converted from the ancient small scale agricultural traditions to the modern, large scale, large profits of cattle production and slaughter.

The housing and business tenants were issued rent rises within days, Maggie's parents among them despite his father's promises. Patrick had taken personal pleasure in delivering that news. He had always been aggrieved by his father and James' softness towards the O'Brien family, and he suspected that it was driven less by commerce than by shameless desire on behalf of his witless brother. True, it was a desire he shared, had harboured since the young hussy, Maggie, has spurned his advances while at their estate.

He was thinking of that occasion as he penned this letter to James. He would take great pleasure in ensuring she, as well as James should pay the price for softness.

For on a mild Spring-day in 1848, while his father was away on business and his mother engaged in some brainless tea party; as his brother James and his beautiful wife Elizabeth were off on yet another holiday in the English countryside; Patrick had found himself alone in the house with the teenager, Maggie. He studied her from across the room as she dusted, his eyes forming dots – a predator's stare. She was indeed as beautiful as his pathetic brother had chirped to him. Startling green eyes. Long brown hair that bounced around her pretty visage. Hips and legs that longed for his touch. Well-formed bosoms, pert and that showed their fullness now as she reached up to dust above the mantle.

She was teasing him he felt sure, she a servant and he the master. His pathetic brother had lacked the guile to show her who was boss; he would not. He put down his newspaper and moved silently across the room, Maggie oblivious to his advance. Then, as she turned around he was suddenly there, his face mere inches from her own, his left arm inexplicably now around her back and pulling her in as his lips parted. His right hand moved up from her waist to her breast and he squeezed hard, pulling her out of surprise and now into alarm.

Maggie was no ignorant girl. She knew how men looked at her - even the old man Thomas had been caught leering at her as she busied herself around the house. Patrick was a large and strong man, larger than James but fatter, and uglier. He had not betrayed any such desires before; she thought he was contented by his own wife and happy with her and their children. Yet here he was, upon her and now forcing her backwards and towards the ground. She realised her stupidity in being alone with him, she recalled the only other servant on duty that day was in the summer house and that she was quite alone. A scream would not save her, no one would hear.

And so she had smiled at him, using his momentum to move her towards the door. As he lightened his hold, pleased at the whore's reaction, she ducked quickly down and then sprung to the door, slamming it as she bolted from the room and the house.

He had had no recourse but to watch her go, and as she glanced back at him as he watched from the window he saw the stark look of fear on her face. But he saw more behind those beautiful green eyes. Even at a distance, he saw contempt. And so he flung it back.

"Dear James

I wanted to send you a personal letter regarding the tragic death of our father. I want to start by saying, he felt no pain and would have gone in the way he wished – silently, without fuss. He died only within weeks of your departure I'm sorry to say, having kept his condition to himself and latterly to our mother alone.

You would know of course that our father had placed the day to day business operations with me, though he was ardent to say you should remain involved in a junior capacity. To this end, I seek your assistance in ensuring a quick end to your arrangements there.

You will need to rely on your personal cash reserves to support both yourself and Elizabeth.

Matters are tight here. I am sorry to say our father left the business interests in a poorer state than he might have led us to believe. Although I have had some good success with conversion to cattle production, our father's heavy investment in the potato enterprise, the minor commercial and residential interests and the silly tourist hopes he held for Blackrock, have proven unsustainable and so I will be shifting those assets in due course. In the meantime I have wisely already increased rents to recoup some of the losses.

To be clear, this is to say I cannot send the further cash you requested from our father. Needless to say, also do not make any further commitments on behalf of our family to avoid undue embarrassment. I expect you will have enough cash left to purchase the most favourable lands and then to return home quickly, where you are most needed. Please take this as intended, a sign of my trust in your ability.

This also means that my support can therefore no longer extend to meeting the additional costs of your handservant, Maggie O'Brien, and again the arrangements for the additional funds that you requested unfortunately cannot be honoured. It is frankly beyond me that our father agreed to such exorbitant wages, and in addition to freezing her parents Blackrock rent.

By the time this letter arrives, I would suggest you may need to quickly dispense with her services.

I will understand of course if you find any of this beyond you and should that be the case I would urge you to return immediately and we will manage matters from afar, together. You will of course always find a welcome here in Dundalk, where I shall also have suitable work arranged for you without delay. You do of course have a share in our own family-owned assets upon death of our mother, but needless to say you will in the interim draw a handsome wage for your efforts to support our joint ventures.

But I doubt any of this will be a bother to you and that your Australian adventure is a roaring success, so I shall look forward to your return soon, and to calling us equal partners, the great Maguire brothers!

Your faithful brother,

Patrick"

James was shocked and felt a pit of anger rising deep within him. Not only had the requested funds been denied, it seemed Patrick was effectively cutting him off from his father's business income, to which he had been promised and had always felt entitled. He could hardly believe his own brother could stoop to such low depths.

By rights he was an equal beneficiary in all their father's assets but with a sinking heart he realised that most of their assets were tied up in business investments which Patrick would never release to the estate. He could perhaps push to liquidate privately owned assets – their Dundalk estate and Dublin manor – but these could not be realised while ever his mother was alive and would come with hefty legal fees that would drag on for years. And he knew enough to know the law would support Patrick in a claim against the estate, should ever he have the funds or time to mount a challenge.

Worst of all, he realised his father's decision to appoint Patrick as Business Manager meant that Patrick would have full control of income.

No, his options were severely limited, particularly this far from home. He tried to push the anger aside and focus on his choices: as he saw it, he had only two. The first and easiest, return home, tail between his legs and live under Patrick's command – no more holidays or parties. He would effectively be an employee of his own family holdings. Patrick would hold the purse strings and make sure he shared the responsibilities, but he doubted he would have any of the decision-making privileges.

The other option was even less appealing. Stay and make a go of it. Finish what he started, see it through. It was intoxicating on one level, but he knew it would not only be hard, but likely to fail. Then he would be left here, on the other side of the planet with little money, no assets – only debt, and worst of all, he would be a failure in the eyes of his family.

He reviewed the positives of the option: He had paid the lease on 5000 acres of Greenough land in advance with the intention of placing his own tenant managers - so he would have a base from which to work. He would also be able to a draw a quarter-share of Cattle Company profits from the Maguire/ Fielding joint family Trust once productive, although he realised this could be some time off.

He had also negotiated most of the Cattle Company shares via a promissory note which would clearly be honoured by his brother and Elizabeth's parents, particularly as it was endorsed by Sean. This meant that he still had some cash reserves in addition to the leftovers of both Elizabeth and his own expenses.

Cash was a rare commodity in those days – something none of them had anticipated at home in Ireland - and because there was still so little cash circulating in the colony, people instead commonly traded in barter, or rum, or land. This had kept land prices low and cash value high.

He had since used a good amount of that cash to purchase most of the supplies needed for his expedition north at a fair price, and they would keep him going for a full year. And he still had enough money left to live comfortably for several months.

The boat building venture was more problematic. He had already paid fifty per cent of his share to Mr Bignell in cash, and thankfully the balance was reserved for production-based milestones. He was hopeful this business would start to return solid income in a few months; but his commitments to expansion were much larger and sooner. For a rash moment he contemplated that if he acted quickly now, perhaps he could commit the remainder via promissory notes, and pass that on to the estate... But he quickly realised that was too risky, as Patrick would only decline them which would surely sink the entire company. But then if he didn't use up his cash reserves on the residual payments, again the entire company could fail...

His best action would be to tell Bignell the truth now, ease back on production commitments and grow the business together as income arrived. But the full balance was not due for a further six months, and he thought perhaps he could stretch that out and pay down the remainder with whatever he had left of his cash at a later date... If not, perhaps he could make some other amicable arrangement to exit the deal ...perhaps to walk away with just his own boat.

And so he decided he would pay twenty-five per cent now, in advance, and delay the final payment until he returned from the north, and simply see how it played out.

Balancing the pros and cons he thought: *Yes, I can make a show of it.* But with barely enough, and it all hinged on the success of his venture North. If he could improve the land himself, he believed he could make sufficient income in a year or so to pay the balance of the boat business, and then simply install tenant managers to the farm and he could return to Ireland triumphant.

His mood lifted a little – *I'll show him.*

Then he realised with a sense of foreboding that success would require that he invest much more than what remained of his money – he would need to dig in himself and do much of the hard physical work building stockyards and huts as he could no longer afford labourers. However he reasoned the convicts should be made available to support his needs, given the importance of that work to the entire venture.

The ember of a new direction now settling in his mind, his attention returned to Maggie. *Poor Maggie!* He would need to continue her wages from his own cash reserves or let her go. His anger mounted again as he wondered what Patrick may have had against her – why had he hated her enough to do this, to make a point of her dismissal. She had driven a hard bargain certainly, but she was a favourite of their father and her work at the Maguire estate had always been exemplary. Their father had even referred to plans of getting her to manage a business, something virtually unheard of for women at that time.

He stared again at the letter in front of him, anger again rising within. Then he noticed something towards the top of the letter – a reverse imprint. He turned the letter over and saw Patrick's letter continued a further paragraph:

"*PS*" it read "*I should let you know that Elizabeth also wrote our father during your little sailing trip. She complained of terrible seasickness – it must have been very hard for you too, I'm sure. But I should bring to your attention that like myself, Elizabeth is also most clearly unhappy with*

Maggie's substandard performance, and that she relayed an intention to sack her upon arrival. This has swayed my decision to cease her wages – I'm sure you will understand."

Elizabeth had made her thoughts about Maggie clear enough to him too, but he wasn't concerned. It wasn't her decision to make and he had spoken to Maggie, who had put in extra effort. It had seemed to work.

None of this was her fault, and he felt obligated to her. The best thing would be for her to return to Ireland, but he doubted they could fund it, even with her own resources combined. *Besides, I will miss her.*

With some dread he realised an even bigger issue - *What would become of the baby...*

Then he realised, there was a second alternative: one to keep her at his side, and to provide a mother for the boy:

He would marry her.

20

Of love and loss

Philomena and Sean were surprised to hear that James was to re-wed – it was less than two months since Elizabeth had died in their very house, and the girl was beneath his station. A mere servant. Worse than that, a Catholic! Beautiful yes, and they could understand the attraction - but one must stay within one's proper class.

Surely it was part of the grieving process, in a way quite pathetic.

But of course they supported the union nonetheless, and they proudly hosted the wedding and reception in their own home in late February, just a week before the planned expedition north. One good outcome of it at least was that Maggie would revoke her horrid Catholic faith and be joined with her husband as a Wesleyan/ Methodist.

The event was well attended by the leaders of Perth alongside their neighbours and most pleasingly, two of the four major owners of The Cattle Company who positively swooned at Maggie's beauty as a bride and engaged Sean and James in private conversation concerning the Greenough lands.

James was introduced to Lockier Burges, one of the Cattle Company owners and the man who would lead the expedition north, having been in the Gregory brothers' original expedition. Burges explained the Cattle Company had already installed 4000 head of cattle and 350 sheep at their headquarters 'Yardarino' on the Irwin River, and that would be their penultimate destination, with settlers to move on to their allotments from that base. Leasees including James would need to quickly install sufficient stockyards and shepherds' huts at locations around their allotments to allow the cattle to be installed, and shepherds would then move the cattle around in rotation, the land being unfenced.

Thinking of his dwindling cash and inability to afford labourers, James assured him of his steadfast commitment to the project, saying that he would personally oversee improvements to ensure they happened quickly. To change the subject somewhat, he announced with pride that this commitment included a temporary abode for his lovely new wife and baby – a prefabricated house built of Brown Mallet that could be reconstructed, with just the addition of roofing, in a matter of days.

James learned from Burges that he and Maggie would in fact be the very first settlers on these Greenough lands, however temporary. As such they had more flexibility to make the necessary improvements, but Burges again stressed that they relied on James installing at least two stockyards and huts before the end of the year, so that the Greenough herds could progressively be moved over as other new settlers began to arrive early the next year. To James relief, Burges estimated it should take him no longer than four to six months.

James was nervous when he had asked Maggie to marry him, only two weeks before that wedding day. He secretly doubted that she would accept – his age, his child… his failure to succeed as had his brother. But he had followed his head as well as his heart, and to his great joy, she had said 'yes'!

They were alone on one of their trips to Perth when he inexplicably stopped the coach, lifted her down from the seat, and guided her to the side of the road. They walked a little way, she confused and wondering where he was taking her, he nervous and not saying a word. After a short walk they arrived at a grassy field with an expansive view over the coastal plain below. She was surprised and eagerly moved forward, straining to see distant buildings along the clear outline of the Swan River.

"Oh look!" she pointed. "Is that Bignell's Maylands yards?" and she turned around to see if James could see it too.

But he wasn't there, not at eye level at least – he was down on one knee directly behind her, so close that she nearly lost her footing. He quickly took her hand, remaining on the ground and then he removed a simple gold ring and held it toward her.

"Maggie O'Brien" he commenced. "You have been my greatest strength these past months, and I almost feel ashamed to say, my greatest dream for many years before. I have always loved you from afar, perhaps you knew this too in your heart? But I have watched you grow, and I have seen with pride as you have developed your own mind, an independent and most intriguing mind that I respect, and yes, rely upon in my own ventures. I have desired you too, watching you develop into a woman of great beauty. Mind and body, I desire them both. I offer you mine. Heart and soul – they belong to you.

Maggie O'Brien, will you marry me?" and he pushed the ring towards her.

The proposal had come out of the blue for Maggie, though she had secretly dared to imagine it may be possible in the months ahead. She hoped it was not desperation on James' behalf, for certainly he had been and was still broken by Elizabeth's death only weeks earlier. But she knew too that James truly loved her – she could feel it in his every glance, every word and action. She had felt it for years, and it had grown over the past months as they connected, a genuine love that she had never felt before.

And she loved him back. Hers was a love built of respect for his kindness; a sympathy for his occasional bumbling; and concern for him as a man, alone in a foreign land with a baby. He was like the older brother she never had, there for as long as she could remember, and he needed her.

In truth, it was also fear for herself, alone and single in a land full of dangerous men. Her experience was that many men – enough to cause caution – would mistreat young women when primitive desire overwhelmed their rational thought. She thought of Patrick and although that was now several years ago it still sent a shiver up her spine, caused hesitancy in her every interaction with men. She no longer thrust herself 'out there', and she took caution in how she dressed and where and when she was alone with any man.

In this, she knew James was not Patrick - that he would keep her safe, and that provided great security. She had seen him looking at her certainly, even as a young woman barely out of puberty. She had sometimes even shamelessly ensured he would see her developing young body, taunting his old man desires. But he had always been a gentleman, never taking advantage of her and she had never felt threatened when she was with him. No, he was a good man – and good men could be hard to find.

She desired him physically too. He was no Declan, no rippling muscle nor the ruggedness of that fisher-boy but he was still fairly young and nor was he fat, or unfit. *And quite handsome*, she thought as she looked down upon his upturned face, pleading for an answer.

These thoughts rushed through her head. Above them all, though she wouldn't admit it, was pride - that she, a humble fisherman's daughter should marry above her class, to a man of means and fine standing. This was what her Ma had always wanted and encouraged.

"Yes!" she said with barely a moment's hesitation, and then knelt herself and took his hands, moved them around her neck and they kissed – long, tenderly and full of suppressed desire.

It was that love for him too that was reflected as they lay in bed later that night, finally together after so many years of both longing for this moment. It felt naughty to them both – yet to marry, no one knew their plans, and she had snuck down to his room in the dead of night, excitement driving her quietly to open his door and boldly enter.

He was surprised and delighted as he saw her unrobe in the moonlight, the curves of her body outlined against the darkness by the full moon beyond: enticing, elusive. And then she slipped into his bed, ran her hands over his chest, unbuttoning, touching lightly.

"Well you can't expect a girl to commit without a test run!" She joked, and pushed her hand downwards.

Then she straddled him, grinding vigorously, groaning in her ecstasy as she approached orgasm and teasing to take him in, but still she did not.

Her form was solid against him, her skin warm and her hips pressing hard against his own as her breasts now thrust forward, their fullness enticing his fingers, calling to his lips. The soft moonlight exposed her beauty as no light could – he was entranced.

She kissed him then, long and well and he mouthed passion and love, falling into her, lost. When she mounted him at last, it was like nothing he had experienced with Elizabeth. Where she had been soft, Maggie was silk. Where he felt excitement for Elizabeth, for Maggie it was passion and yes, love.

He didn't say a thing, and the moment was not long. As quickly as she started, he was done.

"Not bad, Mr Maguire – I shall marry you after all. And you can expect much more of that good sir, while ever I wear this band."

She had grown very fond of his son, Thomas - so named for his grandfather - and she fancied herself now his mother, spending more and more time with him and less and less on her other duties. Thomas had thrived against the odds to achieve a healthy weight for his age and seemed to be past the worst of his premature challenges. She spent hours with him each day and would find herself telling him stories of his mother and of Ireland as he happily smiled up at her. She was, she realised, the only mother he had.

James had decided to say nothing of Patrick's letter to her, nor to his aunty and uncle to whom he relayed only that the letter contained information on Patrick's private family matters. It was hard as he explained how tirelessly Patrick worked at their business interests, and how proud he was of their Australian expansion.

As for Maggie, he didn't want to cause her any stress - he had more than enough himself. However, he told himself he would tell her the full story as soon as the time was right, when their efforts had paid off and he returned to Ireland triumphant, his beautiful Maggie at his side.

And at any rate, he rationalised, the very worst that could happen to her was that the whole sorry adventure should be a failure and that they return to Ireland, whereupon his brother would be compelled to take them in. Maggie could not know his shame.

Instead, he told her that she should travel with him to the north and help him to make the improvements as they cared together for Thomas, raising him as if he were her own. It meant a longer stay than had been planned – longer even than the time he had shared secretly with her back in Perth.

"It will likely be even more than a full year, Maggie. And it will not be easy. It will be as if we were in another world, the first settlers – true pioneers if ever there were. There won't be shops, no stores to get supplies. We'll rely solely on the provisions we bring, and whatever we can grow ourselves. At first there won't even be houses for us or our neighbours – and for that matter it's likely there won't even be neighbours! There will be times I will have to leave you alone, though I promise it won't be for long. And Maggie, from what I understand there won't be any other women. You will be the first European woman in these new lands! It will be hard."

If he expected her to fret, to complain or swoon in dismay as Elizabeth would surely have done, he was to be surprised. For Maggie was overjoyed, the challenge of what lay ahead thrilling her with the fearless excitement that comes only with being twenty.

This was what she had always wanted. To be a pioneer.

Preparations for their grand expedition were finalised. Over the past week wagons full of equipment and people had filed into the Toodyay Farm. There were also a great many cattle, sheep, horses and goats, though the herd was a fraction of the 4000 head that had preceded them.

Wagons were typically packed with supplies sufficient for several months including dried and cured meats, potatoes, carrots, flour, hardtack, rice, fruit and jellies, raisins, molasses, honey, sugar, salt, vinegar, soda biscuits, cornbread along with chickens, pigs and horses. There were also a few dogs, and Maggie was delighted when Philomena and Sean presented to James two one-year old puppies from the litters of their sheep dogs, a breeding pair of fine border collie dogs who had farm work bred into them and with training would be every bit as good as their parents. Good quality working dogs were rare in those days, and to be gifted a breeding pair was extremely generous.

James called them "Chip and Dale" and laughed at his own humour. The pups were placed on leads and travelled in one of their two coaches, never far from Maggie's side.

This was the first of the settler's expeditions, with each of the men travelling to establish a new life. Most were labourers, lacking the funds or ability to either purchase or lease and run their own farms just yet, but planning to do so in the coming months or years. Some had families that would follow in the future, others would set up businesses, livestock stations or hire themselves out to settlers and the Cattle Company as the expected flood of settlers arrived in the years ahead.

There was a buzz of excitement, a grand adventure lay ahead and these eighty or so men and the small handful of women and children with them would lay the foundations for a new beginning not only for their families, but for the colony of Western Australia.

Maggie's presence was like a breath of fresh air for the road-weary and hardened men who had travelled from the Swan. In the middle were 'the old Colony' sons of those first settlers who had battled the elements and the challenges of wild lands to eke out a shell of a future, a dozen now trading their lands for the promises of the north. Some were partners of The Cattle Company and sought to carve out stations along the track at strategic locations, to allow for the settlers and further stock to follow. Some men were travelling on to Champion Bay and the grassy hills beyond figuring the new lead mine, the military command post and the port at Champion Bay would provide a stronger settlement. A number were headed to Irwin River Flats as sub-lease owners or their labourers, expanding out from the base of the Cattle Company's head lease, Yardarino. They carried basic provisions sufficient for only a few months, intending to establish their plots and restock from Yardarino and the nearby Port Denison or Champion Bay.

Nearby were new settlers, several of them retired Pensioner Guards seeking out work and adventure. A few had their wives and children with them, but most travelled alone – an 'advance party' for those to fol-low. As with the 'old colony' group, all would stay around Irwin River or travel on to Champion Bay. Some said they had considered Gree-nough River but thought it would be too remote with no harbour of its own.

Outside their circle but still nearby was a large family of 'the old colony', a family group of fifteen including adults and older children who looked to be adult, but whose giggles and endless demands to 'mum' gave them away – and which ensured they sat at a separate camp-fire. This group had between them six wagons, full of provisions, and a herd of sheep, horses and cattle. They were clearly a well-established and respected family, and Maggie spent some time with the women in the group where she discovered they were all members of the Hamersley family in one way or another. They were major shareholders in the Cat-tle Company and intended to now establish a new family home along the way at a place called 'Woodada' that had been handpicked by the Gregory brothers themselves as a key staging post. It was apparently not far from Yardarino and Maggie's own destination of Greenough River, but the Woodada lease was far bigger - a massive 20,000 acres, the biggest holding in the region. Although they appeared to be in chaos, they were used to hardship of the Australian bush and Maggie saw that they were well accustomed to farming – *more so than the men of that inner circle* Maggie thought.

She flitted in and out of their campfires, providing light refreshments but always great joy to those she encountered, the darting flames only enhancing her beauty. More than a few of the younger men who had arrived in the last week were disappointed to learn she was married – they had imagined her the grand-daughter of the elderly owners of this farm on the edge of civilisation and had foolishly hoped for fleeting moments that they could be the one to win her heart.

Beyond the fires were a more sombre collection of wagons – twenty-five convicts and their guards. That same year a Convict Hiring Depot had been established 5 kilometres upriver from Toodyay Farm, and the township of Newcastle – later renamed Toodyay - would grow around the depot site in the years ahead. These were the first of the convicts to be transported north to provide works along the way but many more would follow. Some would return to the south when their sentences were served, a few would stay on as ticket-of-leave and free men working as labourers and farmhands, themselves early pioneers to the district. Maggie served to them just as to the others and was greeted with cat calls and whistles, the guards yelling at the unruly men to mind their manners. But she showed only kindness and smiles to both convict and guard, giving a kind word to each man as she served him and as she left, each now smiled at her and wished they too, might have won her heart.

Beyond them all, in the stables and an adjacent holding yard, were 200 cattle and sheep, a collection of goats and 70 of more horses, lither and nimbler than the dray horses. A few would be deposited at stations to be established along the track, others would service the settlers once at Irwin station headquarters.

Now, it was the evening before they would leave and she took time to write her parents, a letter to share her news both sad and glad.

My dearest pappa and ma

I grasp at the opportunity to inform you of my safe landing in this little Colony at the bottom of the world, in the best health and spirits and now with the greatest of news to share!

It is March here and the thermometer is often over 100° in the shade although it is now Autumn in this upside-down land – quite the contrast to our cold and wet Blackrock home! The mornings are delightful for taking exercise, but the middle of the day is generally too hot.

I am writing to you from lands on the very outskirts of the Swan River Colony, the tremendously large 'Toodyay Farm', the extent of which I would never likely have seen in Ireland.

Tomorrow we embark on the greatest adventure of my young life, and I tremble to write with an excitement that even now threatens to dislodge my hand from my pen, and this pen from the very paper!

We shall travel overland a distance of several hundred miles, through lands which have barely been traversed before. Thence to lands selected by James Maguire, whereupon we shall reside for a period of some months.

I expect of course this news will come at some shock to you as it is not what either you nor I had anticipated when I left our town of Blackrock a matter of mere months ago. But fear not, I am in good hands and our return to Ireland shall only be delayed, not derailed.

For the first of the news I have to tell you of my journey thence is the greatest of all, so ma be seated and pappa be sure she is! For when I return to Blackrock as surely I will, it will be on the arm of James and we shall be known as Mr and Mrs James Maguire!

That is right Mamma, your daughter has married the master.

The path leading to this event is of great sadness, and in many ways I am probably as surprised as you at this sudden turn of events. But rest assured it is a most happy union, and that I have grown to love James deeply and truly through our treading that very path together.

So, I should start at the beginning – our new beginning that is, with our arrival at the Swan Colony subsequent to the voyage that I told you of in my last correspondence, which as I recall was as we sat in yet another doldrum with naught but the blue sky and endless waves to keep us company.

Well the wind at last sprung up, and now the captain expressed his persuasion that we were drawing near to Rottnest Island, and this news inspired everyone with joy and hope. Then the following day a sailor cried out the long wished-for and glad tidings of "Land ho!" All ran upon deck, anxious to behold land once more. We were overjoyed at the sight and found it to be "Rottnest," which is a rocky barren island, difficult of access on account of a heavy surf. With the coast of Western Australia now in view, we headed for the entrance of the Swan River with colours flying and tied up next to the jetty.

James had made acquaintances with the Captain who told us where to go for a ferry up river, and with the afternoon already gathering we made our way quickly before the others to take a ferryboat. The Swan River was as I had read so many years ago – a long and beautiful stretch of estuary abundant in fish and the beautiful jelly-fish, their colours, bulbous bodies and long tentacles a delightful distraction as we three made our way up the Swan towards Perth. There were magnificent cliffs, long tongues of sandy spit, and white beaches all the way, a true delight as we sailed with a steady breeze behind us towards the capital on a hot Spring day. I thought this place was a slice of paradise, though so very different from our green island home.

For I noticed as we sailed that the wood near the shore, and for several miles up the River, is worth but little, being short and crooked and thus unfit for building. There was little sign of settlement, but I was assured that farms were now established in many parts just beyond those beaches.

I saw then as we sailed and later as I explored many beautiful native shrubs. The lagoons are much filled with the Cats-tail Reed, the root of which is eaten by the Aboriginal people.

The land itself is adorned with curious trees, and pretty shrubs and flowers and so I have studied and learned the names of native trees with the help of a new friend. The beautiful Nuytsia Floribunda attains to forty feet in height and six feet in circumference; it is called Cabbage-tree *in the Colony because of the faint resemblance of its branches to cabbage-stalks: its top is one mass of golden, orange, or yellow flowers. In places where it is swampy in winter there are several species of the beautiful pink or yellow blossomed fringed myrtles. A fine, yellow Calythrix; a yellow and red, and a sky-blue Leschenaultia; a crimson, linear-leaved Calliste-mon; a scarlet Melaleuca; a crimson Calothamnus... When in blossom the Perth-scape provides poetry to the eye.*

You might guess my interest in the colourful plants of this area reflects the colour now in my heart – and you would be right! But there is another reason, and that is that James has made a business of boat making, and due to my own knowledge of the boats that we built together, pappa, I have supported the business much. As the colony has relied so much on imported timber, I was assigned to look at local alternatives, and it is my great pride that a trial boat is now nearing completion – the very first coastal hauler to be built here from a local wood.

Anyway, that venture certainly grew James and I together, but the event which formed our bond was one of immense sadness to him – the untimely death of his wife Elizabeth during childbirth, there being no services to assist. And so I now find myself married at 20, to a man nearly 14 years my senior and an 'instant mother' to his son, a beautiful boy he has called Thomas after his own father. I am enchanted by the boy, and so happy to be now his mother - the only one he has known.

Our wedding was just a week ago and we set off tomorrow on the grand expedition to Champion Bay. One of the servants here will send this letter and by the time you read it, I will be in a new green pasture in a place a little south, called the Greenough River. James has had me under no illusion that it will be tough, but we do have some basics with us. His plan is to reside there to improve the lands before installing tenant farmers, at which time we will return to Perth, and then to you my darling parents!

I may not be able to write you for some months. So, for now, wish me luck! And know that your Little Fish is grown, and swimming strong with its own little school.

Maggie Maguire (nee O'Brien!)

21 |

Journey of the pioneer

As the sun crested the horizon the next morning, the quiet of the night before was shattered. Birds were drowned out of their dawn calls; native animals arising from their burrows scuttled back to bed. Dogs barked, children cried and horses and cattle startled as men made their final preparations.

At the helm was a single guide, Lockier Burges who had accompanied the Gregory brothers on their epic cattle drive a year earlier and was returning now as site Manager, to be located on Yardarino on the Irwin River.

He had with him two Noongar men, who would walk ahead of the group following the signs of that earlier expedition. Both men wore a warm kangaroo skin cloak and a cord spun from the fur of the opossum round their middle. The cord formed a warm, soft and elastic belt of an inch in thickness in which were stuck a hatchet, a kiley or boomerang, and a short heavy stick to throw at the smaller animals. Maggie noticed the hatchet was ingeniously placed so that the head rested exactly on the centre of the back, whilst its thin short handle descended along the backbone and could be instantly attained. In their hands each carried several spears, headed in two or three different manners, so that they are equally adapted to war or the chase.

Maggie studied them, sensing their great nervousness. She recalled Johnston's description: '*The Aboriginal people have their clearly distinguished hunting-grounds, the boundaries of which overlap but in places are definite; trees being often recognized by them as landmarks, and they are very clear to stay in their own areas unless invited by their neighbours.'* It was only the presence of the white men and their guns behind that would allow them to pass.

And so, to everyone's great shock, she approached them and introduced herself, and offered them the last of a large cake that she and Philomena had shared around to bolster everyone's spirits. It was only fair they should get the same treatment, she figured, and she could see they were every bit as nervous as the others, perhaps even more so.

Incredibly, they took the cake and spoke to her, their words unheard to all but Maggie. A little while later she seemed to bid them goodbye, and they her, and she returned to James' coach – all eyes upon her as if she had done some magical thing.

"What did you say to them, Maggie!" James inquired.

"Oh, I just wished them well for the journey and asked them about their home – booja, they call it. They are from south of the river, a long way from here and they're scared and lonely – just like many of these men."

"Well, they seemed to like your visit" James replied, and she looked in time to see them gulp down their cakes and turn toward her, rubbing their bellies and saying an audible "Yum!", much to everyone's delight.

Before long, a horn was sounded and the party made the first jerky movements north. And so the party set out, with laughter and hope. Maggie's simple act had lightened the mood for all, the Noongar warriors among them.

They followed the route taken by the Gregory brothers. It comprised a series of trails and crossings which were quite identifiable thanks to the thousands of hoofs that had passed, but even still they needed to skirt around areas from time to time which had become boggy or had disappeared altogether among rolling sand dunes. Many of the watering holes, river crossings and stopping points that they visited on the long trek north had been shown to the Gregory brothers and other exploration parties by the local Aboriginal community in the past decade.

And again now their own Aboriginal guides lead the settlers and their stock to areas where there was more grass or water, following the topography of the land in a north-westerly direction, which skirted the eastern edge of a limestone ridge between two ancient dune systems, with both the presence of water and the lack of more rugged terrain and poison plants found to their west and east.

This first part of the route took around two weeks, travelling some 170km to Dandaraga Spring where they replenished their water stores. They travelled between rolling hills, and there were frequent small watering holes at which the men would refill canisters before allowing the cattle and horses to drink. They made strong progress, only occasionally needing to stop to help round up wandering livestock, and they travelled for many hours each day, stopping as the light failed. The track was flat, and Maggie and James both delighted in the colourful trees they passed - many of which Maggie could name, much to James' surprise.

They fell into an easy routine, each day a pleasant ride, each evening full of busy-ness as Maggie prepared meals and tended to the child. Effectively still a new-born, young Thomas had quickly adapted to travel, thriving in the warm embrace of his father and mother (Maggie could still hardly believe this was her new title!) and being fed with fresh milk from cows that were happily supplied by the Hamersley family whenever it was needed.

The nights were happy occasions, the stars vivid in the sky and they were blessed by a full moon that illuminated the trees and slopes around them. The men lit a fire, and someone would pull out a guitar or harmonica and they would dance and sing, most of the men drinking from some seemingly bottomless supply.

Maggie cuddled up besides James, holding his arm as they sat by the fire on a log or leaning against their wagon, Thomas often asleep in their arms. It was the greatest of times, everything she had hoped for.

But James was often thinking about his financial predicament. By paying the further quarter instalment to Bignell, he had left himself with little to survive on and he would need to generate income quickly to replenish supplies and hire in labourers. He wondered if he could on-lease some of the land, or perhaps sell some of the cattle to raise funds. But then he would return to Ireland a failure, and this above all he wished not to do. He would rather the boat building business collapse than divest his interests in Greenough.

His thoughts were circular: worry, wonder, worry, pride. Anger. Repeat. Nothing was resolved, no plan made. He was used to nearly bottomless resources and had never really needed to be responsible for outcomes, not really – his father would absorb any losses. But now, for the first time, he was faced with large responsibilities and limited resources, in a land far, far from home. Had Elizabeth been alive, she would of course have insisted they return home immediately, to fall upon Patrick's mercy and leave the Greenough investments to be managed by Sean and his sons. But Elizabeth was gone, their son now his responsibility.

Again, he thought *I'll show him!* – Pride ruling his head.

James was of course entirely unaware of the great privilege he carried with him – his wallet was still more than most of the other settlers who joined them on the trip north could even dream of. He had leased 5000 acres of prime riverside allotment in addition to his share in the company; they had a full year's supplies including chickens; his aunt and uncle supported him with generous supplies which included two fine dogs. And he was part owner of a boat building company...

But none of these thoughts occurred to him, for such is the cost of privilege: ignorance to the plight of others.

And James was not alone in his unrealised privilege. Though wealthier and better educated than almost all the settler party, neither he nor any other stopped to think of the impact of the hundreds of cattle and sheep being driven north on the sacred places of the Noongar and Yamatji tribes. Wells, springs, and soaks on the station properties that were taken up along the route were exploited, modified or rendered unusable. Hoofs that pounded now and for over a hundred years hence had a devastating impact on such places. Stock fouled and drained the waterholes, trampled the surrounding reeds and killed the marine life that provided food, regardless of their necessity for the continued existence of the Aboriginal groups.

Many of these waterholes and places they passed and camped at were also the focus of religious beliefs, and the desecration they witnessed has doubtlessly resulted in a profound emotional and spiritual disturbance.

22

Diamond of the desert

Finally through the hills, they stopped for a day's rest at the Dandaraga gully. As James tended the baby and men rested and washed by the watercourse, Maggie took a chance for a walk and to explore. She wasn't far when she saw a large mob of Kangaroos bounding through the fields and scattered trees, clearly attracted to the abundant fresh waters. As she marvelled at the sight, she was shocked when suddenly one of the great animals fell in mid bounce, and then to her surprise saw Aboriginal warriors appear from the plain, where she would swear just seconds before there had been none. They ran to the kangaroo and quickly gathered it and the long spear one of them had cast with uncanny accuracy, retreating to the tree line before the line of strange white men and beasts saw them.

It was not the first time they had seen white men – once before members of their tribe had shared food. But they knew to keep clear.

As they turned to the dense woods, one of the men at the rear turned toward Maggie. He was at least a hundred metres away, but she thought she heard a word of greeting as the man made a hand gesture, looking directly at her.

She made the same gesture back, thinking it a welcome but then was startled to see the two Noongar men standing beside her, either side and just to the rear. She hadn't heard them approach, and as she turned now she saw them make a different hand signal back to the retreating warrior. Then they turned back towards the camp, encouraging her to join them.

One of them rubbed his belly and said 'Yum' and she laughed, joining them on the short return walk.

Once back at the Spring, the two men approached the expedition's guide, Burges. There was a short exchange and Burges could be seen throwing up his arms, clearly angered or frustrated. Then the two warriors turned without a word, and walked back the way they had come, disappearing into the bush moments later.

Maggie asked Burges what was going on, and he mumbled "They won't go any further, they say this is no longer their country" he replied. "No matter, I don't need them anyway – it's not far to the Hill River and I know the way from there."

 The next morning, they set out early once more. Burges was a little unsure but the track was still evident in most places, and three days later they arrived at the Hill River, a further 55km from Dandaraga without incident. From there they proceeded down that river for a further two and half days to Munbenia Brook.

From there they left the river and skirted along a limestone ridge to a place called Cockleshell Gully, a deep, limestone ravine. Maggie recognised the shells as the same type of cockles from her home of Blackrock. But in this place a stream had gradually worn away at the limestone to reveal thick layers of ancient shells. They were still many kilometres from the shore, and Burges explained to the party that the shells and fossils within the cliffs indicated an ancient shoreline, giving the gully its name.

Beyond the Gully, shrub-covered sand plains stretched before them, a seemingly endless coastal plain covered only by low lying scrubs and banksia trees. It was hot, and people struggled – those that had not replenished their water fully at the Hill River found the going tough, and pestered others for water and refreshment, complaining of the unrelenting sun and heat which would have been close to 35 degrees Celsius.

Maggie and James too found it difficult and spent long hours under the covered area of their carriage shielding Thomas from the worst of it and cooling him with wet towels. So it was a great relief when Burges called that they were approaching an 'oasis' that the previous group had found. James saw now a higher tree line from afar, rising above the rest of the surrounding lower scrub. Maggie identified Zamia palms around the perimeter and as they approached closer could see tall flooded-gums that Maggie said were Eucalyptus grandis, alongside casuarina and wattles. They eventually arrived at a recessed area of limestone caves and rocks – a quiet and somewhat mysterious place.

They again stopped here for a day's rest, and as Maggie explored she found Aboriginal artefacts scattered here and there – spear heads, rocks, broken baskets.

Maggie could sense the magic of this place and as she listened and placed her hand on the walls of the caves, she felt she could hear the memories of song and celebration – she knew this was a place of great significance to the Aboriginal people.

She could see too the evidence of 4000 hoofs that had trampled much of the soft ground earlier, and watched with dismay as the smaller flock with them now did exactly the same.

The convicts were set to work here building timber troughs on the edge of the spring for stock and they marked out an area for stock yards nearby. Three of the convicts were to remain here to clear trees and fence the yards for future settlers.

But for now at least, for one last time this place was one of reverence and intrigue. She sat in the shade, watching the contrast going on around her. A place that seemed deeply spiritual, steeped in Aboriginal lore; now trampled by cattle and men, who bathed from the cooled spring and soon started to drink and swear and to turn it to a place of commerce – a staging post for the European march over the land.

Something about the place reminded Maggie of a famous book from the time, "The Talisman" by Sir Walter Scott. It was a tale of the Crusades that positioned the English monarch Richard the First against Saladin, the Eastern Sultan. While Richard as the Christian and English monarch professed to civilised ways, he showed all the cruelty and violence expected of an Eastern sultan, while Saladin, on the other hand, displayed the deep prudence expected of a European sovereign.

As she witnessed the mysterious place now being trampled and changed forever, Maggie reflected that here again was a clash of cultures, and that 'men of civilisation' were once more those who showed the traits expected of the 'savages' they claimed superiority over. She recalled that the whole sorry saga had come to a head with a great duel at a desert oasis called '*The Diamond of the Desert.*'

"The Diamond of the desert" she mouthed quietly to herself. She was overheard by one of the other travellers, who repeated the name more loudly and before long, everyone was stating the name and laughing at how appropriate a name it was.

And so this oasis of unexpected beauty, midway on the Stock Route that would see the unrelenting flood of settlers to Western Australia's Midwest and beyond, became forever known as 'The Diamond of the Desert' – never attributed to Maggie, nor to the dark thoughts she held in whispering those words.

23

Journeys end

They left the next day, their party again depleted from the convicts and guards who stayed behind. Half a day's march north, they re-watered and rested at Little Three Springs, another water hole. The spring naturally bubbled to the surface here to provide a constant source of fresh water that led into a swamp area where native rushes, flooded gums and casuarinas flourished. This place too would be converted to a stockyard, to support the migration north of the expected rush of European settlers. More convicts and their guards were left here and they and their expected reinforcements would build further stockyards and drinking troughs for the livestock.

Less than an hour further on they found a series of large limestone caves alongside a creek bed with high limestone cliffs. Tall river gums, giant zamia and manna gum lined the edges of the gully floor, while on the upper slopes could be seen brightly coloured wattles, parrot bush and native wisteria. At the end of the creek they found a large limestone cave, some 300 metres long, which the party used as a natural confinement for stock as they camped overnight. It had a sandy bottom and the atmosphere of a large amphitheatre. It was cool and comfortable, and the singing and yahooing of the settlers echoed through the gully. Burges had named it 'Stockyard Gully'.

After this they hit claypan country, never far from claypan lakes and the grassy flats which are found near them. There were several large lakes in a long system, some of them with large semi-permanent pools of freshwater. They stopped at Lake Indoon, a beautiful clear lake where they rested, the lake surrounded by a sandy beach and with large flooded-gums on the banks drooping over the water. The party bathed here and some men swam out a distance, yelling back to the group that they could barely reach the bottom.

Other lakes in the system also boasted rich wetlands and intermittent creeks.

Wells would later be installed at several more sites north along the route to regularly water livestock as they moved north, the convicts with them the first of many to start those laborious works.

They continued northward through the Weelawadgie flats and more clay-pan country surrounded by casuarinas, gums and low-lying heath for roughly 10 kilometres until they reached the allotment purchased months earlier by the Hamersley family, the large and chaotic family that had so helped Maggie and the baby. Here, several single men were also to stay on as labourers to help the family fence and manage the massive allotment of 20,000 acres. It was named 'Woodada' and would be the basis for the Hamersley family's expansion throughout the north and beyond. It seemed an unlikely place for a base, noting the allotment lacked a visible source of water although plenty was to their immediate south. But in the coming years labourers and convicts would dig a massive well measuring six metres in circumference and 25 metres deep, and which is still producing water to this day.

Maggie was particularly sad to part company with the young women in that group, but was told that they were still neighbours, as Greenough was now not too far distant – less than a week's travel.

"Neighbours!" laughed Maggie. "Back in Ireland that same travel would take us across the Irish sea!"

Now depleted in their number and suddenly a lot quieter, the settlers moved on quickly. A further day's march north, they came to Lake Arrowsmith, another beautiful lake with clear water and a sandy bottom set among large swamp gums and paperbark trees, where they rested and replenished.

The next day they set off early, striking out for a watering area that Burges said was a full day's march north, getting there just as the sun set after a hectic day's ride. This area comprised of swamp areas, dried clay-pan lake beds and thick wattle bushland, and Burges set more of the convicts and their guards to the task of digging a well to the north of the swamp, the site identified through the presence of water reliant plants.

They rested here for the night but again left early, the small handful of guards and convicts remaining behind. For Burges was now setting out stridently for his own destination, Irwin River Flats which was to become the headquarters of The Cattle Company in the region and Burges' own new homestead, Yardarino. Most of the remaining settlers and labourers would be billeted to their lands from here, spreading across 56 kilometres of winding bends and twists.

At midday they crossed the Irwin River itself at Milo Crossing before finally arriving at the Flats. As they approached they heard the unmistakeable sounds of livestock across the river plains, and they travelled on through overgrown grass, native reed yangets, casuarinas and flooded gums that lined the banks of the river.

The settlers felt they had arrived in paradise, and mutual congratulations were passed around with handshakes – they were finally at their Journey's end.

The cattle and sheep from the previous stock run had been left here, contained by the river. Only four shepherds and dogs had been left to oversee them and to install stockyards, and they were delighted to see the convoy finally arrive.

Lockier Burges would establish a homestead and headquarters for the Cattle Company here at Yardarino, and from there Cattle Company employees would take settlers on to their allotments along the Irwin or further north. The last of the convicts and several more labourers were to stay here to build a significant headquarters including a house, Shearing Shed, a Milking Shed, a Stockyard and even a post office.

Most of the others remaining in the party would also stay here for a short time before moving to their allotments along the Irwin River, and there was great excitement as they set up their tents and studied maps and charts of the area, comparing their plots and distances from Yardarino. The arrangement was that they would move to their plots and establish stockyards and huts before Cattle Company drovers moved their cattle in. Only then should they commence whatever sheds and permanent accommodations they wished. They had only three months to do the former.

Only a few settlers remained to be settled. James and Maggie were the only two heading on for Greenough, with the other men to continue to Champion Bay and beyond. Greenough lay a day's further march north of Yardarino, and Burges' plan was to help them settle on a suitable part of the river, before continuing with the others to Champion Bay.

The small entourage set out the very next day, Burges keen to return as quickly as possible to oversee the settlement of Irwin River. James and Maggie had with them their two wagons and horses, one tied behind the other as before, but now they also had a single cow that would provide the milk for Thomas as well as them.

The distances here are vast! Maggie thought to herself. *We would have passed through a dozen major towns and more than half of Ireland by now!*

Everyone came to see them off, exchanging words of encouragement and hope. Within months, this group of settlers and labourers would be scattered throughout the Irwin district and they proudly competed that James and Maggie should visit them first, to meet their wives and children, to see their grand houses and lands.

Looking at them, Maggie realised these were the pioneers of the north, and she wondered what history would think of them – and of her. Most would be footnotes in the modern history of Australia; some, would be that history.

"He ya!" Burges called, and the group started forward.

"Don't be strangers!" someone called, and James noticed once more all eyes were on Maggie.

Maggie was nervous as they departed, realising now for perhaps the first time the vast distances in Western Australia, and the knowledge that whether Yardarino to the south, or Champion Bay to the north help and company was at best a full day's ride away should it be needed. She had always wanted to be a pioneer, true – but now the reality of their impending isolation swept over and threatened to overwhelm her. They would be very much alone.

But leaving they were, and with a mix of tears and laughter they travelled on through the coastal heath and trees, through a swampy area called Allanooka where the horses drank deeply and then past another area Burges indicated would be a well, the '8 Mile', and as the sun began to set, they reached the Greenough River and finally arrived at the plot Burges had indicated was now theirs.

Maggie looked across the property and smiled. There were green fields in all directions, almost as if they had already been farmed. The river's edge was shrouded in magnificent trees, and here and there in the fields were stands of trees, and a few rocky outcrops. She could hear a river spring bubbling pleasantly nearby, and beyond that, she could hear the sounds of waves on the shore, judging from the massive sand dunes probably only a couple of kilometres away.

Camp was established quickly near the river's edge, and the already depleted group of remnant settlers heading further north gathered around the campfire for one last time. Although the river was quite dry at the end of summer, the river spring made a lovely, bubbly sound as it pooled over a section of rocks not far away from their camp and men delighted in the pleasant noise, and James in the knowledge that fresh water was here and abundant. Birds sang in the trees, and the sunset that night over the dunes was simply glorious.

A stiff wind blew from the southwest but disappeared with the setting sun. They heard the roar of the ocean, sounding like it was very close, and very angry. Then not far away, a single dingo howled and the men shivered as another replied. Maggie drew Thomas closer to her and snuggled into James as the night fell silent.

Everyone slept a little restlessly that night, the isolation bearing down on them like the darkness of the night itself.

Greenough River runs parallel to the coast from its mouth at Cape Burney for some fifty kilometres south, before sweeping to the east in a series of broad loops that almost double back on themselves in places.

James and Maggie's leased lands were at the start of river's easterly bend, but still only a short walk to the beach. This place was therefore roughly midway between Yardarino and Champion Bay, though they could of course move elsewhere in their plot to establish a base if they wished. In total, they had around 15 kilometres of river side land to choose from for their future home.

Early the next morning, Burges gathered horses for them and conducted a quick tour, leaving the sleeping child with the men. He showed them where he thought would be the best spot for their prefabricated cabin, two or three kilometres further from where they had slept the night before and in a very pleasant grassy area, almost on the river's edge that had the benefit of a small natural spring for year-round fresh water. James agreed, and so they returned to the group and once departed, their wagons and horses were driven to the site.

Once there, men helped them unhitch the wagons one final time, and then the wagons were pushed under a nearby tree – a temporary 'shed' for all their supplies and all the worldly belongings that they had to survive the coming months. Their milk cow was tethered to a tree and would be rotated to other trees for months to come before eventually rejoining the herd when they arrived – once the stockyards were installed. The dogs ran around madly, excited by the work and the chickens clucked loudly in their containers, still on the wagon.

James surveyed the scene, realising that all he could see before them was now all they had.

Then, without ceremony Burges and the men mounted up and headed off once more. James and Maggie were left to watch them go, the reality of the situation now all too vivid. Then, as they disappeared over the horizon James finally said "Well, I guess there's nothing else for it but to make a start!"

Confronted with the true enormity of the task before him, James resolved already to talk with Burges on his return about getting convict help as quickly as possible.

But for now they were alone, and the quietness of those remote Greenough flats was deafening. The chickens and dogs had become inexplicably silent, and the only sound was the ocean, the water bubbling in the river nearby, and the wind moving quietly through the trees. It was beautiful; but to both Maggie and James it was also terrifying. After months of preparation, months at sea, travelling through the Colony, living at Toodyay Farm and navigating the horrid business of that time, and then four weeks of overland travel – they were, they realised, finally arrived.

And for the first time, they were entirely alone.

24

Greenough, April 1851

Maggie made breakfast while James re-pitched the tent. Next, he worked on constructing a chicken coop from local timbers while Maggie collected wood for their fire pit and started to prepare meals for the following day as Thomas slept in the tent.

James worked solidly, but not proficiently. His first attempt at the simple chicken coop fell down. He attempted to remove the prefabricated walls of the cabin and one fell on his foot, and then he hopped around cursing for the next two hours. He dug some foundation holes but soon tired. He chopped the wood, but they were too long for the fire and he would complain of his aching back after only half an hour. And at the end of that first day, he was too exhausted to move.

Maggie would chop extra wood when she had a chance and did whatever else she could to help James over the coming days between caring for Thomas, preparing meals and doing her own chores.

Even an extra half hour chopping wood would help - the rule of thumb was that winter stores of wood should be as big as the cabin in which you lived, so she knew there were many, many days of wood chopping ahead before winter, only a couple of months away.

Maggie milked the cow each day, and there was enough left over that she was able to churn butter. They had with them a dozen chickens, each was laying regularly and the fresh eggs became a welcome addition to the supplies they had brought along.

On the first day she made a type of bread mixed with raisins over the camp fire which they ate with great delight that night. Meals beyond that were equally simple, usually a combination of flour and water to which she added eggs, beans, fruit – whatever she could find. A favourite pudding desert was 'spotted pup', consisting of rice, milk and eggs with a dash of sugar and salt and a few raisins and nutmeg. For her such meals came quite easily – the same typical meals her mother would make back in Ireland. For James, they were the most meagre foods of his life – but possibly also the nicest as he was so tired and ravenous at the end of each day.

On the second day James started work on the cabin and Maggie took Thomas to explore the river. She walked kilometres over the days that followed and became familiar with the sections of river that were deeper, wider, more still. She found a beautiful little section that was well treed but with a wide clearing that shaded a sizeable pool of clear, fresh water, and a log that almost seemed made for sitting on. The river was deeper here, and she could see small fish cutting through stiller water; and yet it was still quite close to their tent. This place became her own place of choice, her private place where she would while away the quiet times reading or writing, with little Thomas asleep beside her. It was also where she would bathe, Thomas on the bank as she sang an Irish lullaby or some other song from home to him.

Lockier Burges returned on their fourth day, a much welcome visitor and to their great joy agreed to join them for dinner and to stay the night. James had prepared a list of items he needed to complete the cabin – although he had brought all of the material he needed, some essential braces and nails had gone missing - admitting perhaps he had built it incorrectly as he had no previous experience in construction, even of such a simple 'kit-form' structure as this. Lockier gave him a smile along with a few tips and promised to send a man back with the few remaining bits and pieces.

As Maggie prepared a meal, James and Lockier inspected the beginnings of the simple cabin, and James took the opportunity to ask about getting convicts assigned to help with the stockyards and other tasks - he wasn't keen for Maggie to overhear. To his delight Burges confirmed that a convict hiring Depot was to be established in Gregory, to the North of Champion Bay, and that he had already lobbied to have some men assigned to the Victoria District. But then to James' great dismay Burges warned it may be a year or more before it was established, and suggested James quickly hire a ticket of leave prisoner or private labourers from amongst those installed along the Stock track once they were available.

He explained the convicts on their journey north, and the others to follow were already assigned to the Victoria District and would soon qualify for their Ticket of Leave. Burges shared James' own interest in enticing them to stay in the area. These men could opt to stay in the district to which they were assigned, reporting to the Police or Comptroller of Convicts every six months. Their pay was capped by law, so they were typically much more affordable than even unskilled labourers, and of course many were experienced tradesmen in their previous lives. They were also able to work privately 'after hours'.

However, again he warned it could be some months before the men who had come up on the journey north were finished their tasks and released to 'Ticket of Leave' status.

"We had wondered why you didn't bring staff..." Lockier said outright. "It is imperative to all of us that the stockyards and huts are quickly installed..."

James cut him off and explained that he had thought the convicts would be rotated to assist, which was true – though he didn't relay that he had very little money left over to employ labourers.

So the best James could do was to give reassurances he would complete the first stockyards and huts himself, and to ask Lockier to please keep an ear out for ticket of leave men that could be assigned to him at Greenough at the first available opportunity. He buttered up his request with a false offer that he would pay extra to keep them here – of course realising that he would be competing against every other settler and every public works project in the District.

Lockier left earlier the next day, and again Maggie and James were alone in the far north, with no one likely to visit for weeks or even months. As he set to work once more on the cabin, James felt trapped and despondent, unsure what to do. He realised the work was quite possibly beyond him, particularly in the short time frame. While he could obtain cheap help it was likely to be some months off. He hit his thumb with the hammer and cried out in pain, cursing Maggie when she rushed to his aid.

As she returned equally angry to her own duties, his accident suddenly gave him an idea: he lacked carpentry skills, and he had arranged for no less than three carpenters to be assigned to Bignell's boat building works. He thought if he could get word to Bignell now, he could have one of those carpenters temporarily assigned to him in Greenough, while he awaited the more permanent arrangements. As the men were effectively employees of private interests, the authorities would not even need to know, so long as he were in Greenough for less than six months.

And so, at his earliest opportunity he left Maggie and rode out for Irwin Station and then on to Port Denison where he delivered a sealed letter to Mr Bignell. He was gone only a day, telling Maggie that he needed some pieces urgently to complete the cabin. But his real mission was to deliver that letter, requesting Mr Bignell provide a temporary loan of one of the carpenters 'for urgent and skilled works'. He enclosed a promissory note to pay the man's wages at completion of the works, which he estimated should take between two and three months.

Fortuitously, one of the Cattle Company's boats was in the port at the time and due to return for supplies, and so it was less than two weeks later that Mr Bignell received the request.

There was one carpenter whom he could release, a very capable young man who had an excellent work ethic. It was a big ask for him to be released, but in truth Bignell didn't yet need even two carpenters as production had not yet reached capacity. And besides, it would be an opportunity for a trial run of The Speculator, which was just about completed.

And so he made arrangements for the convict carpenter to take up the temporary assignment in Greenough. He would leave in less than a week and would arrive in Denison a week after that – only four weeks in total after James had made the request.

Days of the early pioneer

For a further month, life continued on for James and Maggie much as it had those first days. James adjusted slowly to the chores of the farm and worked hard, if not well. They still lived in the tent, but they had grown their camp with the addition of a vegetable patch and chicken coop.

James struggled with the tireless work, but nonetheless they were happy. He worked away on the first stockyard where they had slept that first night, making some small progress while Maggie looked after Thomas, who had grown and was a happy child, now offering them smiles and cuddles.

Maggie loved the sounds and experiences of the bush. Where the silence had scared her at first, now she noticed the many sounds of that silence – birds and insects, frogs and reptiles, as well as their own animals; the bubbling waters of the river; the ocean nearby. All made a constant noise that was to her, the sound of home.

She and James rode around the property when they could, exploring the river, the Flats and the bush. In the evenings, as Thomas slept and only the stars kept watch, they occasionally made love that was sweet and generous. She knew he was sometimes distracted and always tired from his daily toil, but he roused to her attentions and they revelled in each other, alongside the peace and tranquillity of the Australian bush.

When she enquired, he wouldn't tell her what worried him so, but she realised he was concerned about money and time. She assumed he was anxious to get his work done so they could return to Ireland; and she empathised that he was really not that good at it.

The stockyard fencing was hard and time-consuming work. Each post needed to be cut to size, together with longer braces and cross-posts. Each post needed to be dug deep and kept taut with inserted crossbeams. The best wood for this purpose was itself a considerable distance to the north, with long days spent just transporting the wood in the cart, let alone cutting and installing it. It was hard for one man to do alone, and James had neither the experience nor the stamina, and made slow progress. He nearly cried when he realised he needed to build at least two of these plus huts before the cattle could even be moved in and his first income realised.

But they coped, and as each day turned to the next he realised he had made some progress, small as it might seem. Overall, he too was happy.

They had some very scary moments too – a huge snake slithered into their tent one night, and it was only good fortune that it slithered straight on through, directly past little Thomas' cradle. James spent the next day building a barrier around the tent, and Maggie was extra careful as she wandered around the property.

There was a fire to the north across the plains, and smoke and ash settled across their land in the early morning's easterly breeze. Luckily the wind turned and the fire never reached their lands, but James thought how easily that might happen in the long hot months.

So too the dingos that they had heard that first night had persisted, their mournful howls striking terror. They sounded so close. But thankfully they were perturbed by the two collies, Chip and Dale, from approaching the tent. But they seemed to be forever nearby, and James declared they would be a challenge to the stock once installed.

During those happy weeks, Maggie took to bathing regularly in her little spot in the river and was surprised one day as she re-robed to find an Aboriginal woman standing nearby, clearly visible though Maggie had seen no other sign of her before that moment.

The woman said something she couldn't understand and pointed to the baby, making a rocking arm movement. Many other people would have been alarmed, and James said she should have called for help when she told him about the encounter later that day. But Maggie did not feel alarmed. She spoke back to the woman, held Thomas up for her to see, and held him in the rocking motion. The woman smiled at her and then as suddenly as she had appeared, she disappeared back into the bush, leaving Maggie wondering if it had even happened.

Over the next week they both saw more Aboriginal people in small groups, always at a distance and always disappearing as quickly as they were seen. These people seemed different to the Noongar, taller and stronger, more warlike perhaps, but different too in that they had had little contact with white people other than the parties that had travelled through the region.

But they knew too that their presence was well known to the Aboriginals. James saw men looking directly toward him one day as he was out alone in the field. He also noticed that the fires seemed to move around with the Aboriginal people's movements, which concerned him greatly.

And much to his alarm, one morning when they woke up their supplies had clearly been gone through, some flour tipped over and some biscuits missing. Even the dogs had not heard the trespasser, but they could see footprints nearby leading past the river.

James felt threatened and was on high alert from then on, while Maggie was curiously calm. There was something about her encounter with the woman while bathing that made her think these people only wished to avoid them and were not a threat. She suggested to James that they leave out some eggs for their next visit, but James mocked the suggestion and said that the only thing that would be waiting for them next time, was his gun.

He reminded her that the 'savages' had speared explorers that had preceded them, including Governor Fitzgerald himself only two years ago when he had travelled up to the Gascoyne River to view the lead deposits.

"If they're prepared to spear that great man, then you can only imagine what they might do to a lowly fisher girl such as yourself, Maggie Maguire!" he joked.

Maggie thought there was probably a bit more to that encounter than was reported, and that perhaps lowly fisher girls such as herself did not present themselves in quite the same way; but she kept her thoughts to herself.

Three weeks later James finally had the semblance of a cabin installed, though it was still roofless and devoid of widow shutters. James had improvised when Burges had failed to appear with the braces and other items required, so it was a little shaky, but it was protected from strong winds in their little riverside enclave, and it appeared to be strong enough – certainly more secure than the tent, "what with dingos, snakes and savages all around" exclaimed James, proudly showing off his work.

He attempted to roof it with branches, but there were more stars than roof visible as they lay in their beds that night, and the mosquitos took over the cabin so the next day Maggie showed James how to prepare thatches of native reed from the river, using the techniques from Ireland where bundles are tightly bound, and then each bundle secured to the next. They returned to the tent, and in less than a week through their combined efforts finally they had a house – *though really*, Maggie thought, *little more than a shed!*

The completed construction was up just in time, as the very next day the first of the storm fronts of the rapidly approaching winter ripped through, dumping huge amounts of rain and fierce winds and gusts threatening to tip over trees. Seeing the advancing storm, they brought in all their supplies in the nick of time and put large branches over the top of the chicken coop, then all they could do was sit scared and frightened as the storm rolled overhead, thunder and lightning bouncing across the Greenough plains.

But the cabin held, and the thatched roof kept out almost all the rain. When they awoke the next morning the tent was in ruins, a tree limb sitting atop it. But fortunately, their chickens and the cow and horses were all unharmed.

Meanwhile, James continued to fret over his financial situation. The final payment to Bignell was due within weeks, and he was making little progress on the land so any hoped-for income was many months away. If he paid the balance from his reserves, he would have very little left over for them to get paid help; and barely enough to restock food and other supplies. And if he couldn't get the fencing completed, he'd be unable to generate income or install tenants...

A circular problem, and a circular thought process for James: Worry; Wonder; Worry; Pride. Anger. Repeat.

He saw no other option than to pay the final instalment, but then he would be pretty much spent. He hoped and prayed that Bignell had received his letter and would support him by releasing a convict carpenter.

Then, on a cold Autumn's day as James put in another few stockyard posts, and as Maggie sat by the river enjoying the sounds of the bush, his prayers and hopes were answered.

26

Fate arrives

Out of nowhere, a man had appeared unexpectedly in the bush - HER bush, standing in much the same place as the Aboriginal woman had only a week earlier. If before she had been a picture of calm, now she was the opposite.

Maggie screamed, loud and piercing. Without any warning, there was a man before her; in this her favourite and safest of spaces. It was a violation, and she immediately jumped to conclusions about his intention. He was large, she could see that now and as he stood half veiled by shadow and his long coat and jacket, he was threatening. She was terrified for her own safety, and for the baby who now lay between them. Thomas also now cried, alarmed by Maggie's scream and he frantically kicked about in his little carriage, doubling her concern for him.

She grabbed at a large and heavy stick and yelled fiercely at the man, her concern turning to panic as she moved quickly to protect Thomas. Even as she advanced, holding the stick to the side of her body and yelling at him to get away if he valued his life, she wondered momentarily how long had he been there – had he seen her, naked in the cool water minutes earlier? Had he watched her in desire, perhaps even earlier, before now – perhaps for days lurking in the bush awaiting his chance to get her alone.

"Get back you filthy pig!" she screamed, and swung wildly and threateningly at the air before her.

"Whoa there, just hold on!" said the man, with what looked to be a smile upon his face. But still she advanced, and now she was within striking distance and she did not hesitate, swinging directly towards his head. The momentum carried her sideways and when she regathered herself, she turned and he was gone. Amazingly, he was somehow behind her, and again he said "Hold on missus, I don't mean no 'arm!"

But she was beyond reason now, and once more she swung at him, wildly, viciously, intending nothing but harm. As swiftly as she swung, now he stepped deftly to one side and her blow met only the ground.

"Stop!" called the man, holding out his hands, and then he did the most unexpected thing – he kneeled on the ground at her feet and pleaded his case. "I've been sent for!" he said. "I'm 'ere from Bignell's yards!"

She could have rendered him unconscious then, as he knelt on the ground defenceless. But the name 'Bignell' brought her back to her senses.

"What?" she said, the stick hovering and ready to strike. "Who are you, and why the hell are you here?"

"Name's Richard" he replied. "Richard Williams."

Maggie stared at him from the corner of her eye, still distrustful even as she prepared tea for the three of them. James had appeared minutes after their scary encounter, full of alarm for her safety but quickly realising who he was and why he was there. Indeed, he welcomed him like a long-lost brother, ignoring Maggie's distraught anxiety and instead saying "Oh dear God, what a welcome! I'm James, and I'm so glad you're here!"

Maggie put the pieces together as she made the tea. James had recruited help but had failed to make any mention of it to her. This realisation made her even angrier, and she thrust the hot tea at both men with disregard, hoping perhaps it might spill on their lap or genitals.

She listened from a distance as Richard told James how he had sailed up and travelled overland from Denison only the day before. He'd followed the beach and camped along the way and had moved east when he 'figured it was right' to find the river. From there it had been an easy walk across at a narrow point and soon enough he had heard a baby crying, which had brought him to his encounter with Maggie.

Then he explained that The Speculator was to remain for no more than a week in order that James might make his final payment.

"I do apologise for the scare" he said and turned towards Maggie. "I din't mean to cause you alarm."

Only now James thought to explain the situation to Maggie and he relayed how Richard was one of the carpenters at Bignell's yards, and was here to help with the fencing and other essential works.

There was something familiar about the man, but Maggie couldn't quite place a finger on it and then it exited her mind altogether when James announced his next news.

"Maggie, now don't be alarmed but I'm going to go to Port Denison tomorrow to find Bignell's man, the skipper that is, and make arrangements for our final payment which is now due."

He continued to talk, but Maggie heard none of it. She was incredulous that James would leave her with this man, a convict no less who even now stared at her from across the campfire with that stupid smile upon his face.

"..and so you understand I need to go to Denison" he finished, and Maggie realised he was now awaiting her response. But she gave none, instead storming off to their cabin.

"Well, I'll leave you to sort out Mr Williams' digs for the night!" she announced. "Perhaps he can sleep with the other dogs!" and she slammed the door, though without noise or the desired effect as the door fell off its hinges.

"Humph" she exclaimed and disappeared into the cabin.

The next day she was still fuming as James saddled his horse and made preparations to ride to Port Denison. She could still hardly believe he would actually go through with it. She looked around her to find the stranger, but the swag which he had laid out below the wagon was gone, and he was nowhere to be seen.

"He's putting in posts Maggie, in case you're wondering" James said, sitting atop his horse. "I'm sorry I didn't tell you about him, but it's been quite necessary to get help, I'm sure you understand. I can't do this work alone, not out here."

Maggie showed her disapproval by continuing to ignore him, her only response frosty silence and an icy glance.

"Oh Maggie, I'm truly sorry. But he's a good man, one of Bignell's best, and he knows what to do. He's a carpenter Maggie, we're so very lucky to get him. I've set him to work on the fencing, but he can help with the cabin too when you're ready, fix that door you broke for a start, and then there's plenty else to do around this place and beyond."

Maggie still ignored him.

"Well, I'll be back tomorrow. I need to get the payment back to Bignell and hear his news. I'll pick up some extra supplies while I'm there, mind – is there anything you need?"

Maggie's frostiness disappeared as she finally accepted James' intent. She silently thanked God himself that he'd at least only be away a night as she grabbed at his leg, running her hand up his thigh as she said steamily "Hurry back".

And James was sure he would.

27

Tales of the north

But James' visit to Port Denison did not take the path he expected. He arrived mid-afternoon, having none of the encumbrances of their previous journey. Once there, he found The Speculator quickly, the only boat in the bay.

The Speculator was a small and neat two masted Schooner, 44 foot in length and weighing just under fifteen tonnes. James looked at her sitting peacefully in the bay, marvelling at her smart lines and sleek appearance.

He called and waved for the Captain to make shore and soon enough he arrived, rowing the short distance. They made their way to the 'bar' at the still half made port, a poor excuse for a watering hole where a small handful of men drank loudly and fully of a barrel of rum that The Speculator herself had brought in – the first delivery of the first boat built in Western Australia. The grog was expensive and would more than double the skipper's wages.

James was relieved to be back in 'civilisation' once more, if you could call the shack that. He was among the company of other men and he had more than a few drinks, emptying his pockets more than he should and laughing and singing songs alongside the few farmhands and sea men. Again, he felt the urge for sea-life and boats, the adventures and freedom, and they eagerly swapped stories of the boat building and the largely unexplored coast.

Brian Rogers, the skipper, conducted regular runs to settlements up and down the coast from Esperance to Port Gregory, and had jumped at the opportunity to sail The Speculator on its maiden run. He reported she had sailed perfectly, a pleasure to command – fast, sleek yet generous in cargo, large enough to handle rough seas, small enough to get into the smaller bays that others could not. Amidst the songs and laughter, he told James of the remote islands he had encountered, the rugged coasts that no man had set foot on before. To the south of here were a series of reefs and islands protecting the shore from the swells. In several places the islands formed natural bays that would be ideal for harbours, he claimed. The islands and rocky headlands swarmed with seals and the hungry American sealers that had plied the coast for decades had still barely made a dent, such was their number. Fish of every description were abundant, so easy to catch that one had only to cast a line and the fish would climb up it and into your boat! Mighty whales that travelled south to north during the winter months, and then returned for the summer. He told James of the fledgling whaling companies that now also plied the coast hunting the mighty beasts, and just how much money they were making. Their oil is now a new currency, with greater value than the English Pound he said. He had seen schools of salmon, their numbers turning the ocean's horizon to froth in every direction. Crayfish that were even bigger than the lobster ever caught on Irish shores. Tuna and Spanish Mackeral that were so large, a man could not hold them aloft. Sharks that dwarfed those mighty fish and were so numerous they would tear every second one from a man's reel before he had a chance to land. As he continued his tales, happy to have an audience wide-eyed in wonder, he drew silent and beckoned James closer.

"To the near north, or so I've heard from other mariners" he whispered, and looked around as if to ensure no-one could overhear, "there have been discoveries of oyster and pearl, closer to the shore and easier to recover than any of those from the old land. They call it "white gold" and I hear men are already now moving north in the white gold rush, rivalling that other gold rush of the east.

Up there in Shark Bay it's said, barely a few hundred kilometres from here" he continued. "I hear tell men can get the natives to do the work and any diving required and that they are naturals at it, though the waters of those oysters be shallower than any other, close enough that a man can even wade out and pick the oysters from the shore, like daisies from the field! And at night they enjoy the company of the women natives and count their pearls in the dozens!

A man would do well to join them" he said, and looked James directly in the eye, measuring his mettle.

Rogers continued to talk about the seas and islands, but James had ceased to listen. He was dreaming of those pearls, and the money that would flow. A plan formed in his mind – if he had a boat, he could go to those oyster fields before most others and make the money he needed to employ labourers on the Greenough farms. He'd build a large house for Maggie and himself, have servants once more like he did in Ireland. Purchase more land, grow the Australian holdings to rival those back home; and then he would return triumphant, no longer the minor partner, the lesser son.

"Brian" he drunkenly interrupted midsentence, "I think that is where we need to go. I'd like you to tell this to Bignell when you get back: I'll forgo all my claims on the payments I've already made but I'll make no more – the boat building business is his, and I'll make no claim. But in exchange, he'll give me The Speculator, and we'll sail to this Shark Bay as equal partners you and I, and we'll gather these oysters - and by God we'll be rich!"

Rogers smiled a scheming smile and they shook hands, and just like that they were partners.

The next morning James was feeling very ill, and realised somehow he had got out to The Speculator with Rogers and that is where he had slept, the boat anchored near a sandbar and tossing in a gathering sea.

"Right, we're off to Perth then, Jim me lad" Brian said, altogether too chirpy after such a night on the grog.

For a while he thought he was to be the unwitting crew, but as his head cleared he remembered the conversation from the night before. *A pearling adventure to the north!* In the cold light of dawn, he realised he was trading his half share in many boats for this one single boat; but then he rationalised the outright purchase price would be a fair swap. And best of all, he wouldn't need to pay the last instalment – if he had done so as he'd reluctantly planned, it would have nearly broken him. No, in the cold light of dawn and sobriety it actually still seemed as grand an idea as it had the night before, and so they made their plans. Rogers would return immediately to Perth with James' note, handing over all his previous investment to Bignell in exchange for The Speculator. Rogers would reprovision and prepare for the journey north and return to Port Denison in December, and as the summer returned they would sail to the pearling fields of Shark Bay.

As he rode back to Maggie and their Greenough farm, James thought how clever he was, and how well the plan had worked out. He had several months to prepare, and now he had secured this convict, Richard somebody, to support the work on their property for that same period. As he now had money, he'd be able to get other supplies and support in for Maggie to run the farm, and he'd sail north for a few months to earn their fortune!

Rogers was a naval man, who had travelled the world on His Majesty's service. He was one of eight children of poor parents in London and had learnt the hard way that there are no free-passes in life when you're the littlest of the pack; when your father beats you too for your weakness, and your mother screams and throws pots at him but hits you half the time much to your father's drunken delight. He grew up tough, a street thug who would steal from people as soon as look at them. He never had an education, but at just 14 he joined the Navy and that was where his education began, so he would tell anybody who listened.

He learnt that people were not to be trusted, other than your mates and that following orders was all that mattered. Not that he always did – he set up many little side business hustles along the way that the brass would have been none too happy to hear about. But they never did because he was too clever to get caught.

When one of the younger sailors, barely a boy, threatened to tell that Rogers was stealing supplies on the side, Rogers buggered him until he cried and told him there'd be more and worse if he opened his mouth.

When a fellow sailor told him he'd report the illegal gambling that Rogers had set up, that man had inexplicably disappeared over the side.

And when they charged the negro camps in Africa, Rogers was first in line, shouting and killing with a ferocity that gained the commendations of his superiors, and the fear of his fellows who saw not loyalty to King, but madness in his eyes.

At 35 he was discharged from the navy and given a free ticket to the antipodes. He chose the Swan River because it was so new, and he knew there'd be opportunity aplenty for a man of his type. And he was right. He spent his first years working on American sealer boats, where he took a perverse pleasure in clubbing the seals and their babies. For a time he worked as a smuggler, taking illicit goods from Perth to Bunbury. He'd met a girl there and was for a time in love, but when she left him for another, he sought her out in her dark little home and beat her to a pulp, delight in his glare as she begged him to stop.

He had made a good living, though he spent most of it on alcohol and prostitutes. But he had not yet made the money of which he dreamed. He had lacked only a backer, a dandy such as James who looked upon him with respect. And now James was taking the bait as surely as any of the great fish he had hauled up from the sea – instantly, he had a naïve and rich partner that could be taught to become a real sailor, and with the boat a prospect for real wealth in the distant north.

An uncharted, untamed land where he could do anything he wanted and the law would never even know.

28

A stupid Englishman

Maggie had an uncomfortable day and night, forever wondering where the convict was and whether he would pop up behind her like Patrick had that time before, or whether he would try to slip into her bed in James' absence. While she recalled the convicts had usually committed only minor crimes, she did not like the thought of being left alone with such a man, many hours away from help.

She went about her day as she normally would, listening out for him and permanently on guard. But he didn't approach her. She bathed fully clothed when she knew he was far away; and still there was no sign of him. As the night gathered she finally saw him moving back from the field and as she cooked a meal for them both, he silently went about fixing the cabin door. She could see he knew what he was doing, and within minutes it was fixed and stronger than ever before. Then he asked permission if he might fix a few other things he'd spotted, and she heard him tinkering away in the cabin as she laid out their meals.

They ate in silence for a time, until Richard finally said "I got through a few posts today ma'am. Would you like me to continue it tomorrow, or are there other more urgent jobs to do?"

Thinking of the approaching winter, she asked if he could chop wood. "Certainly" he said. "As you wish."

That was all they said to each other that night, though she fretted later when she heard the baby cry and then go silent. She was doing dishes, and immediately regretted leaving the child near the fire, closer to the man than he was to her. So she quickly dropped what she was doing and rushed back to the fire, and there was Richard, holding him and singing a light lullaby. She stopped then, cloaked in the shadows, and watched for a time. Richard held the boy in a tender caress, and looked upon him with care as he sang an English lullaby. He had a lovely voice, deep and resonant, and the child had responded immediately. She thought momentarily that James had not held the boy so tenderly but for a few times recently, he was always so tired at night, so caught up in his worries. And she realised then that Richard showed no signs of tiredness, indeed had done more work after he returned from the field, chopping the wood for the fire, fixing the door and whatever else he had in the cabin. She decided then to hold judgement, perhaps to give him the benefit of the doubt.

"He's a beautiful boy, Maggie" he said then, without even looking up. Maggie realised he had known she was there the past couple of minutes. "You've made a nice little home for him" he continued, and now he looked towards her darkened hiding space, somehow directly into her eyes.

Maggie again felt something else as their eyes connected: a memory of some other time, though she still couldn't put her finger on it. He seemed somehow familiar. But it was a fearful thought - a fleeting passion where none belonged, and again this was an incursion to her private space and security for which HE was to blame. So she walked swiftly to the fire, took the boy from his arms with a glare and turned to the cabin, the door this time closing perfectly behind her.

"Goodnight girl" she heard as she bolted the door and turned on the oil lamp. "Maggie O'Brien."

James returned mid-afternoon the next day, much to her relief. He said little about the visit, only that he had done his business and that The Speculator was a grand boat. "The Brown Mallet wood has turned out a fine craft, Maggie – you would have loved to have seen her at sail!"

Then he suddenly rushed back to his horse and rifled through the saddle bags. "And I got you some things too, Maggie!" he said. "Though you didn't ask for them."

He produced a duffle bag with a handful of items in it and tossed it over to her to inspect. She found various items – some staple food stuffs, oil, a loaf of stale raison bread, a length of cloth and cotton – "For some winter clothes I thought, Maggie" – a box of biscuits and other items. But her eyes and hand were drawn towards one item that lay tangled and twisted at the bottom of the pile.

"Oh James" she said, true joy in her voice. "It's beautiful!"

It was a coil of fishing line and a mix of barbed hooks, and now in her hands she made her way almost instantly down to the river while James and Richard looked on in amusement.

Maggie had seen fish swimming swiftly through the reeds and branches in her river many times since the river had started to flow. Often their fins would cut the still water, and she had watched kingfishers dart into that water emerging with fish of varying sizes and descriptions. She recognised some of the fish, different but same species to those of Blackrock, and she longed to see them up close. She had kicked herself for not equipping fishing tackle.

For bait she simply dug up some grubs, plentiful at the base of the native reeds as she had discovered when she first collected reeds for their thatched roof. Then she sat silently for a moment and chose the spot to cast her line, the subtle currents and movements on the surface telling her where the fish would bite. Before she cast, she said a few words, a 'little prayer to the fishes' she called it, thanking them for coming to her plate.

She cast expertly to a place next to submerged branches but safe from snags and she was almost instantly rewarded – a firm bite which she let go for just a foot or so of line, and then she pulled back, a gentle tug. The fish cut through the water, seeking out the branches and submerged grottos but Maggie pulled it in, smoothly and firmly and there before her now was a large black fish that flashed silver, broad in height and with a narrow body designed for swift turns and speed. It was enough for two, but not three and so she cast again and was rewarded once more, a slightly smaller fish but plenty for the three of them.

She expertly cleaned them with just a few deft movements, discarding only the scales and guts. The rest would go in her 'perpetual soup', a dish that simply grew each night with whatever leftovers were around. Nothing went to waste for an early pioneer.

She caste the guts back out to where the fish had been caught, and as she turned around to leave was curious to hear a large splash. To her surprise, she turned around, and there on a branch over the tree was an Aboriginal boy, a fish bigger than all the others wriggling at the end of his spear. He grinned at her and said something to the fish and to the river, and then disappeared.

How long had he watched me? She wondered, but again felt no fear. His smile alone was enough to put any concerns at rest, though she did think how very easily he could have used that spear on her, had he wanted.

Remembering James' concern from last time, she decided not to say anything when she returned to the camp, the fresh fish ready for the pan.

And so now they had fish and protein, a much needed and tasty change from the simple meals they had endured for many weeks now, and Maggie would ensure they had this every few days from here on wherever there was water in the river. As the daylight gathered or failed, she wandered up and down the river or rode out to the nearby ocean shore and was delighted by different species in different environments. Never did she take more than they could eat; and never did she take a single fish without first saying a little prayer to the waters, and the fish itself.

With James back, the days went much as before but with much greater productivity thanks to Richard's muscle and skill. Where James had installed only one or two fence posts in a day, Richard could do three or four and they were nearing completion of their first stockyard already.

And where James would come home exhausted each night, Richard returned with as much energy as the start of the day.

Maggie noticed that he would disappear for a while each morning and evening, and so she followed him, curious to what he got up to. She stayed well back and quietly watched from the deep forest, shrouded by bushes and trees. To her amazement he started each day with a series of stretching exercises, conducted down by the river with only the trees and early morning stars and birds to witness his movements. They were fluid, almost like a dance, and Maggie couldn't help but think they were beautiful – that they 'fit' this place – and so she started doing them herself the next day.

In the evening, to her amazement and amusement, he exercised! While James was exhausted, Richard took himself back to the same space and furiously exercised: chin-ups on a tree, push-ups, strange lunges, sprints – he would even lift rocks and fallen tree limbs, grunting under the strain. She had to keep her distance so she couldn't see him as clearly as she wished, but clear enough to see he had no shirt on and that he had a very nice body from his efforts. In fact, she wished she could see more of him and more clearly and started forward involuntarily; but she resisted the urge and returned embarrassed to camp.

Whatever does the silly man think he's doing? She wondered as she walked. *Doesn't he work hard enough each day without needing to do more silly exercises at night?*

She put it down to him being a stupid Englishman.

Two days later when the men returned from a day cutting fencing posts, she presented Richard with a surprise.

"Can't have you sleeping under the cart" she said, "there's more storms coming." And she presented him with the repaired and reinforced tent that she had fixed with the strong cloth she bought in Perth when they first arrived.

Richard knew it was a significant thing to do – it would have taken her many hours and the cloth was expensive. She should have kept it for their own needs yet here she was, giving it to him, a convict.

He set it up immediately in a space away from the camp that was well protected from the wind but was not under tree branches that could fall – something James had not considered, and which had resulted in the previous damage. It made a comfortable abode, and he was so pleased to have it - but even more pleased that Maggie had fixed it herself.

While he was busy setting up his new little home, James and Maggie talked about the progress of the work and Richard's contributions. James was effusive in his review, saying that he didn't talk much but was a very skilled and hard worker. Maggie also had to admit that he was polite and kind, looking out for ways to help and often doing them even before she asked.

James was pleased to see she had come to accept him. He had in the back of his mind that perhaps Richard would stay on while he was away. Once he was a ticket-of-leave man, he could opt to do so though James would need to arrange his 'transfer' to the region – something he would discuss with him in the weeks ahead.

Winter, when it had fully arrived, was wet and harsh but short compared to Ireland, and of course it was nowhere near as cold there on the coast and closer to the equator. Bursts of wet weather hit regularly, and so Maggie had made sturdy work clothes for both the men which she had waxed to resist the weather, and which helped to resist the wind and rain. And more importantly, that they had dry clothes at home after a hard day's work. She wore her large coat, the one she had bought in Perth, and though it went below her knees and she would have to constantly draw up the arms, it was as cosy as a warm fire. It was no fashion statement, but both men drew a breath at just how gorgeous it looked upon her nonetheless.

To their great pleasure, Richard had his own little private project when he wasn't working – over the space of a couple of weeks he had built a circular shed with daub and wattle sides and a sloping thatched roof, but with no roof at all over the middle, like a donut. At first they wondered what possible use such a structure would have, but soon enough they realised that no matter the direction of the wind they were always protected, and no matter the rain they could always light a fire. And so the three of them would gather around a roaring fire with the dogs, cow and horses all nearby safe and contained, and they had shelter and warmth through even the most blustery of storms.

In fact, thought Maggie, *the design is quite ingenious – simple, but so suited to the bush.*

They talked, laughed and sang, becoming – to Maggie's great surprise – friends. She realised that Richard was genuine and considerate, and bit by bit she let down her guard.

It was the happiest time of James' life. He had a beautiful young wife, a healthy child, and a good friend who was capable and loyal. He knew these things, perhaps should have been content. But his happiness came from an even deeper place – the conviction that soon, he would make them all very rich.

29

The Yamatji

As winter turned to spring, to Maggie's great pleasure and James' great alarm, they saw evidence that the Aboriginal people were back in the river area. James was on alert and carried his gun, but Maggie sought them out and soon found a small group of women in an area back from the river. As she cautiously approached, dingoes nearby growled at her and the women stood and there was initially great alarm. But Maggie recognised the same woman she had met before down by the river and made the arm rocking motion. The woman smiled a broad smile and said something, and the women seemed to accept Maggie's presence, though they ignored her as they continued talking among themselves. They were gathering a plant with a purplish tuber that she picked up was called 'ajeca' and as they broke off the tubers, which looked like small potatoes, they replanted a small section. Maggie realised they were farming, and here was their crop.

When they had gathered basket loads of the tubers, they walked a short distance and washed them in a deep depression in the ground –a deliberately dug and circular area with accessible clear, clean fresh water that could only be called a well.

She wished she could speak their language and join in, but all she could do was watch. The woman who she had met earlier gave her a few of the tubers and signalled to her mouth, that they were good to eat. Maggie gave a little bow of thanks and could see that the women understood she was thankful. They headed off then, the dingoes following nearby, and so she knew it was her time to go too and she returned to the camp. That night she boiled up the ajeca just like she would a potato and they each had some, James and Richard both commenting that the 'potatoes were delicious', and she had a little chuckle to herself.

Over the next fortnight she sought out the women again and found them twice, each time able to stay with them a little longer. She saw they had large animal skin bags in which they carried water. She watched them as they dug large grubs from the rootstocks of the grasstrees, and she saw them collect bush pears and also zamia nuts which they would bury, though she didn't know what happened with them after that. The women indicated the bush pears would be good to eat, but not the zamia nuts. From those few observations, she had already learned so much about living in this area – she wished she could learn more.

Maggie had Thomas sitting upon her hip, so took great interest when she saw one of the women carried her child fixed in a bag upon her shoulders, which Maggie thought was an excellent design to keep the baby safe and sound without restricting movement in any way. Each woman carried a bag containing digging and cutting tools and a long thick stick with a fire hardened point which they used for digging and poking things out of trees and branches.

On the second occasion, the teenage boy she had seen by the river was with them. He greeted her like a friend, and he gave her a massive grin, much to the delight of the women who laughed and snickered, perhaps thinking they would make a good pair. Maggie laughed too, shaking her head as she said 'James, husband', and the women all laughed. The woman pointed to the boy and rocked her arms – he was her 'baby'.

But then there was no further sign of them. Once though, as she searched much further from the camp she came upon a large collection of huts in a section of woods. The houses were large enough for two or three people, constructed of wattle and daub and each had a thatched roof not unlike that of their own little cabin. Here the houses were in two separate clusters and collectively she estimated they would have housed 150 people – that is, a village. They looked like they had only recently been vacated.

She told James and Richard what she had discovered, reflecting on what she had learned through these few short contacts:

That the people had houses; that they had dug wells; that they had made pets, of a sort, in dingoes; that they sowed and harvested foods in large quantities; that they carried water, which meant they could travel long distances; that they lived in large numbers; and that they had organised villages.

And then her greatest impression - that they lived, laughed and loved alongside each other, in apparent harmony with nature. A far cry from the common beliefs of that time, that painted them only as savages who needed to be westernised and Christianised.

Richard listened with genuine interest – he'd never met any Aboriginal people, nor been exposed to this type of critical thinking. Maggie's perspective was so very different to the brash dogma of the guards and other prisoners, who had really just thought Aboriginals were the lowest of the low.

James listened with alarm.

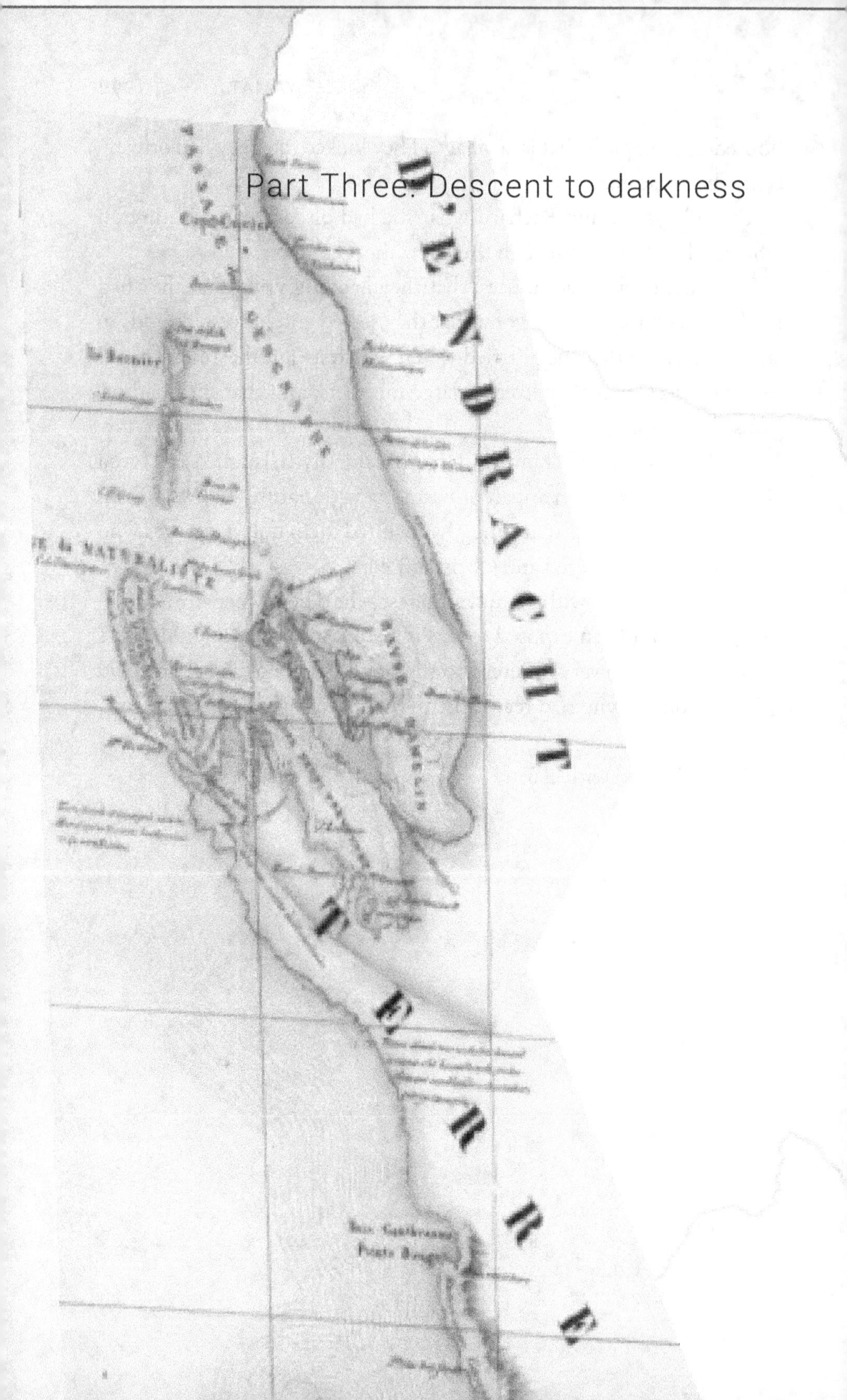

Part Three: Descent to darkness

Greed

In the inward-looking dream of the new world, the great beasts no longer shape the land but rather our own souls.

There are many of them – mighty carnivores such as aggression, hate, and self-interest. Herbivores such as love, kindness, altruism. They roam, clash, conquer.

But all of them pale beside the mightiest of beasts in this new world, the one that rules over them all, shaping the very world as it sits, observes... as it lurks shallowly below your own skin, thinly disguised, awaiting the opportunity that will inevitably emerge.

A greater beast nor blight there has never been, nor ever will there be as long as our gaze remains inwards, surveying only the land that is one's *self*.

If you took away all the systems that support inequality, and challenged all the beliefs that underpin them; if you put in place new systems that ensured equity and equality for all; still the beast will remain and will break through when its chance emerges.

Put aside your pitiful struggles between cultures and colour of skin; between genders; between rich and poor. This is the beast that makes slaves of them all; that turns good people bad; bad people savage; poor people to despair; and rich people to gluttony.

Put aside too your struggles between nations and empires – the beast that lurks is what drives each heinous act and will cause each servant of the greater goal to quickly turn the moment the opportunity presents.

As the dreaming dies and we look inward and shun the land and the stars that gave us birth, the beast seems to be omnipresent, universal, insurmountable... Making us its slave as we allow it to be our master. It is a great and evil beast though we may name it otherwise and will always seek to do so.

Few have even recognised it, and very few have overcome it.

Fewer still have become its master. But some have – rare souls who neither want for survival nor for what they do not already have.

For mastery of this beast comes only when two rare insights combine – when you truly learn how little you need, not how much; and when you learn that true love lies not in being loved nor in any sense of 'possession', but rather in loving and in service to others.

Maggie had named it long ago:

"It is the greed and self-interest of every-man that has caused so much suffering."

But by then James had already rationalised it:

"I'm not so sure it's greed that drives evil into the hearts of men – perhaps each of us is just trying to get by and protect the loved ones around us, and so they want more just to ensure that future?"

James and Maggie continue their different paths.

30

White Gold

As Winter made way for the Spring of 1851, Greenough was variously glorious and wet and windy, but this latter they survived well thanks to the shed and the generous stack of firewood Richard had prepared. He had remained in his tent nearby but out of sight and earshot, though on some occasions moved his swag into the round shed to avoid the worst of the wind. He and James worked furiously and well, finishing their first stockyard and moving on to the second despite the occasional harsh weather.

Alongside this, James slowly made preparations for his departure without alerting Maggie to his intentions. He knew she wouldn't be happy that he should leave, but he thought it would only be for a few months, and she and Thomas were now safe as Richard had agreed to a transfer and would be nearby. He travelled to Yardarino and Port Denison once more, where he met with Lockier Burges and they jointly prepared a letter requesting the transfer of Richard Williams to the district, to accompany Richard's own request. Burges was pleased with the progress made and so he also organised for his six-monthly Police check to be authorised as well, even though he was officially out of district – anything was possible if you knew the right people.

The arrangement was made that Williams would serve out his sentence by completing eight stockyards and huts on the Maguire property so that cattle could be moved in ready for the next wave of Greenough settlers. By having eight stockyards spread over 5,000 acres, cattle could be dispersed quickly throughout the Greenough Flats. Williams would then be joined by other ticket of leave men from the stations and Yardarino itself to build bridges and other public works in the area in the longer term.

The letter was posted, and then James realised he should also write to Bignell to tell him of the arrangement. When he received the letter a week later, of course Bignell was cross that James hadn't even bothered to first ask him; but it was no big issue thankfully – since James had withdrawn from the boat building partnership, Bignell had slowed production and had sufficient staff to do without him.

Mid to late Spring in the district was nothing less than beautiful. Temperatures were warm but pleasant; the river was full and fresh; the bush came to life with flowers and birds, kangaroos, water birds, turtles, and fish. As the season progressed and the temperatures rose, mid-late morning each day without fail, a sea-breeze would come in from the south west, stiffening as the day progressed.

Richard had completed the first two stockyards and huts and told Maggie that he had applied to stay in the area to do other work. She gave him a smile, pleased that he would still be around as she had expected he would leave at any time. He arranged with their permission to build a small cabin for himself around a half-mile away, but he would still join them regularly for dinner. James and Maggie would occasionally drink, but Richard would not – he said simply that when he drank he got in trouble, and didn't want to ruin anything now.

Then one day in early summer, a man arrived. He was very scruffy and rough looking, with wild salty hair, a scraggly, untrimmed beard and his clothes were torn in places. Maggie was alarmed as the men were out in the field, but the man identified himself as 'Brian Rogers' and said James Maguire would be expecting him. She pointed the way, and an hour later they were all back, James and Rogers carrying on like old school chums.

"Maggie!" James exclaimed, and she sensed that he had already been drinking, confirmed by the whisky bottle that Rogers now tried to hide. "This is the mighty Sea Captain, Brian Rogers! The skipper of The Speculator, which I'm pleased to now let you know is entirely mine! Cap'n Rogers is my new business partner and we're soon both to be quite rich!"

Maggie bid the men sit down, but Richard alone complied. She could see Richard had not been drinking, and was looking cautiously at Rogers, positioning himself between the man and her.

"Oh and do you know 'Cap'n Rogers' as well then Mr Williams?" she enquired, attempting to establish the link.

"Well we had a week's company, Maggie" he replied. "He brought me up this way all those months ago, and then kindly pointed the way for me to find you." Maggie could sense Richard's distrust of the man.

James jumped in, already aware of the tension between them. "Ahh, let me explain, Maggie. I'm sorry I didn't tell you earlier, but it's only been Cap'n Rogers return which has brought the confirmation I needed. You see, I've cashed out of Bignell's Boats, and I've purchased The Speculator outright in lieu of the payments I'd made!"

He looked to Maggie expecting delight that he had purchased *her* boat, but he got none. Maggie's look was one of surprise mixed with more than a bit of anger. She was angry that James had made such a decision without even discussing it with her – the boat business was probably the cleverest investment James had made. She also liked Mr Bignell and felt that she had made a big contribution to the business. It wasn't right or fair that James should steal that from her without even a word.

"Ah, yes, well..." he stammered, quickly picking up on her rising anger. "Well, that is done. But Maggie, The Speculator! It's a grand boat, fast and light, able to get in where others can't but still able to take a full hold. And it's mine now, Maggie. You know how much I've longed for sea life and adventure!"

Maggie stood then and brushed her clothes down – in James' experience a sure sign that he was in the bad books. "Ah well, 'may as well be done for a sheep as for a lamb', eh Richard?'" he said. "Maggie, I have more news. First of all, the Cap'n has brought with him Richard's leave transfer – he'll be staying!" Richard was clearly pleased with this news, and Maggie too couldn't supress her smile.

"But I'll be going." Maggie's smile disappeared and now she looked at James with concern. "Just for a wee-while you understand, but we'll be heading off tomorrow, as soon as we have some final supplies from here. We're heading to the pearl fields up north and may be a couple of months. But we'll be back soon enough and we'll be rich, Maggie – it's virtually guaranteed!"

"What the hell are you talking about?" she exclaimed.

James proceeded to explain the whole story, how pearls had been found in the north in rich fields close to shore and that thanks to The Speculator, they would get there sooner and better equipped than others.

"Aye, and we won't even need to do the work ourselves!" Rogers added, and Maggie and James both wondered momentarily what he meant.

Maggie cooked their meals that night in a huff, assisted by Richard as James and Rogers proceeded to get drunk and loud, singing sea shanties and laughing too loud about the wild north and their great upcoming adventure. James was trying to impress Maggie, couldn't understand why she wasn't when he was doing this for their future.

That night, Rogers slept in the tent while James began to wish he had too – Maggie's coldness to him was frosty.

So the next morning when he made preparations to depart, the air between the two was thick enough to cut. Richard saddled up too – he would bring James' horse back.

They couldn't part like that, so Maggie said "Mr Maguire, you'll join me now in the cabin". Rogers gave a haughty whistle - "A goodbye kiss I'll wager!" he laughed.

Once alone, Maggie's mood changed as she grabbed at James and begged him not to leave, to be careful, to not let that horrid man take advantage of him. Soon it was acceptance and the anger turned to sorrow that they should part at such short notice, and she begged that he return soon. They kissed long and well, James gave her reassurances that he would be back soon and again spoke of the inevitable riches – that they would build a grand house, have servants, grow a mighty cattle empire, show his brother that they could make it without his help.

"Your brother?" Maggie stopped him. "What do you mean?"

And so James was forced to finally explain that Patrick had cut them off, demanded that Maggie was herself dismissed, refused his requests for further money to pay off the boat building business and buy further land to the north, as he had expected to do. He was emotional, clearly jealous of his brother and angry at his treatment.

Then Maggie told her own story of Patrick, how he had trapped her and tried to take advantage. How she had escaped only by the skin of her teeth; and how Patrick hated her for this.

James was outraged, swearing to 'kill the bastard!' and declaring that they would get their revenge when he had the funds to return to Ireland and challenge the estate.

Maggie relished the idea. She had come to fear and hate Patrick with an intensity as much, if not more than that James now felt, and revenge certainly wasn't below her.

Again they kissed passionately, and James made to leave, this time for real.

They were partners in a great adventure. They had brought Thomas into the world, together. They had built a business, together. They had travelled the north stock route, together. And looking about, they had built a life as pioneers of Greenough Flats, together. Exactly as Maggie had dreamed, and she was not about to let it go.

"Don't you worry, Maggie" he called, as the horses were spurred to action. "I'll be back soon with riches beyond your wildest dreams, lass! Take care of Thomas."

And then he was gone.

The Speculator

James was excited as they arrived once more at Denison Bay and there, standing now with a number of other boats nearby, was The Speculator. James saw movement on the boat and asked Brian about it. "Ah, my little gift to you!" he exclaimed. "I've brought help."

Richard took James' horse and made to go – James was anxious that Maggie shouldn't be alone with the risk of savages never far from his thoughts. "Take good care of Maggie, won't you Richard?" he said. "I'm glad you'll be there for her, my friend. I promise you well paid work when I return – how does 'Chief builder for the Flats' sound to you, eh?"

Richard laughed, wished them well. "Don't you worry sir" he said "I'll ensure no harm comes to her." To Rogers he gave only a brief nod. "Rogers" he said and turned the horses back to Greenough.

"Now what's this surprise?" James enquired once Richard had gone.

"Ah, you'll see soon enough" Rogers replied. "For now, help me load the last of the supplies to the dinghy, and we'll have a few drinks!"

Much later that night, a heavily drunk Rogers and Maguire rowed out to The Speculator with their supplies. James had saddlebags and a large duffle-bag full of food staples, while Rogers and he had carried a large crate back to the dinghy from the Denison settlement.

"I've already stowed most of what we need of course" said Rogers proudly. "Just needed these last items – take a look." James looked inside the crate and laughed – it was full of rum. "All the essentials I see!"

Once at the boat, James remembered he had seen forms moving about earlier that day, but as they boarded whatever or whoever was no longer to be seen.

Rogers then lit a lantern and holding it ahead of him in the darkness of the sea, he descended down to the cabin, a curious James in pursuit.

The Speculator was well appointed for her small crew, with separate cabins for both the Captain and James. "Of course you have the larger cabin" Rogers said, opening one of the doors to reveal a lovely room "Stick in your gear."

Then they moved forward to Roger's own cabin, and he pushed open the door with a rush to reveal two Aboriginal women, entirely naked and clinging to each other on the bed.

"You'll 'ave your pick tonight. I get first pick every other night."

James didn't know quite what to say, but thinking of Maggie he embarrassedly declined, closing the door to hide his shame from the frightened women.

"As you wish, Mr Maguire" Rogers said without missing a beat, "but you'll change your mind soon enough, when you're deprived of your lovely wife's attentions."

"Who are they? Where did you find them?" James asked, embarrassed but also worried for the women.

"They're Nyoongah" Rogers replied and then curtly added: "And they're ours, that's all you need to know."

They continued down the narrow cabin, and then stopped at bunks, shielded from view by a curtain.

"The women can't swim" Rogers said, and then dramatically pulled back the curtain to reveal two frightened Aboriginal teenage boys, chained to their bunks. "But they can."

James didn't know it, but one of those boys was the same young teenager that Maggie had met on two occasions now, the first time down by the river. His broad smile was no longer there – fear was in its place.

The next morning they set off, The Speculator picking up a good pace in a light wind – exactly as James had hoped.

"About these natives…" James started. He had no wish to mistreat anyone, even if they were just savages. "I don't want to be part of anything illegal."

"Now don't you fret about that, Maguire" Rogers said, with just a slight edge of chill in his voice. "They're free to go."

It was called 'black-birding', and it was an altogether too common thing as the expansion from the British colonies took hold. Where previously the colonies had been restricted in their growth to remain within established boundaries, and Aboriginal people protected by the law as English citizens with the same rights as every other settler, now the boundaries were gone and the locals in charge. Settlers flooded out of every colony, from Van Diemen's Land into Victoria; from Botany Bay into New South Wales and Queensland; and from Perth into the North and East. In time these settlers would move through the Northern Territory and into the Kimberley. Right now, it was the Midwest of WA's turn.

As they spread and developed industry, the need for cheap labour grew. Slavery was outlawed, but getting people to work for food was not; and nor yet was 'black-birding' which was the practice of taking people from their homes to lands where they were alien and isolated. It happened with many Aboriginal groups, and also with Islanders and Malays. The unfortunate Aboriginals would be given their freedom as soon as they arrived in Shark Bay, but they would dare not leave and they would have no option but to do Rogers' bidding – and James'– for nothing more than the food which kept them alive.

"The boys are locals here. They're scared of going out to sea, so I've restrained them for their own protection" he explained.

James mumbled some dissatisfaction but said no more.

The sail up the coast was extraordinary, the mornings allowing a broad reach sail on the stiff easterly breezes that rocketed from the hot interior, the afternoons a strong south-westerly sea breeze that carried them rapidly up the coast. Her shallow draught allowed The Speculator to cruise closer to the coast than other boats would dare, though they still kept well away as there were regular reef breaks hundreds of metres out to sea. Rogers himself had only done it a few times before and was cautious, choosing to make anchor before the light failed each day.

Leaving early from Denison, they sailed to Cape Burney at the mouth of the Greenough River where they made anchor in a little bay, the seas crashing to shore nearby while they sat comfortably behind a small headland. From there they sailed onwards through Port Grey and berthed for the night in Champion Bay, seeing the basic beginnings of the settlement there, the town that would one day become Geraldton but at that time was still little more than a military outpost.

Onwards again they sailed, dropping anchor for the night in a natural harbour that was in the very early stages of building the Convict Hiring Depot of Lynton/ Port Gregory that Burges had told James about. They had hoped to find a settlement and while they saw evidence that surveying the area was underway, there was unfortunately no one in sight.

The next day they sailed on past extensive sand dune systems and cliffs until they saw the narrow mouth of the Murchison River, which Rogers said was the furthest point north that he had ever been before, supplying stores for Francis Pearson at the Geraldine lead mine located some way to the east. Though they still had several hours of light, Rogers recommended they stay the night, in order to arrive at their destination with sufficient light the next day. Although the entry to the Murchison River was narrow and rocky, The Speculator managed it easily, and they enjoyed an afternoon of drinking in the peaceful estuary, lovely and wide with white beaches, and filled with hundreds of pelicans.

They awoke before the dawn the next day and set off, sailing alongside a mighty and tall cliff system that stretched in a straight line to the northwest, with nowhere to land in sight. They made good progress with a stiff easterly falling over the cliffs in the morning that turned south and west as the day progressed, however the seas were particularly rough through the area even as far off the coast as they were, constantly bouncing the boat in all directions. Rogers was baffled at first, but then stated his belief that the cause of the rough seas was that the waves were bouncing off the cliffs themselves and colliding with the incoming seas.

Eventually, Rogers consulted his charts and announced they should be at the entrance to Shark Bay, though they could see nothing but land. Then as they approached, they saw a huge island to the north came in close to the cliffs, and a narrow passage appeared called 'Blind' or 'South' Passage. Taking the passage would save them many hundreds of kilometres, should they otherwise continue around the island – a risk that only a nimble ship such as the Speculator could afford.

Once inside the passage the seas were much calmer and they could see the bottom in most places, waters in the Bay generally being less than 30 foot. To James' amazement, everywhere he looked he saw curved fins breaking the surface. He soon realised they were actually dolphins, but also visible were huge sharks cruising by in the shallow water, collectively giving the area its name: 'Shark Bay'.

The marine charts Rogers had found for the area were badly incomplete, but enough to orient them to the general geography. Shark Bay consists of two major peninsulas, each hundreds of kilometres long, separating the cliffs of the Indian Ocean to the west from the mainland coast to the east over a distance of around 25 nautical miles. The middle peninsula is separated from the mainland coast by a large body of shallow water called Hamelin Pool; while the outer peninsula is separated from the middle peninsula by a stretch of water called Freycinet Estuary, and a smaller bay called 'Useless Loop'. Collectively, Shark Bay has close to 1500 kilometres of internal coastline, although a good part of this consists of rocky headlands and cliffs unsuitable to pearling.

It was to the inside of the Western most peninsula that they were heading.

Once through the passage, they turned north and around a headland and saw their destination directly ahead, the sandy beaches of Wilyah Miah – *The place of the pearl.*

They had travelled nearly 300 nautical miles in only a few days.

They could make out scattered encampments up and down the coast, and soon a foul and overpowering stench reached them. Their Aboriginal 'guests' were terrified by the smell and the foreign lands and wailed in terror, while Rogers looked for a suitable place to anchor.

Wilyah Miah was so named by Aboriginal people in the area, the Mulgana people, and meant simply 'shell place'. The Mulgana occasionally made camp there still, but now there were already several permanent camps of Europeans and Chinese up and down the stretch of beach, each with several workers. Most had purchased passage on boats who only occasionally delivered supplies from Perth, and so there was great excitement that what they thought was a supply boat was arriving now.

Indeed, The Speculator was well provisioned and as they made shore, they were rushed with offers of trade that were too good to refuse.

The camps consisted of tents and a couple of wooden houses arranged above the high tide line, along the beach and to around 20 metres inland. Less than eight months has passed since Shark Bay had been declared 'open' to claims, and here already were 20 or more people scattered around this small section of Useless Loop, and they soon learnt there were other camps scattered around the peninsulas too.

They also learnt there were no other trading boats permanently in the area, and the pearlers relied on fresh water transported across the Bay from the peninsula to their east, which was hard work in row boats.

"Well it looks like we have a business even without stepping foot in the water!" exclaimed Rogers as he wrung his hands in glee, and James enthusiastically nodded his agreement.

They traded some supplies for knowledge as well as pearls. The oyster shell were as plentiful as the rumours had promised, and because of the shallow water it really was as simple as picking the oysters from their sandy beds. Wilyah Miah was the pick of the sites as it contained bigger pearls in deeper waters. They learnt that those shells could only be accessed at a low king tide, and James winked at Rogers, congratulating him for his foresight in bringing the diver boys.

They knew a little about the pearling extract methods, but again the campers were only too happy to share their knowledge and skills.

The means of processing the oyster shells was simple and gathering this 'white gold' was much easier than mining. Oysters were simply plucked from vast sandy oyster reefs and then the inedible flesh scooped into barrels called 'pogey pots'. The flesh was then left to rot in the sun and after a while boiled until any pearls dropped to the bottom of the pot for collection. The odour was sickening and could be smelled for miles around.

Other than that putrid smell, the downside was that there might be just two or three pearls for every hundred shells opened, and of those barely a quarter were suitable for jewellery.

However the lesser pearls still fetched a good price, mostly ground down for facial makeup among Asian ladies.

"Arr, for that pearly glow!" James laughed at his own humour.

And the white mother-of-pearl shell itself could also be sold for use in buttons – a lucrative side product, though more labour intensive as it required each shell to be cleaned of barnacles and then polished.

James again nudged Rogers and commented quietly "Well, luckily we have the women for that!" Rogers winked, glad he was finally catching on.

Yellow mother of pearl shell however was discarded, and there were already vast middens of discarded shell all around the camps.

They were paid in pearls by Wilyah Miah pearlers that night for a simple meal of fresh meat, and Rogers eagerly took orders from them for water and food supplies.

"And if you're still not bothered, Jim" he said "I'll be putting the women to work tonight too."

James did his best to ignore Rogers' insinuation, but he was none-the-less delighted to have made a lot of money within only a few short hours of arrival. If Rogers wanted to prostitute the women, he figured that was his business.

All that remained was for them to find a suitable base for themselves, to make camp and get to work.

The next day they sailed around the area and chose an accessible beach on the other side of the peninsula and some five mile south as their base – close enough for help but far enough to keep away from un-wanted attention. It was in a well-protected area with good beach access for the boat, and there was a large natural harbour a short way south that had a channel entry to store the boat.

The reefs weren't quite as rich as on the other side, but they were every bit as vast, and this was to be only their base – they alone could sail throughout Shark Bay to pluck other reefs and return the shells to be processed here.

They established the camp over a couple of days. James and Rogers had their own tents while the boys and women were set up a short way away, over the dunes - a place where their wailing could no longer be heard.

In the coming weeks as they sailed extensively around the area, they found that Wilyah Miah was on the most western side of one of several smaller peninsulas that extended into Freycinet Harbour. They quickly realised that there were only scattered camps across an almost unlimited coastline, and they alone had the unique advantage of a boat!

That is to say, there were many, many kilometres of beach rich in pearl to be pillaged.

They woke early each day to avoid the worst of the sun and made preparations for the day before setting the boys and women to work as soon as the tides were right. They worked the inner reefs, barely knee deep in water and worked their way out with the tide, whereupon the boys were sent out to the deeper waters where they would dive below to pluck the bigger oysters. The women would be called to come and collect the full buckets of oysters, and they would then scoop out the meat to the pogey pots and clean and polish the whitest shells. The pinker shell was discarded, and within months 'middens' of discarded shell grew in great piles - a monument to their greed and waste.

The days were long, hot and monotonous. But the work was not hard, and the rewards were great. The rarer round pearls sold for 12 pound per ounce; oblong or irregular pearls for less than half that amount, while the polished Mother of Pearl shell could sell for around one a half pounds per ton. In the early days they focused exclusively on pearls, though they still made the women and boys polish the white shells – "for a rainy day" Rogers said.

Rogers would go to the women whenever he felt like it to have his way. James resisted for the first week, but eventually monotony and lust had their way, and he had his. He felt dirty the first few times and worried that he had crossed a line of morality; but within weeks he too no longer cared.

He was becoming like Rogers.

There was no immediate need to seek out other reefs, though every few days Rogers or Maguire sailed across the Bay to the Freshwater Camp on the Peron peninsula, and from there would transport barrels of water back to the Wilyah Miah pearlers for a good price. The Freshwater Camp also developed as something of a trading post, and the occasional supply ships would head there. Their regular visits meant they got the best supplies quickly, and they purchased up others which they would sail back to Wilyah Miah and around to other camps, on-selling the goods for a substantial markup. Payment of course was in Pearls.

On some of these occasions, they also scoped out new reefing grounds all around the Bay and if one was particularly promising they would take the natives and leave them there for a few days with barely enough food and water, threatening to leave them if they hadn't collected big enough piles of oysters before they returned. These times were their own 'holidays' during which they would sail to Wilyah Miah or another camp and drink with the other pearling men, returning to collect the natives drunk and wild.

Each week they would boil the oldest pots of rotting pearl meat in salt water, and when they cooled they would have the Aboriginals fish around with long tweezers to gather the pearls at the bottom of the pots. They had multiple pots on the go at any one time.

Working this way, within short months they were ready for their first cargo. They had already collected three kilograms of A grade pearls, 10 kilograms of B grade and stockpiled many tonnes of polished shell for a later delivery, taking just five tonnes with them now, their first haul. They were likely the most productive pearlers in the entire area.

They had reluctantly agreed it was time to return to Perth and sell their haul. It was too great a risk to leave the Aboriginals there alone, so they decided to close down the operation for a brief recess while they all travelled to Perth and return.

This would also allow James to pop in to see Maggie, who he realised he had now not seen for nearly four months. Somewhere in the back of his mind he remembered a promise that he would return earlier; but he knew she would understand when she saw his vast success.

32

Already Gone

Maggie had eagerly awaited his return, as the weeks turned into months. Richard and she had continued without any issue. She could see in the way he looked at her, late at night as they sat by the fire, that his feelings for her were for more than friendship; but she was equally resolved that should never be. She loved James, and though she also had strong and ever-growing feelings and yes, she could probably admit desires for Richard, she ensured they never had the chance to bubble through. When the fire light found him looking at her longer than he should, she would announce it was time for bed. When she found herself staring at him as they did their morning stretches together, she turned her back.

But it was hard to keep it friendly, alone out there. And as the weeks passed into months she began to wonder how much longer she could resist, and if James would ever return.

The first of the other landowners had moved into the Flats in early January of 1852 as planned, and were delighted to meet Maggie and Richard, commenting they were a lovely couple. Richard snickered his delight and rather than cause Richard any embarrassment, Maggie went along with it. So as other settlers moved in that month and beyond, they were introduced, and became known, as Mr and Mrs Maguire.

Richard's ticket of leave transfer had been approved and listed his base and primary employer as 'Maguire property, Greenough Flats'. However he was now free to move anywhere within the district and to work for wages for others 'after-hours'. So when his work requirements allowed, he was often found helping many of the new settlers - often for no pay at all.

With Maggie's help he wrote to his father via the local Betley church, who would be able to relay and read the letter and help Daniel to make a reply. He told him he was well and in the employ of a 'wonderful couple who mean everything to me' and that he intended to stay in the area while serving out his ticket of leave period. He enclosed 5 pounds – a lot of money in those days – with the request that it go towards support of his father.

Before the autumn of 1852 arrived, Richard had finished fencing five of their own eight stockyards and shepherds' huts across their lease, and they had already installed their own herd of cattle and sheep who were thriving on the lush green lands. With plenty of meadow on which to rotate the herds, The Cattle Company staff began moving the first herds of cattle and sheep of the new settlers to these plots as well, for easier access of the new settlers.

Richard remained in his hut nearby but helped out the new families across the district as they arrived. And with other convict and paid help arriving, stockyards and huts across the rest of the district was progressing rapidly with Richard's skilled help. It gave them a little extra cash, and more importantly a way to greet the new arrivals.

Her comfortable cabin by the river became the focal point for Sunday socialising, with up to a half dozen families visiting mid-morning and often not leaving until the dusk. It was a festive picnic atmosphere in their well-tended garden by the prettiest part of the river. Maggie would take the children aside for an hour or two to provide bible reading classes, with the help of some of the mothers. Of course, the children needed to be taught to read first, and so the bible itself rarely made an appearance.

And so it was that Richard became known as Mr Maguire, an excellent carpenter; a man of faith; a much respected pioneer and tireless farmer - and an outstanding family man with his beautiful young bride and child.

Late on a Tuesday in early April, when Richard was away some-where and Thomas was asleep, Maggie was busy with her thousand usual chores when she looked up and there was James. For a second she couldn't quite believe it was really him - so many times she had hoped to see him but never in four months had he appeared. She had begun to wonder if he would ever return, and had fretted that he was injured, or worse. He had said it would be 'weeks' but it had turned slowly into months.

And now he looked different – browner certainly, perhaps older than she remembered – but something else too she couldn't put her fin-ger on. She immediately noticed however that he was well dressed in fine new clothes, and that he had with him large parcels of clothes, foods and gifts for her.

She ran to him and leapt up, wrapping her legs around him and very nearly pushed him to the ground.

"We're rich, Maggie!" he said without welcome, laughing at her exu-berance. "The pearling, the boat and cargo - they've all worked out bet-ter than I ever dreamed! And we're rich! Over 1500 Pounds and plenty more for us too!"

Maggie didn't really care for money at that moment, though she wel-comed that the money would allow her to purchase different food sup-plies. All she cared for now was James, and she unwrapped herself and dragged him into the cabin.

Fifteen minutes later he was exhausted and laying naked on the bed, happy in both the moment and his great pride.

"The place looks different" he said absently, and then took a better look around.

"Windows!" Maggie said. "Richard put them in as a Christmas gift to us, and there's more too, don't you see?"

James sat up properly then and looked about, but without realising that the cabin had grown, a lot. Richard had done extensions and their little cabin was almost double its previous size and there was a stone fireplace installed, and a store room.

But James barely even noticed.

Maggie looked at him uneasily – he literally wasn't in the room. She had instantly sensed a change in him, and even as they had sex James was distant from her and aloof.

"I have everything I already need right here, James, don't you see? Everything but you."

"Ha, soon you'll live in a mansion, Maggie and this little place will be our doghouse!"

But Maggie still couldn't work out what was different about him – there was something in his eyes. Yes, a distant look, a distraction that signalled that while he was here physically, in his mind he was elsewhere.

She tried to reach him, to connect again. "James, forget the riches for a moment and come be with me. Where have you been? Why were you gone so long? Will you stay?"

At that latter, James came back to the moment – but his own moment, not Maggie's. "That's right!" he said. "I need to go! I'm sorry I can't stay Maggie, but our camp and claim is at risk if we stay any longer. We already lingered in Perth too long."

"How long were you in Perth?" Maggie enquired, desperately trying to engage him in a conversation. "Were you with Rogers?" She remembered her dislike for that man, worried at the influence he was having.

"Yes, Perth where we sold buckets of pearls for cold hard cash, Maggie." He was gone again. "I'm leaving you plenty now, enough to look after all your needs for a long time I would think, and to hire shepherds and labourers and anyone else you need. I've banked the rest. I'll be back soon though I promise, with plenty more!"

"James!" she exclaimed and now took hold of his head, directing his eyes to her own. But he barely looked, and it was then that she realised that was what had been different – he hadn't looked her in the eyes for more than a second since he'd arrived. Something else was going on. Something deep. Something dark.

"Forget about the money, James!" Now she pleaded with him. "James, the camp and your pearls can wait a while can't they? Tell me about your trip. What's happened to you up there?"

But James was already on his feet and dressing to leave.

Somewhere in the back of his mind was a guilt that could not be shared. But above it and now prompting his retreat was more - greed. He had the lust of white gold, and he wanted more, and more.

"I'm sorry Maggie, I have to go. But I wanted to see you, let you know I'm alive and that everything is working out just fine. I'll be back in a couple more months I promise."

And then he whirled and left the cabin, mounting his horse within seconds.

"Check the package, Maggie" he said as he turned the horse toward Denison. "You'll find enough money and pearls there to keep you going for quite a while, and to pay Richard too. Tell him I'm well, and that I hope he'll stay to look after our interests here. We expect to trade in Perth regularly, so I'll be back again soon enough with more money for you.

I love you Maggie."

And he set off at a gallop.

Maggie called out her love to him and her concern with it. "I love you James, come home!"

But he was already gone.

33

Always a price to pay

Rogers was waiting at anchor, ready to go. He had the boys in chains once more, and had managed to find another, purchased from a second ship stopping in the bay on her return trip to Perth. This lad was younger than the others, perhaps 10 or 11.

"From the Kimberley I'm told" Rogers said. "We got him for an excellent price."

James looked at the scared boy, and the other lads who fought against their restraints. Then he took the boy's face in his hand, moving him to inspect teeth and health.

"Excellent, Rogers" he said.

The darkness was now absolute. James Maguire's soul had gone and in its place were a thousand pearls of greed.

They moved about the Bay, plundering, growing their pile of pearls and their mountains of shell. The reefs were vast but accessing the larger pearls in deeper water meant travelling, and as more and more pearlers moved into the area it became harder to find sites. An inspector and military detachment had been sent to the area to chart it properly and to assign claims for which the squatters already there also had to pay a fee. But they had staked many of the best sites already and happily paid to keep others from sharing in their wealth, and over the course of time, thanks to The Speculator Maguire and Rogers became incredibly rich.

James thought with relish how he would return to Ireland soon and challenge his brother, great resources at his beckon call. The power he would have that came with such money; how everyone would admire him and wish to be like him.

And if the courts don't do their job, I'll do it myself! he thought with some relish at the prospect of killing the man.

These thoughts filled his everyday for years, and little by little he grew crazy with them.

By mid-1853, the continuing influx of people to the Bay was starting to have an impact on the amount and quality of pearl, and the police presence was increasing, making it harder to work outside their licenses. Soon there were upwards of twenty sites each with several camps, and also several other boats working the area. Although there were still rich pickings in the shallows, increasingly they had turned to diving in deeper waters, which returned the bigger shells and pearls.

Unfortunately they found the Aboriginals were not good at it – although good swimmers, they had no need to dive to any great depth traditionally and as they went deeper and deeper, several died. Both of the original boys were among them – one had died from a shark, and the other drowned. But they were easily replaced. Rogers had some source through his earlier sealing and smuggler days and more than a dozen Aboriginals were traded as their workings grew.

By late 1853, there was also a very good source in the Mulgana people themselves, who were gradually being displaced from their land by emerging cattle and sheep stations. Without access to traditional hunting grounds and water, their political and economic systems collapsed, and they presented themselves for paid work wherever they could find it. Some became station hands, some worked the reefs – women were prostituted by their own elders. Maguire and Rogers only needed to pay them in alcohol and some food and water.

When the Colony administrators passed laws requiring monetary payments for Aboriginals, they turned instead to professional Malay divers, who were more capable. They found ways around these payments though – the isolation of the Western Australian coast meant men could literally get away with murder, and the Malays were often kept for far longer than their contracts allowed and were forced to live in abject conditions.

And so, while their returns were never quite as big as that first haul, each run to Perth netted them over a 1000 pounds each; and they had made several trips already.

In what? James thought to himself. *Probably only a few months?*

But it had already been well over two years. And while he had more money than he needed to challenge his brother, still he wanted more, and more.

In fact, James would never have quite enough to satisfy his white gold lust. Greed had taken over. And greed has its own price that must be paid.

34

Darkness descends

They made fewer trips to Perth as the Bay's population grew. The trading post at Freshwater camp had become something of a general store, with supply boats now arriving frequently. They could then negotiate sales directly with the supply merchants – they would get a little less, but it meant they could continue to pearl longer.

All of this meant their profits were somewhat reduced, although they were both by now already very rich. They tucked much of the money they made through trading into jars which were kept hidden away around the boat, and on their occasional trips to Perth they banked it. James had created an account in his own name and when the bank had required it, nominated Maggie and Thomas as joint beneficiaries in the event of his death.

James had become a competent sailor as he worked around the Bay and so now only one of them needed go at a time with a small crew while the other remained to supervise continued operations.

It was June 1854, though he had no idea, and it was James' turn to make that run now. He exchanged another three kilograms of pearl at Dalgety's, visited the brothels and drank himself silly at the Fremantle hotels for three days before setting out on the long return to Shark Bay.

On the spur of the moment, he decided to stop into Denison harbour and visit Maggie. He had entirely lost track of time by then and didn't realise his previous visit had already been over two and a half years ago, thinking it was perhaps 'a few months'.

Of course, he first needed to have a few drinks at the harbour shack that still stood much as it had before. It was there that he learnt the local Aboriginal people were becoming more and more aggressive. As their lands were increasingly taken over by settlers, their access to hunting grounds was restricted and their water holes were now trampled by cattle. The men at the bar told stories of how cattle and sheep had been killed, land had been set ablaze, and last week, a shepherd had been speared which had caused everyone great alarm. Someone stated that Lockier Burges himself had tried to reason with them but had got a reply along the lines that 'they would kill the sheep and cattle whenever they wished'.

The group were already angry and talking about keeping the natives in their place. This was an issue and response as old as British settlement in Australia. Even while the colonies were contained by British policy and the Natives afforded the same rights and entitlements as every settler, still there had been conflicts of this nature. James vaguely remembered his aunt Philomena talking about incidents in the early days of the Swan Colony, and recently he had seen similar things starting to emerge in Shark Bay as well. A swift and decisive punishment was essential – as Stirling himself had said: "They need to fear us before they can love us".

In his own mind, Aboriginals were less than human, good only for work to support development and occasionally for sex. And so he was forthright with the gathered men, and told them it was time to act now or they would have even more trouble down the line. The men listened to him eagerly as the grog flowed, and the conversation became rowdy as men now shouted their calls to act decisively.

Soon, the Deputy Superintendent of Police, John Drummond, was summoned and the group swelled, with other settlers marching down to the waterfront and over a few hours, there were now 50 men, many drunk, all angry and calling for action.

One of these men said he had heard reports that the offenders had been killing sheep around the Bootenal Springs area of the Greenough River, not far from James' and Maggie's own lands. The Aboriginals knew this as Boolungu, 'the place where pelicans rest', and frequented the springs for corroboree. And so it was hastily arranged that under Drummond's lead, a group would ride upon the area the following morning to round up the ringleaders.

Early the next day, the heavily armed group set off parallel to the coast and made their way silently up towards the river at the Springs. There, Drummond directed the group to split in two in order to create a pincer movement and stop the real troublemakers from escape.

James led the second group, figuring it wasn't too far out of his way to return to his own farm when the business was done. He was to await Drummond's signal and only to prevent the men of the tribe from escaping, while Drummond and his group approached and called on them to surrender the men who had killed sheep, and also the man or men who had speared the shepherd the week before.

As Drummond and his men emerged from cover, the large group of Aboriginal people broke into panic, and men, women, children fled into the bush, away from Drummond but into James' group, who had fanned out about the area. At first they stood and yelled at them to go back, but one of the men raised his spear and suddenly, all hell broke loose as the first shots were fired. Perhaps those first shots were into the air as some men claimed, but perhaps not – nobody really knew. For now the Aboriginals tried to fight back, throwing their spears and rushing towards men standing alone, hoping to break through. This only heightened their alarm as now the men shot wildly at them.

Men, women, children. Amongst the chaos of the scene the bullets of those men did not discriminate, and soon many Aboriginals lay dead, others wounded. James himself shot three Aboriginals, one of them a woman who reminded him of one of his own whores at Shark Bay, who he had grown to despise even as he had raped her. He took satisfaction in seeing her fall and when a child ran up to her, he didn't hesitate to shoot the child as well.

Amidst the carnage, no one really knew who did the killing and who did not, and so charges were never laid on anyone. But the Aboriginal people would never recover. Any men who survived the massacre were arrested and transported to Rottnest Island, charged with stealing. This was a successful practice of the colonisers in the 1850s and for decades following – arrest the largest and strongest in the tribe on charges real or made up, remove them from their lands so that they wouldn't cause any trouble.

The settlers were in shock at what had occurred. Nobody had intended to kill anyone, not really, but here now before them were the slain bodies of dozens – the Aboriginals themselves said as many as 300 – men, women and children, some who were still dying and calling out in pain. After the arrests were made and they returned to their homes and wives, nobody spoke about what happened, and the Police report noted only that 15 Aboriginals were killed after resisting arrest and attempting to kill the white posse.

James however was non-plussed, if anything glad that action had finally been taken and that his lands and livestock would be safe.

As the group dispersed, he made his way back towards his own lands, only a couple of hours ride away. It was now mid-afternoon so he decided he would have a night of fun with Maggie and then leave early the next morning for Shark Bay.

35

Black Heart

His spirits rose as he approached the bend where he recalled the little cabin would be, and once there, he stopped by the cover of trees to have a look and surprise Maggie.

But what he saw left him confused and devastated. Maggie was there all right, and she was nursing a baby. Initially James thought it was Thomas, but then Richard appeared nearby followed by a toddler. Confused, James realised that the boy child was Thomas who was now around three years old, and he saw now that Richard moved to Maggie and wrapped her up in an embrace.

His blood boiled. He could hardly believe what he saw – he was betrayed.

"Whore!" he yelled and stormed out of the bushes towards them. Richard immediately stepped in front of Maggie and the children and held out his hands to placate the enraged man.

"James?" Maggie called out. She couldn't believe it was him. "I thought you were dead!"

"Oh no, quite alive which must be a disappointment to you, here in your little lovenest!"

He was putting new bullets into his gun as he approached, and Richard then told Maggie to take the children and get away quickly, as far as she could.

It was her quick action that saved them both, as James took aim at her and let off a shot as she ran to cover, the shot hitting the cabin just inches away from her head.

Richard was already in action by then. He dived forward and even as James was readying for a second shot, grabbed the gun and pointed it upwards, the shot harmlessly discharging.

Deprived of bullets, James swung the gun itself at Richard but the younger man was too fast, too strong and instead James found himself on the ground, disarmed with the irate Richard looking down on him. There was a wildness in Richard's eyes – that this man should threaten Maggie and their children – and he was preparing to finish him.

But then Maggie reappeared and pleaded with Richard to stop. He did so, but kept a foot on James' right shoulder, pinning him down.

"I've been gone for a few months and already you've shacked up with this convict scum!?" James yelled as he struggled to stand.

"Months? James, you've been gone for over two years! I thought you'd drowned or ship-wrecked or worse!"

James calmed a little then – could it really have been so long? It felt like months...

Richard released his hold, and James rose up, dusted himself off.

"I've been out there, working for you and our Thomas!" he yelled at Maggie, his anger rising once more. "And you're here, with that convict scum and now with your own little bastard too!" and he pointed at the baby, Daniel, still in Maggie's arms.

"Oh James, if only you'd made some contact, a letter, a message..." she tried, but James would have none of it.

"You're nothing but a whore!" he yelled and pushed past Richard, making a retreat.

But once away from Richard, he again ran at her, bare fists ready to strike her and the bastard baby. But Richard had the gun now and with a swift hit, the hilt of the gun smashed into James' face and he tumbled down, blood pouring from his nose.

"You'll be seeing more from me!" he yelled at Richard, grabbing at his bloody nose.

And he disappeared into the bush, heading back in the direction he had come.

Maggie and Richard stood motionless for a moment, in shock at what had just occurred. Both the children cried, and as Maggie moved to them Richard took off after James.

"Don't hurt him!" she called after him.

"Just want to make sure he leaves" Richard said coldly, and he tossed the gun aside.

He found James staggering along the side of the river shortly after, seeking out his horse. He was walking as fast and as furiously as he could, but Richard caught up quickly.

"James" he said and when James didn't respond he moved in front of him, blocking his way.

"James" he repeated, commandingly. "I'm sorry it's turned out this way, but it ain't Maggie's fault. For more 'n a year she waited here looking for your return. She went to Denison every single week asking for news, asking mariners to take you messages.

She thought you were dead, fair and simple."

James pushed past, anger still burning in his eyes.

"I need to know Maggie and the children are safe, James. I need you to say you won't be back, that you won't cause her any more trouble."

"Oh I don't want to know anything more about the whore or her bastard child, I'll guarantee you that!" James replied shrilly. "But she'll get no more money from me, rest assured. I'll see to it that you get nothing, and that you're soon gone from your little love nest here - in my own home no less! I'll see to it she's ruined, that I can guarantee!"

"Oh you'll ruin me will you?" a voice suddenly sounded from behind them. Maggie had caught up, the children left in the cabin. "You've already done that you son of a bitch! Your precious money ran out a year ago after we had to pay the lease, and it's only been Richard's work that has kept this place going and kept food on the table for us all.

But if you really wanted to ruin me, don't you worry – you did that when I thought you were dead!"

A semblance of his soul returned to him. "Oh Maggie..." he started.

But Maggie wasn't finished yet. "Here's what is going to happen, James Maguire! You're going to leave here now and you're not going to cause any strife for any of us. You're going to go back to Perth, to your aunt and uncle and tell them what's happened, and then you're going to return here and manage this farm! Richard and I will be nearby and we'll help though God knows why we should even care! But I do, James, I do care, and wherever you've been these last years, whatever it is that has so darkened your soul, you're going to leave that too, and you're going to make a proper life for yourself once more, here, with us and your son and in time you'll find your own wife James, and though I'll look upon her with envy just as you do now to Richard, I'll be happy because I'll know you're back from the hell you've been in and you're happy once more!"

James stared at her then, wondered for a brief moment if that were possible. But then the darkness descended upon him once more and he had that faraway look again, the one Maggie now knew was greed.

"Bah!" he said "and bah! Very good then Maggie, I'll go - but not with my tail between my legs back to my aunt. And yes I will be back. And then you and Richard and your little bastard will leave, and Thomas will stay and I'll have the biggest house here, and you'll go back to the slums where you belong." And he pushed past them both, that one final time.

For weeks after his rampaging visit, Richard and Maggie lived with an edge of fear that James or his hired help, or perhaps lawyers would arrive and bring their world crashing down. Maggie knew that he had great wealth behind him, and that if he wanted to divorce her he would take everything from them out of revenge.

But he did not. They heard not a word.

Rather, the only talk in the community was of the events of Bootenal Springs, where Aboriginals had risen up and tried to kill the policeman Drummond, and that 'a handful' of their own had been killed as a result. There were reprisals around the district for weeks after, but only ever minor – a sheep missing here and there – and none of the men had an appetite to do anything about it anymore.

Someone mentioned though the wild man from the north who had come to town and bought everyone drinks, and who had been the one and only of them to shoot at the blacks that day as far as anyone could remember. Maggie put the dates together and wondered, could it be…

Part Four: A Future

A future, together.

If greed corrupts the soul and drives the darkest deeds of humanity, what then explains the great achievements of its people, the great beauty and joy that we see through the gloom every day, providing us the light and energy to shine despite the darkness of greed that surrounds?

Connection.

As much as some might like to think otherwise, not even the greatest achievement of any one person is solely their own – we each stand on the shoulders of giants.

Each act of any individual is built upon the discoveries and toils of hundreds, thousands who came before and who even now share their knowledge and strength.

The worker who goes the extra yard to ensure a quality product. The person who would drop everything to go to the aid of a stranger in distress. The smile on a face walking by. The parent who would put their life at risk before seeing their child come to harm. The lover who would forsake their own needs for that of the other, bound through love. Each of these acts is driven not by greed, but by our respect and commitment to each other.

Connection.

When we realise we are all connected, indelibly to each other, to those who have preceded, and to the world that we each share – then we can realise too that there is an even greater and more powerful driver than greed: each other. When we finally act for others, that beast Greed has no place to insert its teeth; no weakness that will be exposed to its claws. Call it love if you will, but 'connection' is the realisation that we are each a part of the greatest tapestry ever created, the human experience - that which binds us and that which gives sense to the universe.

It is absolutely love, but more – it is conscious thought itself, a choice, a realisation that *without others I am nothing*.

Connection is the single and greatest beast of all that shapes this new world. It is all around us yet people act blindly of it even as they go about their daily lives with acts of love and kindness.

Greed has no power over it and so that great and powerful beast merely walks away, looking for weaker and more vulnerable prey to stalk and overcome.

Slowly, we are coming to remember once more this truth of connection, to turn away from greed and to instead look towards a new future bound in collective hope and aspiration.

Slowly, we are coming to realise that in demanding Truth-telling, Aboriginal people are not demanding guilt nor shame but rather, reconciliation.

Because behind every big lie is an even bigger truth, and it is only the truth that can set us free.

36

True Love's bloom

It was mid-Spring 1853, but the night still carried the winter's chill as Richard stared unashamedly at her across the fire. Though he knew it made her uncomfortable, he was entranced once more, the dancing fire enhancing her beauty ten-fold if even that were possible. He wondered, doubted, that she would ever be his, but it didn't matter for he was already hers, had been since he saw her on the deck of the Hashemy three years ago.

He felt it was Fate that had brought them together then; and Fate that had sought to cement their bond when he was sent to her by Bignell. For what else could explain this coincidence other than Fate; that they were meant to be?

And so, he had been patient, knowing that one day she too would release herself to true love's bloom.

Perhaps it was fate too that had resulted in James leaving nearly two years ago, and other than a fleeting visit, that Maggie now had no idea whether he was alive or dead. She had relayed her fears to him, described the many attempts she had made to contact him over the months – none of them successful. All she knew was that James had gone to a remote and wild area a great distance north and accessible only by sea. She had heard many tales of shipwrecks, drownings, murders and Aboriginal uprisings since that time, and she expressed her belief to him that James too had fallen foul.

For a time, she had moped about sick with the worry and dread of her loss. She couldn't even tell the other women who had become her friends – they all thought Richard was her husband. And so Richard was her rock, her only confidante, her truest friend. He stayed with her when she needed him, left her when she required it. But he was always there and inevitably, their friendship deepened until this night as he stared too long at her in the firelight, and she did not look away. She did not make excuses to leave but rather, she asked him to hold her.

And she convinced herself that tonight, that was all she needed, and it was enough for Richard. He moved to her side and he held her warmly, firmly, tenderly and all he felt for her was love.

It seemed inexplicable that he felt this way – certainly she was pretty but so were many other girls that he had known and cast aside. But Maggie had drawn him in, attached herself to his very soul when she locked eyes with his those years ago. If fate had forged their past, it was nothing less than love that had shaped their future.

He loved the way she smiled. How she put others first, even he a lowly convict. He loved that she worked so very hard to meet their needs. He even loved that she loved James and the baby Thomas so truly and deeply. And he loved that she was a child of nature, as happy catching fish by the river or delivering a calf into the world as she was in her little home. That alone had made her stand out, he thought.

But most of all, he loved the way she thought. Hers was an inquiring mind; a sharp intellect that did not take the things that 'were' as things that 'should be'. She questioned authority, caused others to question their understanding. He's never known a woman like this before. But he's seen it in her time and again – a mind that steps outside convention to pose new realities based on what could be, not what is.

And he'd never loved someone for their mind before – it felt like a true connection, beyond physical attraction, beyond even sexual intimacy.

And most perplexing of all, he wasn't scared of these feelings. He realised that it really didn't matter if she never loved him in the same way – this was about her, not him.

If only we could all give such a love.

And now, he held her and the perplexing love, his untamed, unfulfilled love only grew deeper, and he sunk into her as did she into him.

Eventually, as the fire died and no one dared separate to fix it, he simply picked her up and carried her to her bed in the cabin. And then he did the most perplexing thing of all, and left.

Maggie was mystified. She would have welcomed that he should stay, would have welcomed that they should strip bare and continue that warm embrace. She wondered then if perhaps he didn't feel the same way, that perhaps he had other female companions among the new settlers that had flooded into the District. Lord knows she had picked up that many of the young things and their married mothers had thought he was the most desirable thing in several hundred kilometres!

She felt the same, and only her loyalty to James had prevented it. That they had therefore grown to become friends, confidantes, partners in this farm and as surrogate parents to Thomas had made their bond all the stronger, all the more sweet. Now she was finally resigned to James' death their only barrier had been removed, and as she lay there and saw Richard backing out the door, she felt a wave of unfulfilled desire that threatened to overwhelm her. She had two choices – be angry or accept his act as misguided kindness.

She was left on her own, gravitating between these extremes. A woman scorned. A woman loved. The coward. The hero.

Until she realised there was a third choice.

She got up from her bed, put on her sexy bed clothes, a beautiful patterned and light petticoat direct from Paris that she had found in James' own gift to her, and that had felt like a slap when he had deprived her of an opportunity to wear it. But she realised that opportunity was here now, perhaps had been for months before this moment.

Then carrying a lantern, she made her way to Richard's own cabin and let herself in.

"I'm not finished with you" she said. And Richard quivered.

She hung the lantern on a hook and stood back a little, as if to show off her lingerie and the curves it held to their fullest. Then she turned down the light, knowing the full moon outside would provide the illumination they needed. Her form was outlined against the light of the open windows, her breasts full and nipples erect, her hips and waist like perfection itself. Richard gasped at what he saw as she now moved towards him.

She pulled back his blankets and tugged eagerly at his pants.

Then he took control. "Maggie" he said, standing now before her in that same moonlight. Maggie could see his body in its full glory, leg and arm muscles shining against the backlight; his abdominals flat and like a washboard; his manhood standing firm.

"Maggie" he repeated "I've loved you for a very long time. I've desired you every night, every moment you moved before my lustful glance. But if we're to do this now, you'll need to put aside your needs while I meet my own. This first time is for me. The second time is for you."

And he pushed her down to his bunk, diving upon her and before she realised it, her petticoat was a torn mess on the floor. He moved up her body sucking and teasing her nipples and then he was in her. She groaned and thought *if this one is his and the next one mine, I might not survive to enjoy it!* For he rode her with a passion and an expertise that she had never experienced before. She orgasmed once, then again while he flooded into her but even then he didn't stop as she lay beneath his body and strength, not prepared to withdraw.

With a firm movement he wrapped her in his strong embrace, and now somehow she was on top while he still remained inside, and then they talked, joined now and maybe forever.

Minutes later, he roused again and now if it were possible, it really was her time and she grinded into him, finding her pleasure both within and without. She rode him then, long, slow and hard and fast and they both groaned, lost in the pleasure and lost in each other's eyes and souls.

Eventually, reluctantly, they separated and returned the short distance to her cabin and to Thomas who lay blissfully asleep as they coupled again; and that was how they remained for hours until finally they agreed they needed to move.

There was no going back from that moment, only going forward, together. At the height of their passion, Richard had finally revealed that they had met before he arrived at the farm and he described the way he felt when they had first locked eyes, on the Hashemy. He poured out the truths of his life and his belief that it was fate that brought them together, but true love that would keep them together now.

They shared stories of their past lives, their passions and hopes for the future. They were, now and forever more, finally, as one.

37

A sweet revenge

Six months after James' rampaging visit, Maggie found herself sitting across from Lockier Burges with tears welling in her eyes. Richard was working away and Burges had brought devastating news.

James had exacted his revenge after all, from afar. Back in Perth some short time after that visit, he had taken two simple acts of bitter revenge: he immediately opened a new bank account with new beneficiaries in place of Maggie, and he had presented a letter to the Cattle Company's head office. As he left, James had wrung his hands in glee as he plotted that Maggie would soon be both homeless and penniless.

That short letter, now before Burges, had instructed simply that James wished to sell the Family Trust's shares in the Cattle Company and cease the continuation of their lease immediately.

Maggie realised it was a simple act of revenge, intended to hit her where it hurt the most - to evict her from the Greenough lands, just as he had threatened to do.

Burges had asked for James when he first arrived, but Maggie had quickly explained he was still away somewhere to the north. She realised that like others across the District, Lockier too was unaware that James and she were estranged.

Burges looked quite upset himself, not just from seeing the beautiful young woman in distress as he read the letter to her. He was being pressured from all sides to either take up the option to buy the land of the Cattle Company's extensive lease, or to release it to sale to the many others now interested in those lush lands. James' decision had put the most important lands of Greenough at risk.

"You didn't know?" Burges inquired as he finished reading the short letter to Maggie.

"No" she replied, choosing to continue the readily accepted lie. "James has been away for months now, and though I've tried to contact him I've not had a response."

Well it's the truth she thought, *albeit out of date...*

"I see. Well unfortunately this presents quite a dilemma to us both" Burges said matter of factly as he eyed the letter once more. "The annual lease of your lands expired a month ago. I'm afraid that unless you're able to make the lease payment now, you'll need to leave".

Maggie suppressed her tears and looked back at Burges with a steely resolve. She had no intention of leaving - though had no idea how she might stay.

"But that's not what either of us want" he continued as he now looked in her eyes. Maggie felt a glimmer of hope as Burges continued. "You've done a tremendous job improving the lands and helping us to move in cattle these past years, and we recognise that and we're truly thankful to you both, despite this letter. Everyone we speak to talks highly of Mr and Mrs Maguire, and report to us how much you've both welcomed them and helped them settle in.

I hear you've even been running a little Sunday school!"

Maggie blushed at the compliment – *If only he knew the 'Mr Maguire' to which they referred was none other than a convict!*

"Thing is, we're being pressured to either buy the land or release it for sale to the general public" Burges continued. "It's these river lands you see – their potential is now well known in the south and everyone wants their slice of our pie... We're under a lot of pressure to cease our lease!

So I was hoping, perhaps you could convince James to buy the land instead of withdrawing his investment?" he offered, the true intention of his visit. "A bargain at just 1 pound per acre, so we can be assured of your continuing partnership with us..."

Maggie was pleased to hear there was an option for sale, though she realised instantly that of course there was no way she could ever find 5000 pounds.

Maggie shook her head. "No, unfortunately the investment is held by a Trust and James is only a part owner" she reminded Lockier. "I'm afraid we simply won't be able to raise the funds to afford the 5000 acres".

Burges again looked despondently at James' letter. "I understand" he said, remembering James' inability to hire staff, and reasoning here was just another family in financial trouble like many others across the District. *What else could explain James' decision to sell his shares in the burgeoning Cattle Company?*

He hesitated a moment before making another suggestion – something the Cattle Company partners had only recently discussed as a means to get the authorities off their backs, and to make a nice little profit to boot.

"There's another possibility" he started hesitantly, "and I'll need to be honest with you in this. Our lease gives us a pre-emptive right to purchase the land freehold off the Crown. There's mounting pressure for us to do just that now, or to release the land back to the Crown for sale to others" he said.

"So, we've been thinking of getting in quick and buying land off the Crown, and then breaking it up for on-sale as smaller lots.

If we did that, could you perhaps buy a smaller plot? We do want you to stay!"

Maggie hesitated for only a while before making her reply.

"At 1 pound per acre? We'd be foolish not to!" she declared, before adding more modestly: "That is, James would want that, I'm quite sure!"

Burges left soon after, explaining he would clear the deal with the other owners. Their plan was to buy nearly all of the land that the Maguires had developed, sit on it for a while, and then sell it to new settlers in smaller lots as they arrived - a more manageable size that they felt would appeal to the influx of new settlers to the Swan and make the Company a nice profit to boot. If breaking up the Maguire property for sale worked the way he hoped, they'd buy more land across the District and do exactly the same.

Maggie of course had a plan of her own though it was of a much smaller scale than the cheeky scheming of Burges. Its success, she relayed to Richard later that day, relied almost solely on a calculated gamble to install wheat crops across just 60 acres – the maximum she felt they could afford.

It was already clear to them both that cattle were destroying the land, as the once lush grasses and springs of the Flats were trampled by the hoofs of cattle and sheep, and both dingoes and the local resistance of Aboriginal people had taken a toll on the stock.

"But it's possibly an even bigger risk swapping to wheat now" she admitted to Richard as they contemplated it over the following week.

Wheat at that time was a time-consuming and costly product that was very expensive to export compared to wool and meat. Even as she considered it, she had serious doubts.

"But when I think back on the fields in County Louth, I'm sure the rich Greenough River soils would be ideal for wheat, and most of those farms were much smaller. And if the population continues to swell across the Victoria District as well as Perth, I'm sure it will soon be viable to supply locally..."

But her voice betrayed her nervousness - she was attempting to convince herself as much as Richard, and she knew there was every chance her plan would bankrupt them both.

"Maggie" said Richard as he held her shaking hands, "my fate lies with you now, just as it always has. Your plan will work, we'll see to it.

And if it doesn't, what does it really matter eh? As long as we have each other, we have the world."

Burges returned a week later and it was formally agreed that they would purchase 60 acres from the Cattle Company as soon as they had negotiated the purchase. For now, she – James that is - would need to pay only 6 Pounds tillage rent of their sixty acres for the next year, and then a further 60 pounds within a year to secure the freehold purchase of their chosen plot.

Ownership of the land of course would be in James' name as women were not allowed to be landholders; and as James was still away and un-contactable, Burges said he would negotiate the title transfer himself, directly upon payment.

The price was an excellent discount on the likely market rate - the same price per acre that the Cattle Company would itself pay the Crown. But even as she paid the 6 pounds rent from their meagre savings, realising how long it had taken to save just that amount Maggie fretted if she could realistically raise the 60 pounds required in less than a year. It was nothing for the likes of the Maguire family, but it was a huge amount for her and Richard who had subsisted on much less these past years, and it all relied on her untested hope that wheat could provide the future they sought...

As it turned out, the timing of Greenough's very first wheat crop came in at exactly the right time for Maggie and Richard, and the gamble paid off. It was a struggle and they had both worked tirelessly, but by the time the sale was due they had scraped together the money required; and only days later Burges relayed to her that the title had been transferred.

But while they had parcelled up other less productive river side land for on-sale, the Cattle Company saw the success of Maggie's wheat crops and so appointed Richard to install and manage further cropping across their own adjacent holdings. As a result, it wasn't until 1867 that the Company finally sold that land to the Hamersley group – part own-ers of the Cattle Company and that very same family from Woodada that had so impressed and helped Maggie all those years ago.

The land was now theirs and the wheat crop was flourishing. They weren't rich by any stretch, but still they had all they needed. Between wheat sales and their incomes from odd jobs, Richard and Maggie were surviving fine.

Richard had extended the cabin further to now be a comfortable family home, and he had cleared the land around it, in which they had installed fruit trees and extended their house crops which were doing well in the rich riverside soil. And there were plenty of fish in the river and sea. Lately Maggie had also started to go offshore in her own little boat that she and Richard had built and left in the dunes by the coast, and now she was catching even bigger fish!

Ironically of course, that little slice of land was henceforth in James' name, and all she could do was hope he would never find out. But rather than stress and dwell on what might be, as ever Maggie focused on what she had now.

She thought back on the truth of her father's words:

With true wisdom, you realise how little you need, not how much.

For just as Richard had said, she realised it didn't really matter even if they were kicked off the land; for they were young, in love, and in a land of immense opportunity.

If it were possible, the plan worked out even better for Burges and his colleagues. The Cattle Company knew the Greenough lands well and inspired by the success of Maggie's arrangement, they purchased the best lands for themselves, breaking up much of it just as Burges had planned.

Attracted by the small plots just as they had gambled, a flood of settlers began to flow from 1856. As a result, the population of Gree-nough boomed and within just a few years it was one of the biggest settlements outside of Perth. Soon these new arrivals started noticing the wheat fields and started planting wheat on the lower flats as well. Within a short time the region became the major producer for the colony, servicing Perth and even exporting overseas as it grew. The Greenough community thrived and continued to grow around them, and with it a townsite as commerce, industry and trade took hold.

Ironically, James had triggered a whole new future for Greenough and his plan to destroy Maggie had failed spectacularly.

It was a sweet revenge indeed.

Building a community

They never heard any further from James, ironically living under his very nose on land he didn't even realise he owned.

As the years passed, Maggie knew that she couldn't divorce James, and unless he divorced her or was now truly dead as she suspected, she knew too that she and Richard could never marry. And of course, maintaining the façade of her marriage to James had enabled them all to remain on her beloved farm.

And so they carried forward the difficult, and easy decision made years earlier into a land title, and continued the lie that each of them carried the name 'Maguire'.

The lie had started almost by accident those years ago, when the new settlers simply assumed Richard was 'Mr Maguire'. Then when their first-born, Daniel had arrived back in 1853, first he, and then all three of their children were named 'Maguire' on their birth certificates as the registry happily assumed that the father, of course, was Mr James Maguire, married to Maggie Maguire as confirmed by their marriage certificate, and father to the oldest son, Thomas Maguire as confirmed by his birth certificate. Neither Maggie nor Richard had protested.

Richard – 'Mr Maguire' to the locals – was well known and well respected in the growing community of farmers. Nobody knew or suspected his convict past - although by now so many of the settlers were convicts that nobody really cared to discuss it either.

Neither of them had enough money to return to the old land. Richard had learnt that his father had died not long after he had been transported, and so there was nothing for him to return to now. The Betley church had replied to his letter and relayed that they had tried to contact Robert as Daniel's health deteriorated but he never returned, and so the parish had gathered round Daniel to help with meals and to do all they could. The priest reported that Daniel had died after only two weeks bed-ridden, and that nobody held any blame for Richard in this – that his father's ceaseless defence of Richard's character had assured he should hold neither guilt nor remorse. Reading the letter to him, Maggie estimated that Daniel had died around the same time as Richard had arrived in Greenough.

And as much as Maggie would have liked to send more money to her parents and family back in Ireland, she simply had none to give. They got by frugally, nearly devastated by floods and the great cyclone of 1857 that destroyed both their cabins, but making enough money from other paid work and the sale of wheat to rebuild and get through each year.

But while they continued on much as before, their companionship took new directions as they built not only a life for themselves, but for their community.

Their passion for life was unbounded, freed through love. Maggie had continued her little school for the children, as there was no other. At first there had been only a small handful of children, but it was growing every week as new settlers arrived, and she loved taking them through the simple lessons. The student's ages varied, but none of them had had any form of education so she started at the beginning, by teaching them to read.

"Education is our future" she told their parents.

"If you can read, your mind is set free" she told the children, and reveled whenever either a parent or a child grasped that central truth.

39

The Hedge

One day in late 1858, Richard took her and their children across the wheat fields to a small section of land that had been shielded by thick trees and left to virgin forest. She remembered that she had been there before, loved it in fact, but it was far from the river and she'd had no reason to visit it again; so she wondered where he was taking her to now.

He led her around a path that seemed to have been well used and she momentarily wondered why that was so, and then he stopped and asked her to put on a blindfold.

"I've been doing me own little project the past few years, Maggie" he said, leading her further along the path "and I've worked harder at it since the cyclone. Now I can finally show you.

It's been a hobby you understand, something I always wanted to try back when I was an apprentice to both carpentry and to me own dad, a stonemason you'll recall." They stopped, but he bid her to keep the blindfold on.

"Well anyway, what I wanted to try was to merge the two you see. Bit of stone, bit of wood, see what it was like I guess. Anyway, I guess I've finished."

He took off the blindfold and there before her was a building. It wasn't large, but nor was it small – probably only a little bigger than their 'extended cabin'. But it was solid, with a raised stone foundation and tall walls made of cut limestone. Some room extensions were made of wood, and in some places there was an odd collection of both. There was a shingle roof, wooden window shutters, a wooden balcony that swept the entire perimeter but with a stone balustrade, and a stone garden wall beyond. There was a hand-drawn well nearby to supply all their water needs, and around the building was a pleasant garden with some established fruit trees and wildflowers of all descriptions - a colourful, spaced and peaceful garden that added to its curiosity.

If it was odd looking, it was also completely practical. The wood was perfectly cut and straight and constructed with all of Richard's skills. The inside was unfinished but she could see potential. For a start it had large rooms that could become bedrooms, and a sitting area with a large wooden table and chairs already installed. And there was also a large country kitchen partly fitted out at the back - *benches of wood, oven of stone* she laughed.

Adjacent to the kitchen was a large space that was separate to the rest but directly accessible from the kitchen. It had a thatched roof and was made entirely of wood and at first glance looked unfinished with only two walls and a low hedge along one side.

"I thought maybe you could take classes here, Maggie? Sorry, it's all a big mess I know…"

Their newborn Margaret balanced in one arm, Maggie wrapped the other around Richard's neck and drew him in to kiss him tenderly. "I love it! I can't believe you did it? When did you do it? …HOW did you do it??"

"Bit o' this, bit o' that; Bit o mine, bit o' we won't mention!"

Richard explained the locals had been getting him to help so much that he'd made a substantial store of leftovers and had purchased a few other bits and pieces with his earnings. He had gone up here whenever he could, particularly since the cyclone and put it together with stone he cut himself from a nearby outcrop, and wood from the cleared trees.

"I started it six years ago as a place for you and James, but I guess now it's just yours, Maggie".

Maggie stood and admired the place, reflected on the rambling design that worked so well. It was like his round shed in many ways – unusual, but somehow suited to this unusual place. He had put his own money into it as well as Lord knows how many hours of his time, but more than that - he'd invested his own soul, the dreams of his youth, of the time he'd spent supporting his father and the wasted years as a convict.

"Well, let's keep it our little secret for a while longer then too" she said. "We'll pop down and fit it out, and it can be our own private place for a time.

But I like your idea of that room as a school..." she mused "A lot! Yes, a school..."

She stroked her growing belly, their third child growing inside. "Our children, their children" she said, waving her hand wide to encompass the entire Greenough community "will need an education if this place is to work. It'll be a school for everyone – Aboriginal children, Catholic, protestant, none of that matters here. What matters is the future, and the future is education."

A few months later, they revealed the new house in the woods to the settlers. The families had arrived at their usual place by the river on a Sunday morning, and then Maggie announced there was a change of venue today and marched them all the half-hour to their new house.

Parents commented on the unusual design, noting it was sturdy and well protected there in the woods.

"I'd like to thank you all for sending your children to my little school these last years" she said, quietening the group. "Today, I'm pleased to show you all our new home, and a new school room for the children!"

There was a buzz about the group as she continued. "Back in Ireland, we had the National School available to all, though it was only a few short years before the Famine put an end to it. So I was one of few who benefitted from my own little school, Mullaharlin".

As she spoke, she led the group around the side of the building, towards the wooden hall. "One day, Western Australia will set up schools for everyone too, instead of only for the rich. But in the meantime, I'd love to keep teaching our children here" and she opened the door to reveal a classroom, with rows of desks, a blackboard, and benches.

"Before Mullaharlin, some of the parents got together and ran 'hedge schools'. So here, Richard's gift to the Greenough community, is "The Hedge"!"

Parents and children clapped at the beautiful room, and at Maggie's enthusiasm. Few of them had gone to school themselves, but they knew the children of rich parents in Perth were getting educated, and the idea that their own children could now receive the same gave them all a 'special' feeling, like Greenough offered a new future.

"I can't offer much" she said "but I would very much like it if the children could attend here on Wednesday mornings for reading and writing lessons, in addition to our Sunday morning picnic class. And I'm wondering if other parents could also help? It would be great to see classes in other skills too... Mrs Button, perhaps you could teach needlework? Mr Smith, maybe you could teach mathematics? I know you're good with numbers! My husband has already offered to teach carpentry. Anyway, it's just a thought but I wondered if maybe by joining forces, we could offer the children of Greenough a future and one day, get a full-time teacher here."

There was a good deal of discussion, and a handful of parents put up their hands to do some classes as well, and before she knew it she had teachers and students signed up for a full day of classes every Wednesday.

"It's not much" she confided to Richard later that day. "But it's a start."

40

Flying Foam

Maguire and Rogers plundered the oyster reefs of Shark Bay for a further ten years after his rampaging visit to Greenough, until at last the fields were barren. For those ten years they drank and abused their staff, whether paid or not; they abducted, tricked and coerced their workforce; and they continued to make large profits - though never quite as large as those early years.

They made occasional trips to Perth to sell their best produce and to enjoy the luxuries their great wealth afforded them, but James vowed never to return to those Greenough lands where his world had come crashing down.

His anger at Maggie's betrayal still fresh in his mind, on his very next such return to Perth James had created a new bank account with the disbursal authority going to 'Patrick Maguire of Dundalk, Ireland' in the event of his death. He took perverse pleasure that the riches he had gained would not benefit Maggie if ever he died before her, and simultaneously that his brother and relatives back in Ireland would finally realise the extent of his success. He could imagine his brother's shock at realising just how much he had underestimated him.

Then he sought the ultimate revenge - to have her evicted just as he had said he would. All it took was a short letter to the Cattle Company saying he wished to cash out the Family Trust's investment and discontinue their lease. The investment had tripled the original cash in only three years, but he didn't want a cent of it. It was chicken feed against the wealth of his pearls; and again he took pleasure in the fact that his brother and Elizabeth's parents would each realise just how wrong they had been about him. He didn't offer any reason, relishing the thought that Maggie and the deceitful Richard would be evicted within months.

And as for his own son, well Maggie could keep him along with her other bastard child.

In 1863, as the Shark Bay leases were nearly picked dry and they had finally begun to wonder at their own futures, Rogers heard from a buyer that new pearling fields had been discovered in an area much further north, nearly double the distance again from Perth. The new cattle station owner at Point Samson, William Padbury had reported that decorative pearl shells from *pintada maxima* was being worn by local Aboriginals, the Ngarluma people.

Padbury had landed stock in an estuary at the mouth of the Harding River and named that landing 'Tien Tsin harbour' after the barque that had carried him there. His report sparked a 'pearl rush' over the next decade greater than the Shark Bay rush of the decade earlier and which would soon turn the harbour into a significant town, Cossack, with boats and men arriving from both north and south.

Already, Rogers learnt, people were moving in to stake claims. Like Shark Bay, in the early days these considerably larger and more valuable pearls could be collected from the shore and shallow waters, but with much bigger and better pearls at greater depth off-shore.

So Rogers had acted quickly, buying a second schooner to service the operation and taking out a massive lease. He was to remain in Shark Bay to finish up that lease while Maguire was to head immediately to Tien Tsin to secure the new sites, arriving before the multitudes of pearlers just as they had in Shark Bay. Rogers would come later when the Shark Bay operation was no longer viable.

Maguire chose to take his beloved Speculator to the new fields, crewed by a handful of Aboriginal convicts and Malay divers.

When he arrived, he was initially disappointed to find there weren't as many shore-based oysters as Shark Bay. But they had a huge lease and the *maxima* pearl was bigger and more prevalent, such that his first haul produced more valuable pearl and shell than even their earliest from Shark Bay.

James Maguire wrung his hands in glee and sent word to Rogers to come as soon as he could.

There were more pearls here than he dreamed, and his greed meant that he could not slow down the operation lest some other person should benefit and his own profits reduce. Perth was simply too far away to make his own runs. So he sold only the inferior pearls and shell with traders entering the harbour, and kept all the best pearls in his own cabin in jars which gradually filled the room. Maguire would take pleasure in their glow and would scatter a handful in his bed each night.

They worked the Cossack claims for a further ten years – a total of twenty years of monotony in which they had built a vast wealth, beyond the reaches or comprehension of any other.

Five years after he arrived, in May of 1868 Maguire found himself involved in another Aboriginal massacre at Flying Foam passage. The passage was so called as it was a narrow strait between islands and the mainland of Burrup Peninsula that saved hours of navigation but was extremely dangerous – foam of the wild waters literally sweeping through the narrow entrance at the changes of high and low tide.

Up to 60 Juburara people of the Burrup Peninsula (Murujuga) were killed over three days at that place after the Police constable William Griffis apprehended Coolyerberri for stealing flour from a pearling boat.

Nine Juburara men carried out a rescue, killing Griffis, a pearler, an Aboriginal police assistant and a pastoral worker. Robert John Scholl, the Government resident in Roebourne, arranged two small parties of men to round up the offenders, 'dead or alive'.

The parties travelled separately overland and by sea in the familiar pincer movement, seeking to ensure the wanted men should not escape. But of course, they did – seeing the white men and their guns arrive, the tribe ran in all directions - including over the Flying Foam passage to take refuge on the islands beyond. James was part of the naval assault on his beloved *Speculator*, and again took pleasure as the scene descended to chaos and violence. Maguire then personally took charge of the 'mop-up' operation as he and his men wandered the adjacent islands and shot every Aboriginal they found.

Eight years later to the day, James Maguire, now aged 60 was with Rogers on The Speculator. They were finally returning to Perth with the massive store of pearls that now filled up much of the hold, and then they would retire. James planned to return to Ireland to live out the rest of his days in wealth, and where he would also finally challenge his brother.

As they sailed through the Dampier Archipelago to the west of Point Samson, Maguire chose to show off his sailing skills by navigating the notoriously dangerous Flying Foam passage.

As they flew down the strait in the ripping current of a five-metre king tide, there was great excitement as The Speculator reached the fastest speeds she had ever achieved. The men laughed and Rogers cheered as James pointed to the nearby islands where his part of the massacre occurred, and he proudly told Rogers of his place in that event; how he had personally killed no less than 10 Aboriginals, including several women and children.

Then suddenly, without warning The Speculator dipped violently into a great whirlpool which had formed as the tide peaked at the same moment they rounded an intersecting channel, and inexplicably the

Brown Mallet of which she was formed creaked and splintered under the stress, and then tore with a mighty crack.

Rogers and Maguire looked at each other in alarm for only the briefest of moments before the boat tore and began to go under. Rogers was swept from the boat and quickly disappeared. James swore to the sea at this great injustice and tried, even as the boat whirled into the eye of the maelstrom, to get to his cabin and retrieve just a jar or two of his precious pearls. But it was too late, and the last sight he saw before The Speculator disappeared into the hungry mouth of the whirlpool was the Island, and the exact spot he recalled even now that he had shot down a pregnant woman, thinking in his rage that he should prevent another bastard child from entering this world.

The Speculator disappeared without trace, Maguire and Rogers the only crew; their only cargo a massive haul of grade A *pintada maxima* pearls, expected market price: 200,000 pounds.

The shipwreck was reported months later when they failed to show in Fremantle Harbour, their filed destination. A report of the missing men and schooner was filed and two years later, as was the requirement of that time, the Police Gazette reported they were missing and declared dead.

41

A visit in the night

The bank that held Maguire's thousands acted soon after the Gazette notice was published, discovering two beneficiaries across two separate accounts: Maggie and Thomas Maguire of Greenough; and Patrick Maguire of Dundalk. Whether James had forgotten amidst his anger and self-obsession - or perhaps it was a sense of responsibility that dwelled somewhere deep in his dark soul - he hadn't closed the original account, which still bequeathed the money he had made in those first three years to Maggie and Thomas in the event of his death.

And so in June 1876, as the winter bit hard and residents of the Greenough community sheltered in their houses, an ageing Mrs Maggie Maguire and her partner, Mr Richard William Maguire were chilled to the bones in their stone and wood cottage, set among the trees. Amidst the howling wind and rain, they were surprised to hear a knock at the door and let in a shivering man who rushed to the fireplace. They gave him a mug of hot tea, and eventually, he identified himself as a representative of the Bank of Western Australia.

"Can I firstly please confirm that you are Mrs Margaret Maguire, nee O'Brien, and adopted mother to Thomas Maguire also of this address?" the odd little man said after collecting himself.

"Yes, that's right... Why do you need to know?" Maggie replied and was then invited to present identification. She found her marriage certificate and her passport, the same one she had used on the Hashemy. She also found and presented Thomas' birth certificate.

"Is Thomas here?" enquired the man, looking around the odd stone and wood house.

Maggie explained that Thomas was working some kilometres away. "Oh", said the man, shivering at the thought of a further ride on that cold night. "Well I'm sure you can deliver the message to him? Please sign here."

"Get on with it, man!" said Richard, who had had enough of his officious nature. "What is she signing? What has happened? Are we in some sort of trouble?"

"Ah, no, not at all" he replied, and then read from a sheet of paper that emerged from his inner pocket.

"It is my duty to inform you that the bank has foreclosed on the accounts of James Maguire, subsequent to the listing of his death in the Police Gazette." Maggie let out an audible gasp and sat down weeping.

"I'm sorry to have brought you this news, Mrs Maguire. But it is my duty to inform you that Mr Maguire nominated yourself in joint with your son Thomas as the beneficiaries of his savings.

We have taken the liberty of already splitting the money into two to avoid any bother or embarrassments." Then he opened his suitcase and took out two folders.

"Here is your bank account, Mrs Maguire." He opened the file to the first page and drew her attention to the figure at the top. "You may withdraw up to this amount at any time, although we ask that you kindly provide at least two months' notice should you wish to close the account, given the quantum of money - I'm sure you will understand."

Richard and Maggie looked at each other in confusion and bewilderment, and then both took in the figure at the top of that page – their new and unexpected wealth.

Even as she reeled at the news and the sum before her, Maggie realised it was of course less than the riches accumulated by the likes of the Maguire family, nor the vast wealth of the emerging Western Australian moguls; but still to her and Richard it was a staggering amount.

The clerk presented Thomas' chequebook of the same value and asked that it be given to him and that he then present himself with it at the bank for his signature.

"We'll do better than that!" Richard exclaimed, now excited. "Have another tea – Maggie, give him a brandy. I'll ride out and collect Thomas now, so you can explain it yourself."

Half an hour later they were back.

Thomas was now 27 years old and a fine and handsome young man. He looked like James when Maggie first knew him, those years ago on his visits to collect the rent in Blackrock. But unlike James, Thomas had inherited Maggie's sense of calm reflection in life – he was at peace. Richard had taught him well too, and he was a fit and capable man who had the eye of every young woman in the District.

But now in the odd stone and wood cottage as the storm raged past, Thomas was briefed, and the clerk collected his signature and sealed both documents into his case, then bid them each good night and reluctantly made his way outside.

The three sat quietly as they stared at the folders by the fireplace, and each contemplated their newfound riches.

42

Awaking from a dream

Fifty thousand pounds.

It was more money than most people could even dream to have, the equivalent of nearly $8 million today.

After a couple of day's deliberation, Thomas declared that his share of the inheritance needed by rights to be shared equally with his three siblings.

"I never knew my father or mother" he explained to Maggie and Richard as they beamed with pride. "But you have always been my parents and they have always been my family - so I figure it's ours, not mine".

As James' rightful heir, Thomas had quickly confirmed that the sixty acres of Greenough land would also pass to him, and Maggie was proud as he declared his intentions to continue to manage it alongside his brother Daniel, but that they would install a manager and travel around Australia for a while.

Maggie realised the truth of his words as he said they would never have an opportunity like this again – young, independently wealthy and in a land they knew would never be the same again in only a few short years.

And Maggie relished that in the longer term, Thomas said that he would travel back to Ireland and England to meet his mother's family, and to claim his birthright from his uncle, Patrick Maguire.

Their own first born, Daniel, was 23 and managing some of the nearby Hamersley properties, and in great demand by both the local landholders and their daughters! Daniel looked the spitting image of the young Richard and was every bit as capable. He and Thomas were both very competent in farm work, and regularly helped each other out. They had become the closest of friends even as they competed for the eyes of the local girls - of whom they each had many, many admirers.

Their other two children had moved to Perth and were getting on with their lives. Their youngest, Richard, was already 18 years and had recently taken up work as a carpenter at one of the now burgeoning ship building enterprises that dotted the Swan. There were no grandchildren just yet, but Maggie and Richard knew it wouldn't be long: their only daughter, Margaret - a 20-year old girl with long brown hair, green eyes and every bit as stunning as her mother - had recently announced her engagement!

So Maggie and Richard also decided to move to Perth to live out their final days and to be near their younger children and grandchildren. They purchased a large stone house in Guildford – far too big for them alone, but of course she had plans.

Once installed, she set about doing more of the things that she loved best – helping others.

She had kept in touch with family in Ireland and knew that her parents, now in the 70s, were in poor health. So, the very first thing she did was send a very large cheque to them that would ensure the best of services and would give her brothers and sisters, and their children, security for the future. She left it up to her Pappy to decide how best to use the money.

Next, she sought out Hazel, the mother she had helped on the Hashemy. Soon enough she found her and her husband Henry managing a bar in the centre of Fremantle. The town had grown and now had some pleasant buildings, and the streets were at least a little less unkempt than those years earlier.

Before she went into the hotel, she went to the nicest dress shop in town and bought the most expensive dress she could find. And then she contacted the proprietor of the hotel Henry managed and made a little deal.

Hazel recognised her instantly when she opened her door and gave her possibly the biggest hug she'd ever had.

"Maggie O'Brien!" Hazel exclaimed in delight. "Now there's a face I'll never forget"

Maggie presented the dress box to Hazel and bid her to put it on.

"Whatever do you mean?" said Hazel, confused.

"Well" Maggie replied, "you promised me that the next time you saw me, you'd be wearing a fancy dress and would be the lady of the house…"

"Oh don't be mean Maggie" Hazel said, a little hurt. "We ain't got much to show for our lives of hard work, but you were right that it would be better than London! We've had a good life."

"Yes, I can see" said Maggie. "But you'll also need a good dress now you ARE the lady of the house."

To Hazel's confused look, she explained the owner had accepted an offer too good to refuse and would be there to present the deed to the hotel to Henry and her in just a short while.

Hazel was stunned.

"But I do think the place needs a bit of improvement, don't you?" said Maggie.

"It's a bit of a shithole, true enough!" Hazel replied and they laughed.

"So, here's a cheque for a thousand pounds. Should be enough to make it the most respectable place on the block, don't you think?"

Hazel broke down in tears – this was like a dream.

Her final task, for now, was her favourite of all.

She sought out her old and best friend Caroline, from the Hashemy. She remembered that she had worked for the Bruce family in Guildford and easily tracked them down, but they admitted with just an ounce of shame that Caroline had been 'mutually dismissed' a few years ago, stating that she was now simply too old for the tiring domestic work.

After some sniffing around, Maggie found her and her husband managing a property towards Mandurah. Caroline was delighted to open her door to Maggie and recognised her instantly. Caroline looked a lot older than her 46 years and told Maggie of her ill-health and aching bones. Over a cup of tea, she explained they were doing okay for now, but she was very worried about their future. Aside from her own health problems which prevented her doing much more than essential jobs around the house, her husband had war injuries that had increasingly bothered him as he grew older, and he was now also struggling to keep up on the farm.

She cried as she admitted there was a real risk he would be replaced soon, and then she didn't know what they would do.

"Well" said Maggie, with a grin that lit up the room. "I'm glad you don't have lots of plans then!" she laughed. But Caroline didn't share the humour.

So Maggie asked if Caroline and her husband might come back to her new house in Guildford and take on the roles of head of house-keeping and gardening.

"Of course, your main role will be to support the young girls we have there already. I regret there won't be an awful lot for you to do, but helping me to manage and train those girls would be a tremendous help if you wouldn't mind? Your husband is much needed too, helping with the grounds, and the couple of young groundsmen need a bit of training and support too."

Caroline was so surprised she nearly dropped her tea.

"But there is one other thing Caroline, and I'm sorry to have to ask you this, but I'll need you to first go find Patricia wherever she is in Melbourne and give her a gift." She presented a cheque for a thousand Pounds. "Oh, and here's your own too."

As Caroline stared at the huge cheque, she looked at Maggie with wide eyes and many questions not far behind them.

"Here's the thing, Caroline my darling friend" Maggie explained. "I've come into a bit of money and the best thing I can think to do with it, is help the people I love. So I guess what I'm asking is if you and your hubbie might please come live with us, and this cheque is intended to ensure that you don't have to.

So if you do, you won't be coming as a servant – you'll be coming as my friend, and your only job, if you even want it, is to help the young girls that we once were develop into the women we are now.

Oh, and have cups of tea with me." And she looked to Caroline for an answer.

"After you've holidayed in Melbourne as long as you want that is. Oh, and here are your boat tickets for that – first class this time."

Caroline's worry and fears faded instantly from her face, and she once again looked like that beautiful 20-year old Irish girl who danced on the decks of the Hashemy, sweeping up all in her joy for life.

"Oh Maggie" she said "Are you feckin kidding me? We'll be there tomorrow!"

They kept enough money to meet their own and the households needs, and yet still they had more than they could spend. She remembered her Pappy's words:

I'll never understand why people want more than they need. Why have two houses? You can only live in one.

And so they arranged a meeting with the Wesleyan Church for the purposes of building and staffing a new school.

Maggie's only condition: that all children irrespective of religion, ethnicity or class, should be supported to attend.

"Because" she told the shocked administrator as she presented the cheque for 10000 pounds, "education leads to truth, and it's only the truth that will set us free."

---ENDS---

*W**ho am I anyway?* – **Perth, 2020**

The family was in an uproar – not generally something too unusual, but today's topic of conversation was certainly a novel one.

Our 90-year mother had been researching her family tree for years, and she'd found something big, an un-truth that could upset not just her relatives today, but affected two generations before her and would cause everyone to question, *just who am I?*

"It was what *wasn't* said" she'd explained to me as her research unfolded. "Some family secrets that the older people clearly knew but wouldn't discuss if ever it was brought it up. I was only a child, but I remember the raised voices between them that would hush whenever we entered the room.

I knew there was something there that no one wanted to admit."

And recently, she had found the link.

Using a simple DNA test, she was able to show the genetic mix of her heritage, but more than that – when the results came back the website linked her – and all of us – to people and families with no apparent connection, separated by many years but with high levels of accuracy.

Through meticulous enquiry to these people – our long lost cousins - and inquiry to stitch together names and dates, she had tracked back her questions three generations, to a single lie.

Some of the family refused to believe it, others like me were simply intrigued.

She was pleased to prove not only an Irish heritage, but also that there was a convict ancestor. It was 2020 now and with the separation that 170 years afforded, people today were only too happy to wear that most Australian badge of honour. But she was also cautious, I thought because some of her older generation still carried honour close and would not want to admit to a shady heritage – British tradition and prejudices still ran deep.

"It's not that surprising to me" I'd said. "Nearly half the West Australian population in the 1850s and 60s were convicts".

But her concern was much deeper that that - she was alarmed that the family might not be so ready to accept the implications of her research – that their family name itself was wrong and had been for three generations.

"This is about identity" she said. "You grow up with a set of beliefs about your past, and then to find out those assumptions were wrong – it might affect some people too much. That you're not who you thought you were...

Perhaps it should be kept a secret?"

But I, and all of the new generation were clear that secrets had no further place in our lives. We'd been brought up with too many lies already – the lies of colonisation, of white Australia, of the English prejudices that had coloured our views.

And finally, after all these years those prejudices were being challenged. For the first time, as a population we were finally hearing about the pre-history of Australia, as if previously there were none and that this great land had only come into existence in the 1829 act of colonisation.

We were challenged to hear of great atrocities that had been carried out in the name of Great Britian and Christianity, and in the name of future generations. Of racism, and pompous disregard for our fellows, people judged only by their class, their religion, the shade of their skin. Australia was finally coming into the 21st century and we were now big enough to challenge those beliefs, to declare NO! They will no longer define us!

A new and well-educated generation had found it challenging to be sure, but most were able to accept that lies had been told, and chose now to define ourselves by the *truth* of the past, and thus enlightened to take hold of the future. A shared future, of truth.

But challenging it most certainly was, and when the extent of a lie goes down to the level of your very own name - well, then you really know it's personal.

For our dear mum's research had uncovered that back in those early days of Western Australia, a lie had been perpetuated and future generations had carried forward a family name to which they had no legitimate claim. All to avoid a connection to a convict - or so it was thought.

And so in trust that people could both handle the truth and were entitled to it, our dear old mum had blasted out the truth, even to the extent of changing her own name. And the family was in an uproar.

She of course needn't have worried about the implications - some refused to accept it, and others simply chose to ignore it; but most really didn't care. Family trees often only become interesting to people when they have the time to examine their family line in the context of their own mortality, an existential quest that most people have neither the time nor patience to undertake as they go about the busy business of raising children and having careers.

But some of this new generation embraced it. Because behind every big lie is an even bigger truth; and it is only the truth that can set you free.

What was the background to this new truth, emblazoned in the very DNA of scores of descendants?

The idea of a lie carried forward over more than one and a half centuries, through three generations – to me, it was intriguing. And so I researched it further and uncovered not just the full extent of the lie, but the greatest of truths that underpinned it all:

A love story, embedded in the very birth of a nation.

Author's notes and acknowledgements

Maggie's story is based on a piece of family folklore, where my dear old mum did indeed uncover a lie in her family name centred around a very young Irish pioneer and a convict in Western Australia's midwest. Her research and 'thoughtful curiosity' into that lie inspired both the story and many long conversations exploring possible histories.

But alas, of course there is no real way of knowing the actual truth behind her discovery. The reality of family history that many will be familiar with is that research can sometimes lead to little more than a dead trail. The great reality is that within 100 years, all your efforts, your wealth and accumulations, all your living will be gone and mostly forgotten with little else to show than four or five facts: born; died; married; children; and if you're lucky 'lived at'. So think of that next time you deliberate too long over your worries and cares!

Diamond of the Desert tells one possible truth, which allowed me to explore and relay the actual history of the early colony 'warts and all'. As I said to my many supporters along the way, this is a story that needs to be told.

Firstly, my thanks to the brave handful of Beta-Readers who have taken and transformed this tale from its earliest form. I was inspired to hear their feedback - that they enjoyed the tale certainly, but in particular that they had learnt much of Western Australia's settlement and about the pre- and post- invasion history of the many Aboriginal nations. The feedback of these 15 brave souls has resulted in a much changed and I must say a much better tale – as ever, I am reminded through their efforts that connection and co-design with others *always* produces a better product!

Part of my inspiration, it must be said, was the travesty of truth that was the horrid movie, 'Australia' wherein a cattle drive from Katherine to Darwin in the NT went past both Uluru and Purnululu... Boy did they get lost! Oh, and whereupon arriving the Japanese had apparently landed foot soldiers on Australian soil!

No, I wasn't keen to tell an *alternate* history, as tempting as that has apparently been these past 200 years. I wanted Maggie's story to be a true one, reflecting the actual events and circumstances of the day.

And so I stumbled into the literary world of 'historical fiction', where I found a single paragraph could often require two days research... I found lots of great information out there, but it was often conflicting and frankly, none of it painted a coherent whole.

This is where fiction comes in - to paint the whole, and make it live once more through its characters.

So while key characters are entirely fictitious, to the best of my ability key dates and events in Maggie's tale are accurate - including many minute details that should keep any history buffs busy! Other minor characters are based on real people of the time, however may not reflect entirely accurately (for example, Johnstone Drummond died in 1845, a few years before his imagined flirtation with Maggie).

But as to the truth... well, what became clear as I read and explored was that the real history of nations is its people. That is, a nation is really nothing more than its people; and as much as we like to blame 'someone else' for the wrongs of the world, in fact it is all of us who create history and equally, all of us who can change the future now.

The truth is certainly not one we've been told, nor one that many may want to hear. Again, I draw inspiration my dear old ma's words: "It was the things that weren't said; the hushed voices when younger people entered the room". For this is the reality of our upbringing too – things that were never said; lies that were perpetuated through hushed, silent voices.

Some of the early surprise discoveries included the measures designed to protect the original inhabitants. Enlightened Victorian philosophy acknowledged the reality that this was an invasion. So, the British Government had made Aboriginal people instant citizens (not that they wanted it) with all the rights of the British. The WA Constitution even set aside 1% of GDP for Aboriginal advancement (not that it's ever been acted upon). British policy also constrained the Australian colonies from rapid expansion – perhaps a case of 'minimising their guilt', but largely driven by an unshakable belief that the British way was right and proper and that the natives would 'convert' soon enough (not that they did).

For the truth of colonisation in the 1830s and 40's, and the expansion of colonies in the 1850s and beyond is not a pretty one. There were terrible policy decisions that reflected the culture of the day and enabled suppression and injustice: Stirling and Irwin's decree: *They have to fear us before they can love us* (a stance even approved in the Supreme Court); the outcomes of policies based on the philosophy that *the poor are the cause of their own poverty*; along with the alignment of church and state. But perhaps most of all, the simple *turning of a blind eye* to the brutalities of expanding the settlement after 20 years of constraint, in which both law and morality were cast aside, alongside the truth.

Diamond of the Desert contends that this is a history not of British imperialism, but foremost of *individuals* failing to transcend the culture of their time – failing to use their own judgement of what is right and what is wrong. The policy frameworks allowed and to some extent even encouraged it, sure - but the hardest truth of all is that we can't blame the British Government.

Maggie's wisdom summed it up:

"So, it strikes me that now just like then, our troubles are very much the fault of every single one of us who refuses to stand up for and to do what's right. Every person who knowingly perpetuates inequality.

It is greatly convenient for us to reduce it to a single cause, to point the finger of blame. But the blame isn't just with the English, not solely, though it suits us to say so. Yes, English policy has shaped, allowed and even aggravated poverty and inequality; but it is the greed and self-interest of every-man that has caused so much suffering."

Maggie's Truth - education - provides her with the unique ability to see culture for what it is: a map for collective survival; and a set of constraints on individual freedom and thought. Only Maggie could see beyond the constraints of greed, apathy and indifference that dominated the culture of the day.

That was Maggie's truth; but there was no greater truth in this book than one line, referring to Richard's great discovery when he realised unconditional love:

'If only we could all give such a love.'

Please note that I very deliberately used the word *give* here, not *receive*.

A huge thanks to the people and agencies who keep our history alive. In writing this tale, I drew on the written records that have been kept or researched from scratch by a wealth of people. For Part One (Ireland and England) I visited Blackrock itself and drew on excellent resources published by the County Louth Archaeological and History Society such as Susan Mullaney's *Poor Law Relief in Late Nineteenth-Century County Louth: A Social and Economic Analysis* along with a range of books and online resources such as John Arwel Edwards' *The Landless in Mid-Nineteenth-Century County Louth*. The Carlingford Heritage Centre and the Blackrockvillage.ie also provided additional content on detail - such as how to build a Curragh boat!

The Perth and Western Australian content also drew on a wide range of agencies and individuals such as the Australian National Museum 'Defining Moments' series; the Australian National University for biographies; and Henry Reynold's excellent books *This Whispering in Our Hearts Revisited* and *The Other Side of the Frontier*. Other great resources include Louise Tilbrook's *The first South Westerners: Aborigines of South Western Australia*; RH William and Tom Stannage's *European-Aboriginal relations in Western Australian*; Paul Hasluck's *Black Australians: A Survey of Native Policy in Western Australia, 1829–1897*; Fiona Bush's *The Convicts' Contribution to the Built Environment of Colonial Western Australia between 1850-1880*; and Bob Reece's *'Prisoners in the own country: Aborigines in Western Australian Historical Writing'*. Map images are from excellent user contributions to OldMapsOnline.org. Information regarding WA Educational history primarily drew on an excellent resource from Edith Cowan University by B.T. Haynes (Ed.) 1976 *Documents on Western Australian education 1830 – 1973*.

Of course, there is no better source than the firsthand accounts afforded through newspaper articles of the time, and letters sent by the early pioneers themselves. Of note, the newspaper article by William Nelson appearing in Chapter one is actually from the Goldfields Reporter nearly two decades later (1850), and the letters in this novel are adapted directly from sources including James Backhouse's *A narrative of a visit to the Australian Colonies 1839* and J. Giles Powell's *The Narrative of a voyage to the Swan River*.

Aboriginal Nation and skin-group names are largely drawn from the Australian Institute of Aboriginal and Torres Strait Islander Studies resources, and my sincere apologies for any information I have either missed or wrongly interpreted.

Information on the Western Australian regions, locations and events including the Northwest Stock Route, Irwin, Greenough, Champion Bay, Shark Bay and Cossack drew on publications from the Heritage Council of WA; the Australian National University; The City of Greater Geraldton; and Greenough Museum along with 'niche' interest groups such as The Redcoat Settlers; and Australian Historical Towns. My particular thanks to Gary Martin of the Greenough Museum and Gardens for his time in conversation filling in gaps and reviewing the account for accuracy.

Information on the Greenough and Flying Foam massacres primarily came from the University of Newcastle's tremendous new resource index as well as accounts linked from that resource. The WA Parliament also lists a detailed Inquiry into the Flying Foam massacre – harrowing reading that shows how easily self-righteousness can turn to violence.

Information on Shark Bay and Pilbara pearling came from WA Museum resources and key publications including Ronald Moore's *The Management of the Western Australian Pearling Industry 1860 to the 1930s*; and J.P.S. Bach's 1935 *The Pearling Industry of Australia: An Account of its Social and Economic Development*.

And finally, most proudly, my deep thanks to Associate Professor Rohan Collard of Curtin University and Dooga Waalitj Healing for his review of content through a cultural sensitivity lens. As a proud Nyungar man and emerging elder, Rohan's review and comments resulted in a number of changes and gave me confidence that the story being told was both as truthful as possible, and as sensitive to the Aboriginal people and nations of this great state as I could make it. Reading the accounts of massacres, rape, blackbirding, desecration and more is traumatic for Aboriginal people and I'm sorry for that, and thankful to Rohan for sticking with it. But I'm also aware that many non-Aboriginal people today simply have no idea of such things, so I'm not sorry if relaying the occasional horrors of that truth has shocked while it educated – as I've said before, *this is a story that had to be told*.

Finally, I'd like to say that I hope the book has left you with a sense of hope. Not just the simple hope of Maggie and Richard's love and new-found wealth nor the things they did with it; but the hope of building a new future on the basis of two simple truths: Education, and Love.

Because in order to build something new, you sometimes need to pull down the old. What our forebears did in the name of England is a great shame we must acknowledge and carry forward, and we can each honour that truth by accepting it and vowing to never allow it to happen again. Once we learn to think for ourselves we can find our own truths; and once we do that we can truly respect others and seek involvement to further our knowledge - and then we can go forward together. Then we have a future.

"Because behind every big lie is an even bigger truth, and it is only the truth that can set us free"

I acknowledge the Aboriginal people of Western Australia as the true custodians of the land on which we live and prosper. I pay my respects to all the elders past, present and emerging of the Western Australian nations, and I relay to them my enduring hope that through truth and love that we will walk forward together on this great land, and that we will once more learn the truth of connection.

A story that had to be told

An engaging and easy-to-read tale of adventure, love and greed spanning 40 years and half the globe - the first fiction to tell the true history of The Swan River colony as it expands to become the state of Western Australia.

...'for one last time this place was one of reverence and intrigue. She sat in the shade, watching the contrast going on around her. A place that seemed deeply spiritual, steeped in Aboriginal lore; now trampled by cattle and men, who bathed from the cooled spring and soon started to drink and swear and to turn it to a place of commerce – a staging post for the European march over the land.

Something about the place reminded Maggie of a famous book from the time, "The Talisman" by Sir Walter Scott. As she witnessed the mysterious place now being trampled and changed forever, Maggie reflected that here again was a clash of cultures, and that 'men of civilisation' were once more those displaying the traits expected of the 'savages' they claimed superiority over. She recalled that the whole sorry saga had come to a head with a great duel at a desert oasis called 'The Diamond of the Desert'...